IN
PLAIN
SIGHT

IN
PLAIN
SIGHT

BARBARA BLOCK

KENSINGTON BOOKS

KENSINGTON BOOKS are published by

Kensington Publishing Corp.
850 Third Avenue
New York, NY 10022

Copyright © 1996 by Barbara Block

Library of Congress Card Catalog Number: 96-076016
ISBN 1-57566-059-8

First Printing: August, 1996

10 9 8 7 6 5 4 3 2 1

Printed in the United States of America

DISCLAIMER

Although the city of Syracuse is real as are some of the place names I've mentioned, this is a work of fiction. Its geography is imaginary. Indeed, all the characters portrayed in this book are fictional and any resemblance to real people or incidents is purely coincidental.

ACKNOWLEDGMENT

I would like to thank Bob Hutchison and Richard Hehir
for their time and patience.

For My Father:
I wish we could have had more time together.

IN
PLAIN
SIGHT

Chapter

1

It was four o'clock on a dreary Friday afternoon in mid-April. I was standing near the cash register, watching the rain streaking down the windows, wishing for a Scotch, and trying to figure out how I was going to pay all my bills this month, when a figure from my past walked into the store. Time had definitely not been kind to Marsha Pennington, I decided as she closed her umbrella and came toward me. Fifteen years ago she'd been a young, thin, bubbly blonde; now she was an overweight, middle-aged, stoop-shouldered brunette.

"Robin, remember me?" she asked uncertainly as she tucked a strand of limp brown hair behind her ear. "The Crestville. Apartment 2B." I guess I must have looked shocked because she added, "I know I've changed."

"No you haven't," I lied, trying to make up for the thoughts she'd read on my face.

Marsha sighed. "We had some good times back then, didn't we?"

"Yes we did," I agreed, though what I mostly remembered were the endless hours I'd spent listening to Marsha chatter on about her china painting class or the flowers she was planning on stenciling on her bathroom wall or which grocery store had the best sales this week. Ten minutes into the conversation and I usually found myself struggling to stay awake. By the time I'd left the complex I'd taken to avoiding her whenever I could.

"I tried calling after you moved."

"I know." I hadn't returned them. "I'm sorry. I just got busy." Then I flushed, embarrassed by how I sounded.

Marsha smiled sadly and changed the subject. "So this is your store?"

"As long as I can keep paying the bills." Which these days was becoming more problematic. Thanks to a snowy winter and a soggy spring our receipts were down by thirty percent. I kept hoping the weather would take a turn for the better, but so far all it did was rain.

She pointed to a hyacinth macaw I was baby sitting for a customer.

"How much for that?"

"Twelve hundred dollars if she was for sale, which she's not."

"That's a lot of money."

"It's a lot of bird."

Marsha wiped a stray drop of water off her cheek with the back of her hand. "I've read about you in the papers," she told me. "I guess that makes you a celebrity."

I gave a dry little laugh. "Not quite." I'd solved a couple of homicides in the past two years and the papers had given the cases some play.

"Well, nobody's ever written about me." Her voice contained a hint of envy. Then she gave me a long, hard look. "You've changed, too." Her tone implied it wasn't for the better either.

I did a quick mental inventory. Maybe time hadn't been kind to either of us. When Marsha had known me my red hair had been bobbed. I'd worn short, straight skirts, silk shirts, blazers, and tons of makeup. I'd been an up-and-coming reporter at the *Herald Journal*. Now my hair was a little duller and my wardrobe consisted almost exclusively of jeans and T-shirts. As for makeup—I didn't wear any at all—not even lipstick. But the animals didn't seem to care and neither did I.

"I'm sorry to hear about your husband," she continued.

Undoubtedly she'd read about that in the papers, too. Murphy's demise had gotten a lot of ink. I nodded but didn't say anything. I still don't like talking about his death. ODing on cocaine is not my idea of a graceful exit, and it certainly doesn't lend itself to idle social chitchat.

Marsha glanced around the store. "I like this place. I like the name, too. Noah's Ark. Very clever. Was it Murphy's idea or yours?"

"Mine."

"I figured as much. Murphy never was very good with words." Marsha patted her hair again. The overhead light picked up the strands of gray woven through the brown. "I have two dogs you know. Shih Tzus. You want to see a picture of them?" And before I could answer she reached in her bag, fished out her wallet and opened it. "Here they are," she said, a proud parent passing out photos of her progeny.

I glanced at it. The picture looked as if it had been taken professionally. The two small dogs were sitting side by side in a green brocade armchair. Their top knots were both held together with gold bows. They'd been groomed to within an inch of their lives.

"They're why I came." As she took her wallet back she looked at the photograph and smiled. Her face lit up. For a second I saw the old Marsha. Then the glow was gone. "Is there someplace we can talk? Somewhere private?" she asked as she put her wallet away. "Somewhere I could sit down?"

I shrugged. "Sure. Why not?" I mean it wasn't as if I was exactly overrun with customers. I had the time. And I was curious about what had brought her to the store.

I took Marsha into the room that passes for my office. It's a small windowless space, ten feet by twelve at the most. At one end is my desk and two chairs. Fifty-pound bags of pet food, cedar shavings, and cat litter take up the rest of the area. As I walked in Zsa Zsa, my cocker spaniel, jumped down from my desk with a sample box of pet food clamped in her jaws. The twit. When I tried to grab her she ran through my legs and scooted out the door. Marsha laughed. For a few fleeting seconds her face was animated again, and then as quickly as it had come the sparkle was gone.

"So what's up?" I asked after she and I were seated.

She fiddled with the cuff of her yellow-green blouse. The color didn't do much for her complexion. Neither did the ruffles around her chest and neck. They made her look heavier than she really was.

"I teach ESL at Wellington High now," Marsha informed me as she shifted her weight this way and that trying to get comfortable in a chair that was too narrow for her. When I'd known her she'd been working as a typist out at GE. "It's nice teaching English to immigrants. I like it."

"I'm glad." Whatever it was she'd come to tell me, it certainly wasn't this, but that was okay. I could wait. To pass the time I took a Camel out of the pack in my pocket, lit it with my new toy, a gold cigarette lighter, and exhaled. I figured as long as I was waiting I might as well smoke, but Marsha didn't see it that way.

She frowned and coughed and ostentatiously waved her hand in front of her face. "Do you have to do that?" she complained.

I told her I did. After all, this was my office and my time she was taking up. To emphasize the point I took another puff and put my feet up on my desk.

"Merlin smokes, too," she said, her face a mask of disapproval. "I could never get him to stop. Even when he said he had, he was lying. I could smell the tobacco every time I got into the car." She started plucking at the cuff of her blouse again. "We're getting divorced, you know."

"You've been married a long time."

"Too long," Marsha spat out. "I should have done this years ago."

Actually I was surprised she hadn't. From what I remembered, Merlin was a soft, squishy man who drifted from job to job always complaining that everything that went wrong was somebody else's fault.

"Years ago," Marsha repeated to herself. "But I'm doing it now," she said to me.

"Good, but what does this have to do with me?" I spun my lighter around with the tip of one of my fingers. In truth, I really didn't want to hear about her lousy marriage—it made me think of my own.

"It's the dogs." Marsha leaned forward. "He's suing for custody of Pooh and Po." Her eyes narrowed. "And I won't let him have them. He thinks he can take them from me, but he's wrong. They're my babies." She pounded the desk with the palm of her hand. "He hates them. He comes in and kicks them out of the way. He doesn't walk them. He doesn't feed them. He doesn't pet them. The only reason he wants them is because he knows how much I love them. But I won't let him have them. I won't. They need a special diet. I make them hamburger and rice every day. And Po has to have his heart medicine. They need me and I don't know what I'd do without them." Suddenly Marsha's face crumpled. She bent her head, opened her pocketbook and began rummaging around for a tissue. "You must think I'm very silly," she said a moment later as she dabbed at her eyes.

"Not at all," I assured her. "In my experience sometimes dogs are nicer than people."

Marsha smiled weakly at that and started plucking at the ruffle around her collar. "I just can't bear the thought of what Merlin would do to them." Then she squared her shoulders and looked me in the eye. "Hell will freeze over before I let him have my babies."

I took my feet off the desk and leaned forward. "I can understand the way you feel, but what I don't understand is why you're telling me this."

Marsha put her hands on the desk and leaned forward, too. "I'm telling you this because Merlin is doing something dirty. I want to find out what it is."

I ground out my cigarette in the glass I was using as an ash tray. Guess there was no sense in suggesting mediation. "What you need is a private detective."

"No," Marsha said emphatically. "What I need is you."

"But I don't have a license," I protested.

"I don't care. I've already been to two detective agencies. They thought this was funny." Marsha's mouth quivered in indignation at the memory. "They thought I was some nutty middle-aged broad."

They were right. She was. But so what? Everybody has to have something to love. Why should it matter if the objects of her affection had four legs instead of two? I started fiddling with my lighter. "What you say may be correct," I replied slowly. "But an agency will still do a better job than I will. For one thing they have more resources."

"It doesn't matter how many resources they have. They'll just take my money and sit around and have a good laugh at my expense. Please," Marsha begged. "Merlin can't get my babies. He just can't. You have to help me. Will you?"

Looking back, I think I said yes because I felt guilty about the way I'd treated her all those years ago. Marsha was always happy to collect the mail and water the plants when Murphy and I were away. When she'd baked a pie or a batch of cookies she'd always given us some. All she'd wanted to do was become a friend, but I'd been too bored by her endless chatter, too self-involved to see how lonely she was.

Marsha beamed when I told her I'd take the job. "I knew you wouldn't let me down," she burbled. "I knew it. You were always good that way. Now they'll be safe." And she continued talking about her dogs as she reached back in her pocketbook, a scratched black leather job big enough to fit one of her Shih Tzus in, and took out a crumpled white envelope.

"I have three hundred dollars in here. I hope that's enough," she exclaimed worriedly.

"It's fine," I reassured her as I opened the envelope up and took out the money. The bills were all worn twenties. Cookie jar cash. I put the money back where it had come from and slid the envelope under a pile of catalogs. "Okay," I said, getting back to the business at hand. "You said you thought Merlin was dirty."

"I think he may be cheating on his taxes."

"What makes you say that?"

"Because of these. I took them out of his desk." And Marsha opened her bag again, put her hand in it, and began rummaging around. "Damn." She peered inside her bag. "Where are those papers? I know they're here." Her rummaging became more frantic. "They've got to be," she muttered as she dumped everything out of her bag onto my desk and began pawing through folded pieces of paper, blue exam books, old playbills, and a bank statement or two.

"Maybe you left them someplace," I finally suggested when it was apparent that wherever the papers where they weren't in her bag.

Marsha went through everything again. "No. I know they're in here."

"They're not," I pointed out. "Why don't you just calm down and think."

"You're right." Marsha swept everything back in her pocketbook. "Of course you're right." And she began gnawing anxiously on the inside of her lip.

Another moment, I remembered thinking, and she'd dissolve into a puddle of tears. "Maybe the papers are in your car," I suggested after a minute of silence had gone by. "Or maybe you left them at work."

Marsha clapped her hands. "Yes. Work. That's it. I cleaned my bag out right before fifth period." If this was clean, I would have hated to see it before, but of course I didn't say that. "The papers must be on my desk."

Well, at least we were making progress. "Do you want to go back and get them now?"

Marsha looked at me as if I was stupid. "Nobody is there." I'd forgotten. It was Good Friday. Schools had the day off.

"Then what about tomorrow?" I suggested.

She shook her head again. "School will be closed till Monday. And even if it wasn't, I couldn't get the papers. I won't be here. I'm going down to Jersey to see my mother in a little while. She hasn't been feeling well lately. Her arthritis is acting up again. I promised her I would drive down for a visit with Po and Pooh. We won't be back till Sunday." Marsha sighed. "I don't know what's wrong with me. I can't seem to get anything right anymore."

"You're just having a bad day," I said, trying to make her feel better.

Marsha gave a short bark of a laugh. "I'm having a bad year." She pulled the corners of her mouth up in a lousy imitation of a smile. "I'll come by on Monday afternoon with the papers. We can talk then, if it's okay with you."

I reached for another cigarette. "Hey, you're my client. Anything you want is fine with me. Within reason of course."

"Thanks again," Marsha said, and she got up to go. She was halfway to the door when she turned around and came back. "Promise me you won't let anything happen to Po and Pooh," she said.

"I promise," I told her. Given the circumstances what else could I say?

"Good." Marsha heaved a sigh of relief, turned around, and left.

It was the last time I saw her alive.

Chapter
2

Twenty minutes after Marsha left, Enid Garriques walked through the door. It was turning out to be a busy day after all.

"I've been expecting you," I told her as I watched her calibrate her smile to the requisite degree of social correctness.

"Well, it *is* that time again." For the past three years she'd come in to buy her husband a birthday present. "Any suggestions?" she asked after we'd exchanged pleasantries.

"He's been admiring the retic." And I pointed to the back where Monty, our reticulated python, was living.

Enid pursed her lips. The movement made her chin look even smaller. She was one of those short, dark women who have a brief moment of beauty and then quickly balloon into a fat, plain middle age. "I was thinking more along the lines of a salt water tank. He's been talking about starting one up."

I did diplomatic. "Either would make a nice present. How many gallons were you thinking about?"

"Fifty."

"That will run you some money." Not that she couldn't afford it.

"I don't mind." In the three years Enid had been coming in, she always bought her husband something big and expensive. I'd heard she'd bought her husband as well. "Why don't you show me what you have?" she asked while I wondered if the rumor was true.

I spent the next half an hour helping Enid put together an attractive package. We had just finished pricing the items when Tim came in. He'd been with the shop ever since Murphy had opened it and knew everything about reptiles there was to know.

"Mrs. Garriques is thinking about getting her husband a salt water tank," I told him.

"Nice choice," Tim said and moved off to the other side of the store.

It was better that way. Although Enid had never said it, she'd let it be known that she preferred doing business with me. I don't think she approved of Tim's shaved head, earrings, and tattoo.

Enid tapped her fingers on her expensive brown leather clutch. "Let me think about this for a while."

"Go right ahead." If past experience was any indication, she'd come back three or four more times before she bought anything.

"Think she'll get him the snake?" Tim asked after Enid left.

I shook my head. "She doesn't like snakes. I'm putting my money on the fish."

Tim reached down and scratched Pickles, the store cat, under his chin. "You know my mother never got me what I wanted when she bought me a present. She always got me the things she thought I should have."

"Mine, too."

"I wonder why people do that?"

"I don't know."

We were still discussing the subject when Manuel barged in. The kid's breath was coming out in ragged gasps. Drops of rain ran down his cheeks and off his chin. His shirt was plastered to his body. It looked as if he'd run all the way here. As he hurried toward me I noticed that he was wearing two different sneakers.

"The police chasing you?" Tim said.

Manuel shot him a dirty look. "You got no call to say that. None at all."

"So what's the matter?" I asked, intervening before an argument got started. The constant rain had made everyone cranky and out of sorts.

"The matter is there's a bat in my bedroom. I woke up and picked up my pants off the floor, and this thing flew out and started flapping around the room."

"So you ran?" Tim said.

Manuel flushed. "Hey. I could have been bit. It could have sucked out all my blood when I was asleep."

Tim pulled in his cheeks and did a bad Bela Lugosi imitation. "Come into my castle," he intoned, "and let me suck your blood. Give me a break."

Manuel gave Tim a venomous look. "They can do that. I seen it on a TV show."

"The bats you're talking about live in South America and attack farm animals," I gently informed him. "The ones we have here eat bugs."

Manuel scratched the tuft under his chin he called a goatee and looked down at the floor. "I don't care," he muttered. "I don't like them anyway. Can I hang out here till it goes away?"

"How about I get rid of it for you instead?"

Manuel brightened. "Will you?" he asked me.

"Yeah, sure," I replied. "Why not?"

Taking twenty minutes to catch the bat seemed infinitely preferable to having Tim and Manuel at each other's throats for the rest of the day.

Tim rubbed the top of his head. "This is the third bat sighting we've had this week."

"I know." When you run a pet shop people figure that you know everything there is to know about anything that crawls, slithers, trots, or flies. Both of the other calls had been equally panicky. Most people don't like bats, especially bats that are flying around their houses. I'd removed the bats from the other places as well. I'd done it partially as a favor to the people, who were my customers, but mostly because I'd felt sorry for the bats.

"Don't you think that's odd?"

"Yes I do."

"I wonder what's going on?"

"Why don't you call the zoo and see if they know something?" I suggested as I took my butterfly net out from underneath the counter and reached for my work gloves. They were made out of four layers of heavy cotton. Over the past week I'd become extremely fond of them. Bats are mild creatures, but any animal will bite if they're under enough stress; and since being pursued by a large-net-bearing human constitutes stress it seemed wise to take precautions, especially since there was a rabies alert in effect in Onondaga County. If I did get bitten, I'd have to take shots as a precautionary measure, and even though the series now consisted of seven shots in the arm instead of twenty-one in the belly, it was something I'd definitely like to avoid if at all possible.

"I'll be back soon," I told Tim as Manuel and I headed for the door.

The rain was still falling and Manuel and I dashed to the car. Another week or so of this and I'd get to see if my store, Noah's Ark, would live up to its name and float, I thought as I stepped in a puddle and cursed. Manuel stopped in front of my Checker cab. Murphy had found it when he was visiting a friend down in Brooklyn. It was one of the few nice things he'd ever done for me. When he'd bought it it had 50,000 miles on it. Now it had over 150,000. I loved it even though it was hard to start when the temperature got down below twenty, and the left signal light had a permanent short that no one could find, and the heater didn't always work. Oh, well. I guess the things we adore are never perfect.

Manuel sneezed. "This weather really sucks."

"Tell me about it," I replied as I opened the door and slid behind the wheel.

Manuel got in on the other side and closed his door. It didn't shut all the way.

"You have to slam it hard," I reminded him. "It sticks."

"I forgot." I heard a whomp. The car shook.

"Not that hard," I snapped as I turned the ignition key.

The motor grumbled and caught. I turned on the headlights and the windshield wipers and eased out of the lot. Ash was deserted. So were Pine and Oak. The only person I saw was a wino leaning against the wall of a scabby-looking liquor store called The House of Fine Wines, fine in this case meaning Thunderbird or Ripple.

A couple of minutes later we pulled up in front of Manuel's mom's place. It was a yellow, nondescript, run-down two-story colonial that housed the always changing parade of people that constituted Manuel's family. The porch sagged and the postage-size front yard was filled with discarded Big

Wheels, jump ropes, balls, and crumpled up Big Mac bags. Surprisingly no one was home. Usually the house was full of playing children and chattering adults.

"Where is everyone?" I asked Manuel as he hurriedly led me through a hallway cluttered with bikes and basketballs and sneakers.

"They went to Rochester to visit my great aunt," he explained as we stopped in front of what had once been the den and now served as a bedroom for Manuel and his two cousins.

"You mean they left you alone for the holiday?"

He shrugged. "I didn't want to go. I hate it there. Especially at Easter. There are all these little kids running around all over the place and we got to go to church and then we hafta to sit at this table and eat all this food."

"Sounds horrible. When do they bring out the bamboo splinters?"

Manuel narrowed his eyes. "Yeah, well, maybe you wouldn't like it so much if you were sitting there and everyone kept asking you what you were doing with your life."

"No, you're right I wouldn't," I replied softly, remembering a few of those meals myself. It was tough being in that position, especially when you didn't have an answer to give them.

"Okay then." Manuel swallowed and pointed to the door. "It's in there."

When I opened the door Manuel jumped back. Nothing flew out. I poked my head in. I didn't see anything flying around.

"The bat probably went to sleep," I told Manuel as I stepped inside.

I looked around. The room was so cluttered it was hard to move. Each wall had a bed pushed against it. The walls themselves were covered with posters of heavy metal groups. Piles of clothes and towels carpeted the floor. The room smelled of incense and pizza and socks that needed to be washed.

"Have you got him?" Manuel called out from the hallway two seconds later.

"I don't even see him." I put my net down on the floor and took a more careful look around the room.

"Where is he?"

I started poking around. "Probably burrowing in one of the dirty piles of clothes." This could take a while. The bats most commonly found around Syracuse are small enough to work their way into tiny cracks and crevices in the walls or along the baseboards. Fortunately this one hadn't been that ambitious. I found him in the first pile of laundry I looked through.

"Now, aren't you embarrassed?" I asked Manuel as I walked out of his room, bat in hand. I'd wrapped the animal up in a grungy Metallica T-shirt. I hadn't even needed my net. I'd just dropped the T-shirt over the animal and scooped him up.

"Not really."

"He's tiny. You want to see?" I asked, holding the bat out toward him.

"No." Manuel backed away from me. "What are you going to do with it?" he demanded once we were outside. The rain had gone down to a drizzle. "Kill it?"

"Hardly." I put the T-shirt under a scraggly laurel bush by the house and stood back. "I'm going to let it go." In a little while the bat would fly away. "Bats eat lots of insects. Some species eat as many as six hundred mosquitos an hour. So you can see why they're good to have around."

Manuel did not look impressed. "That's not what that guy says." He indicated a blue van parked down the street.

"Naturally that guy wouldn't." I'd seen the van around the neighborhood a fair amount in the last couple of months. Its sign, M & M Exterminators, painted on the side in big, white block letters and outlined in yellow was hard to miss. "Look at what he does for a living."

Manuel hitched up his shorts. "He said bats carry rabies."

I stepped around a puddle. "A few do. Most don't." A gust of wind blew rain drops down from the tree I was standing under. I wiped a few off my nose.

"He told my mother he could set up some kind of sound system in the attic of our house to make sure we never got any."

This was sounding more and more as if this guy was running a scam. "And how much did he want for this service?"

Manuel shrugged. "I don't know. Six, seven hundred, a thousand dollars."

I whistled. "That's a hell of a lot of money. I hope your mother didn't give him any."

"No, but Mrs. Chan did."

"Jesus," I growled. "That's ridiculous."

Manuel hitched up his pants. "Hey, the thing works. Mrs. Chan don't have no bats now."

"Did she have them before?" I demanded.

"Uh." Manuel started fidgeting. "I don't think so."

I began tapping my foot on the sidewalk. Stuff like this really made me angry. Not only was this guy killing things he had no business killing, but he was taking money from people who didn't have any to do it. I knew Mrs. Chan. She was a sweet forty-year-old woman with a husband on disability and a mildly retarded twelve-year-old daughter. The woman needed every cent she could get her hands on.

I was trying to decide whether I should get involved or just forget about it when the door on the driver's side of the M & M Exterminator's van opened and a skeletal-looking man dressed in black stepped out and strode up the path to the house in front. He had spiked platinum hair and dead white skin. With a scythe and a hooded cloak he could have done a perfect stand-in for the Grim Reaper. Maybe the man just scared the bats to death. As I watched he knocked on the door. A beach-ball-shaped woman dressed in purple answered. She listened for a minute, shook her head, and slammed the door in Grim Reaper's face. He was marching back toward his van as I got in my car.

I guess even Dr. Death can't win all the time.

Chapter
3

Business had been bad over the weekend and it wasn't doing
too much better on Monday. I was going over the accounts
and thinking about whether or not I should just close up the
shop and try and get my old reporting job back at the *Herald*
when Gregory Garriques came into the store. As he loped toward the counter I reflected he still moved like the ex-cop
and prizefighter he'd been rather than the high school principal he'd become.

"I don't think your wife is going to go for the snake," I told
him, putting my pen down.

"That's okay." He readjusted his tie. It was an expensive silk
paisley. Garriques was always well dressed. Despite the scars his
two years in the ring had inflicted on his face, he was a hand-
some man, and it was easy to see why Enid had wanted to
marry him. It was less easy to see why he had wanted to marry
her. "I didn't really think she would. So what is she getting me?"

I suppressed a smile. "I'm not telling you."

He cocked his head to one side. "You're not mad at me, are you?" he asked. "Is that why you're not talking?"

"Why should I be mad at you?" I asked, genuinely puzzled.

"Because of Marsha."

"Marsha?"

"Marsha Pennington," Garriques explained a little impatiently. Somehow I had the feeling he thought I should know what he was talking about. "It's just that we were chatting before the staff meeting on Thursday and your name came up," he continued.

Understanding finally dawned. "That's right. You're both at Wellington, aren't you?"

He gave an ironic clap and I countered with an equally ironic bow. What could I say? Sometimes I'm a little scattered.

"I didn't know you knew her," Garriques continued.

"She was my neighbor when I first came up to Syracuse."

"That's what she said." Garriques patted his tie. "Ordinarily I don't talk about personal matters with my staff, but she seemed so upset I asked her what the matter was." Even though he didn't say it, the slight furrow between his eyebrows told me he was sorry he had. "Everything just spilled out. Frankly I didn't know what to say, so when she asked me what I thought about her coming to see you I was relieved. I said it sounded like a good idea to me."

I couldn't help interrupting. "Excuse me, but aren't you the one who told me you didn't approve of amateurs mixing in police business?"

Garriques grinned. "I changed my mind. That's what makes me such a good administrator. I'm pragmatic." He leaned over the counter. He was close enough for me to smell the peppermint he was sucking on. "In fact, Marsha's one of the reasons I'm here."

"You're interested in her marital problems?"

He laughed. "No. I decided to follow her lead. I was hoping you could help me out with a problem of my own."

"And what's that?" Despite what Garriques had just said, I was surprised he was asking for my help.

He straightened back up. "One of my students is missing. I was hoping you could help me find her."

I reached for a cigarette. "Why don't you just go to the police?"

He fingered the scar on his chin. I wondered if he'd gotten it in the ring.

"Ordinarily I would," he replied.

"But?"

"It's not that simple." He hesitated for a minute. "She and her aunt are illegals."

I raised an eyebrow.

"From Mexico. Times being what they are, I'm afraid if I go to the cops and they find the kid they'll end up turning her and her aunt over to INS. Then they'll be deported." Garriques popped another mint into his mouth. "I guess you're wondering how I come into this?"

"The question crossed my mind." Pickles jumped on the counter and rubbed his head against my hand.

"The kid's aunt cleans house for my wife. Ana Torres has worked for us for the past two years. With Enid not being well . . ." His voice trailed off into some private well of sadness. Then he rallied. "Anyway, Ana is frantic and she's making Enid crazy, so I . . ."

"Thought of me."

"Yes. You seem to get along with the kids and you speak Spanish."

"Not very well."

"Well enough for this."

"True," I conceded. "What's the girl's name?"

"Estrella Torres."

"Pretty," I murmured. Then I lit my cigarette and took a puff. "What else makes you think I can help?"

"Her friends hang out around this side of town. I know you're on good terms with some of the kids that live around here. I was hoping you could talk to them and get a lead."

"You haven't talked to anyone?"

"I tried, but I haven't gotten anywhere. She's tight with a girl called Pam Tower. She wasn't at school today. I called her house and she's not there either. Who knows, maybe they've taken off together."

"How long has Estrella been gone?"

"Since Friday."

"That's not that long. She's probably staying at a friend's house."

Garriques sighed. "I know. But try telling Ana that. She called us at three in the morning on Friday. The poor woman's hysterical. My wife went over on Sunday to try and calm her down."

"Do you know why Estrella ran away?"

"Ana won't say, but my guess is they had another fight." Garriques shook his head. "Estrella is fifteen going on thirty."

"I understand," I said, thinking of Manuel and his friends. "What about the girl's parents?"

"What about them?"

"Are they around?"

"I don't know about the father, but I get the impression from what Ana says that the mother is a migrant laborer. My grandfather did that," Garriques said suddenly.

"Did what?"

"Worked as a bracero. He swam the river to get here. I guess maybe that's why I feel a responsibility." Garriques tapped his fingers on the counter. "I just thought if you could keep an eye out, maybe we could get to Estrella before she gets herself into even more trouble than she's already in."

I told him I would. I didn't mind making a few phone calls and keeping my eyes open. Plus the man *was* a good customer.

"Do you have a picture of her?"

"I have a copy of last year's yearbook in the trunk of my car. Will that do?"

I nodded. The man had come prepared.

"Good. I'll go out and get it."

He was back a moment later. The picture he showed me was of a round-faced, plain-looking girl staring sullenly out at the camera. Her bowl-cut hairstyle accentuated her big nose and plump cheeks. Definitely not the cute cheerleader type. I was willing to wager she wasn't having a good time in high school. Girls who look that way usually don't.

"She doesn't seem very happy," I observed.

Garriques studied the photograph before replying. "She doesn't, does she?"

"No." Of course, at that age I hadn't been very happy either. "Can I keep the book?"

"Of course." He closed it and handed it to me. "Thanks again," he said. "I really appreciate it." He took my hand in both of his and held it a moment longer than was necessary. He was about to say something else when he glanced at the clock on the wall. His eyes widened. "God, is that right?"

I told him that it was.

"I didn't realize it was so late. I've got to go."

"Meeting back at the school?"

"No. With a real estate agent."

"Are you selling your house?"

He shook his head. "No. Enid has some property in the

country—actually it's her mother's—but somehow I got put in charge of selling it." With that he strode across the floor and went out the door.

Why couldn't I have married someone like Garriques instead of someone like Murphy?

Because I'd been dumb that's why. Murphy was all flash and I'd fallen for the packaging. There should be a truth in advertising law concerning men.

I sighed and put the yearbook on the counter.

Tim looked up from sweeping the floor. "What's the matter?"

"Nothing." I didn't feel like explaining.

"By the way, I called the zoo about the bats," he said. I gave him a blank stare. "You asked me to, remember?"

That's right, I had. On Friday. My mind was definitely starting to go.

"I got this guy Remington on the phone," Tim continued as he moved behind the counter. "He said three sightings this time of year were pretty unusual."

"Did he say anything else?"

"Not really. I got the feeling he really didn't know that much. He did tell me, though, that the best source of information about bats in this area is a book called *Bats Are Our Friends* by a guy called Porter. Unfortunately it's hard to find. It was one of these self-published jobs. The guy put it out ten years ago."

"Has he written anything else?"

Tim shrugged. "I don't know. Remington said he dropped out of sight soon after the book came out. You want me to try and find out?"

"No. Don't bother. We've got too much other stuff to do to worry about this."

I stubbed out my cigarette and glanced at my watch. It was

later than I thought it was. Marsha should have been here an hour ago. Oh, well. Maybe she'd gotten held up. I went into the bird room and started cleaning cages. At six I called her house to see if she was coming. Nobody answered. I left a message on the machine and went back to work. She didn't return my call. I decided maybe she'd changed her mind about hiring me and she just didn't have the nerve to tell me.

I called the school at nine o'clock the next morning and was informed Mrs. Pennington hadn't come in. She hadn't come in on Monday either. I left a message telling her to call me and hung up. I twirled a lock of my hair around my finger while I thought. The most likely possibility was that Marsha was still down in New Jersey with her mother. She'd told me her mother wasn't well. Maybe she'd taken a turn for the worse. Maybe she was in the hospital. Nevertheless Marsha could still have called to let me know what was happening. Did she want my help or not? It would be nice to know because if she didn't, I'd have to return her money which meant I couldn't pay off the full balance of my account with Reptiles Inc. and The Pet Food Company. I didn't want to write the check if I didn't have enough money in my account. These days bouncing checks was an expensive proposition. I called her house again at four. This time a man picked up.

"Hello?" he said. I recognized the voice. It was Merlin, Marsha's husband. But I asked anyway just to make sure.

"Yes it is," he replied. "But whatever you're selling I don't want," he snapped.

"I'm not selling anything," I snapped back. "I'd like to speak to Marsha."

"Well, she's not here."

A twinge of unease shot through me. "Do you know where she is?"

"No, I don't. Why?"

"We were supposed to meet on Monday afternoon."

"Who is this anyway?" he demanded suspiciously.

"A colleague," I lied. The last thing I was going to do was tell him who I was or what Marsha and I were going to talk about.

"I wish you people would stop calling," Merlin whined. "I already told you I haven't seen her since she left for work Monday morning." He sounded about as upset as a man talking about getting rid of a wart on his hand. Then before I could ask anything else, he hung up.

I reached for a chocolate bar. This wasn't good. It wasn't good at all. I went through the rest of the day with a bad feeling in the pit of my stomach. I called Marsha's house again at nine o'clock before I left the store. Merlin answered. He didn't sound happy to hear from me. I asked if he'd spoken to Marsha's mother, and he said of course he had. When I asked for her number he sounded even more aggravated. What was I implying? he demanded.

"Nothing," I told him, which was of course ridiculous because I was implying plenty.

For a moment I thought he wasn't going to give the number to me, but he did along with the information that he'd already filed a missing person's report and that he was doing everything he could and he'd appreciate my butting out, or words to that effect.

As soon as Merlin hung up I dialed Marsha's mother's number and got a nurse with a heavy Jamaican accent who informed me that Mrs. Wise was sleeping now and that if this was the police again, I'd have to wait till she woke up.

"Actually I'm a friend of her daughter's," I told her as I lit a cigarette.

"I don't care if you're the Pope himself. I'm still not wakin' the poor dear up. After all she's been through she needs her rest."

"Perhaps you can help me then," I suggested, figuring I didn't have anything to lose.

"Maybe I can and maybe I can't," the nurse replied.

I suppressed a sigh. This lady wasn't giving anything away. "All I want to know is when Marsha left."

There was a short pause while she considered my question. "I guess there's no harm in that," the nurse finally allowed. "Mrs. Pennington left here the same time she always does— early Sunday morning."

This time I put the receiver down first. I was tired of getting hung up on.

I made some other calls over the next few days, but none of them panned out. Marsha had disappeared.

I was hoping she'd run away with a lover.

Or just run away.

But somehow I didn't think that was going to be the case.

And it wasn't.

Marsha surfaced on Thursday.

Or rather her body did. It was found floating in the LeMoyne Reservoir.

Chapter
4

Marsha Pennington's death was the lead item on the eleven o'clock news. It was probably on the earlier edition, too, but I'd missed it. According to the Channel Five anchorman her body had been found by two hooky-playing high school kids. They'd been fooling around when one of them had spotted what they thought was a log floating by the shore. Then they'd realized logs don't have hands, and they'd freaked and called the cops. Bet they won't be cutting classes for a while, I thought as the anchorman rustled his papers and stared straight at the camera.

"The police are investigating," he informed the audience, "and an autopsy to determine cause of death is planned."

No shit.

I clicked off the TV as the anchorman began discussing a proposed rise in city taxes and stared out the window. I felt bad and I didn't know why. Even though Marsha and I had been neighbors, we'd never been the best of friends. In fact, there had been many times when I thought that if I heard one more description of what her coworkers were wearing I'd strangle her. Slowly. I clicked the TV back on. Now the weatherman was saying something about rain. What else was new? I tried to pay attention, but I couldn't. I kept seeing an image of Marsha rummaging through her pocketbook looking for the papers she'd left behind superimposed on the screen. I got up and started pacing around the living room.

No matter what I told myself I couldn't shake the feeling that there was something I could have done to prevent Marsha Pennington's death. You want guilt, I thought sourly, call Robin Light. I ran on the stuff. Even though I didn't want to, I started thinking about my mother. Our relationship was the kind therapists make lots of money off of. She'd clawed her way up from a tenement in Hell's Kitchen to a co-op on Park Avenue. She'd wanted me to continue the climb by marrying rich, living on Fifth Avenue, and spending my afternoons at the country club with her and my stepfather. Of course I hadn't. I'd gone off to live with Murphy instead.

We'd had a big fight when I told her I was moving in with him. She'd called me a slut, an ungrateful loser who would never amount to anything, and I'd called her a money-grubbing social climber who'd screwed her way up to the top. She'd run out of the apartment and gotten hit by a car as she'd crossed Park Avenue. At the hospital, before she'd gone into surgery, she'd looked up at me and said, "This is your fault." My stepfather had added, "See what you did to your mother" as they'd wheeled her into the OR. I knew what they had said wasn't true, but a part of me felt as if it were. I guess I still do, especially when I see her limping along. She's had seven operations since the accident and she still doesn't walk right. I sighed and looked around. Suddenly the house seemed too quiet, too empty. I didn't want to stay in it anymore. I wanted to go where there were people and lights and Scotch, lots of Scotch. I looked at Zsa Zsa, who was now chewing on a piece of rawhide.

"Want a beer?" I asked her.

She wagged her stump.

"Good." I slipped on my shoes and started looking for her leash. It was time to go to Pete's.

Pete's is a neighborhood bar located over on Westcott Street. The place is strictly low rent in terms of decor, but it does have a good selection of beers, it's nearby, and most importantly my friend Connie tends bar there. I liked the other place she'd worked at better, but when she changed over I'd followed. Most times Pete's is overrun with Syracuse University students, but not tonight. Tonight no one was there except Connie and a couple down at the other end of the bar. Too bad. I could have used the distraction. I sat Zsa Zsa and myself as far away from the couple as possible on the off chance that they were conversationally inclined. Just because I wanted to listen to strangers talking didn't mean that I wanted to talk to strangers.

"Where is everyone?" I asked Connie as I ordered a shot of Black Label and a Samuel Adams.

"Spring break," she replied, reaching under the bar.

A moment later she set a saucer down in front of Zsa Zsa and poured a little of the Sam Adams into it. Then she plunked the rest of the bottle down in front of me and went off to get my Scotch. By the time she'd come back Zsa Zsa had lapped up the beer and was woofing for more. I fed her some pretzels instead. Too much beer is bad for a dog's kidneys.

Connie set my Scotch down in front of me and pointed to Zsa Zsa's collar. "Very elegant."

"I think so." It was jeweled—pearls in a rhinestone setting. The all rhinestone one had seemed too gaudy.

One of my neighbors had said I must have chosen Zsa Zsa because her fur color and my hair color matched. I never bothered to tell them that when I'd found her huddling under Mrs. Z.'s porch she'd been so dirty there was no way of telling her coat was red.

"I bet she's embarrassed," a gravelly voice behind me said. "I know I would be if I had to wear something like that."

I half turned. My friend George Sampson was standing there. As per usual I hadn't heard him come up. Despite his size, he was 6´4˝ and weighed almost three hundred pounds, George moved more quietly than anyone else I knew.

"Where'd you come from?" I asked. "I didn't see you at the bar."

George nodded toward the back. "I was talking to Sal."

"I see." Although Sal was ostensibly a cook, he spent most of his time making book out of the back room of the bar. "I thought you weren't going to do that kind of thing anymore."

George's eyes narrowed. "We were just talking," he informed me, his tone daring me to say something else. I guess he was still touchy about the four hundred he'd lost on The Final Four.

I sniggered. "About world affairs no doubt. I hear Sal's a real expert on NATO politics."

George's eyes narrowed even more. "Heard from Ken lately?"

"No, but I'm sure I will," I lied. I'd lent the guy five hundred dollars three months ago, and he'd skipped town without paying me back. It was still something I didn't like to discuss. Which George knew. Which of course was why he'd brought it up. I decided it was time to switch to a more neutral topic of conversation. "You look very elegant," I told him.

"Thanks. I'm trying." Mollified, George surveyed his khakis and the pink oxford cloth button-down shirt that emphasized the black sheen of his skin. Since he'd quit the police force and gone back to grad school for Medieval History, he'd abandoned his hightops, sweats and T-shirts and gone prep. I was still trying to get used to his new look. And his new persona. I had a feeling George was, too.

"Another Dos Equis?" Connie inquired.

George nodded and sat down next to me. Zsa Zsa wagged her stump by way of a hello and pawed at my hand to let me know she was ready for more beer.

"So how's campus life?" I asked as I poured a smidgen more into Zsa Zsa's saucer.

"It's okay," he answered, even though his face clearly said that it wasn't and he didn't want to talk about it. He started drumming his fingers on the counter. "So what's up with you?"

I took a sip of my Scotch and rolled it around my mouth for a few seconds before answering. Then I swallowed and told him about Marsha Pennington.

"Yeah," Connie said as she plunked George's beer down in front of him. "I heard about it on the news. Poor lady. She always looked as if someone kicked her in the teeth. Then last month she started looking happier. And now this." Connie gave a little shake of her head. "It just proves you should get as much as you can when you can."

"You knew her?" I asked, pointedly refraining from commenting on Connie's latest rational for sleeping with every guy she could.

"Sure." Connie ran a hand through her cropped, magenta-toned hair. "We get a whole crew from Wellington in here most Friday afternoons. She was always one of the ones that came early and stayed late."

"Was she in this past Friday?"

"You mean Good Friday?"

I nodded. Maybe she'd stopped off here after she'd been to see me.

"Sorry. I couldn't tell you. I had the day off." The door in back of me creaked open and then banged shut. As I half turned my head to see who had come in Connie leaned over and whispered, "These guys look like live ones. Talk to you later." And she plastered a big smile on her face and cruised toward the three men now sitting in the middle of the bar.

George took a pull on his Dos Equis. "She break up with whatshisname?"

"Ed. How'd you guess?"

"I was a policeman, remember? I know these things."

I laughed and fed Zsa Zsa a pretzel. I fed her another and ate one myself, and while I did it occurred to me I hadn't had dinner yet and that I was hungry. Then I wondered if Marsha had ever forgotten to eat. Somehow I didn't think so. I shook my head. For some reason I just couldn't seem to get that woman out of my mind.

I took another pretzel and began flicking the salt off it with my fingernail. "George," I said as I gathered the coarse grains up and licked them off my fingertip. "Do you know where the LeMoyne Reservoir is? I can't find it on the city map."

He took a sip of beer. "It's off Thompson Road. Why?"

"What's it like?"

He shrugged. "I don't know. I've never been there."

I ran my finger around the rim of the shot glass. "I wonder why Marsha was?"

"You said she was an ESL teacher at Wellington, right?" I nodded. "Maybe she was looking for one of her kids. I hear the reservoir's supposed to be a Wellington hangout."

"Maybe," I said, trying to picture Marsha doing something

like that. But I couldn't. When I'd known her she'd been a strictly paint-by-the-numbers sort of person, and something told me she hadn't changed.

"You don't sound convinced."

"I'm not." Suddenly I felt an overwhelming desire to see where Marsha had died. George's statement hadn't allayed the suspicions I'd been fighting since I'd heard the broadcast; it had inflamed them. "Exactly where on Thompson is the reservoir?" Obviously it was near or on the LeMoyne College campus, but try as I might I couldn't remember seeing any large or even small body of water in that area.

George drained his beer and threw a couple of dollars on the bar. "Come on. I'll show you." He laughed when he saw the expression on my face. "Don't look so surprised. I told you. Now that I'm not on the force I can afford to help you. I couldn't before. Not when I thought I was going to make it a career. It wouldn't have been right. But now that I'm not . . ." He let his voice drift off for a second, and I wondered if he regretted his decision. "And anyway," George continued before I could ask him, "I could use the break. I've been sitting in front of my computer screen for too long." He stood up and stretched. "I'm going home to change. I'll meet you back at your place in twenty minutes."

"Thanks."

He smiled. "I'm looking forward to this." Then he left.

I picked up Zsa Zsa and waved at Connie as I headed toward the door. Not that she noticed I was leaving. She was too busy showing off her cleavage and making goo-goo eyes at the three men. Personally I didn't think any of them looked real good, but Connie's standards were more elastic than mine.

I stopped off for gas and cigarettes on the way home. Then I walked Zsa Zsa around the block. I was just unlocking my door when George pulled up in his three-year-old Taurus.

"Ready?" he asked.

"Be right there." I put Zsa Zsa in the house and jumped in the car.

George took off as if he were driving at Watkins Glen. He'd driven fast when he'd been a cop and he drove fast now. As he squealed around the corner I glanced over. His face was expressionless as he concentrated on the road.

"So how's your paper going?" I asked. It was his first research paper and I knew he was nervous.

He frowned. "Badly."

"Why? What's the matter?"

"I don't know." We turned onto Thompson Road. "I just sit in front of the screen and stare. The words don't seem to want to come."

"Maybe you should start out with a pencil and paper. That always worked for me when I got stuck." George didn't say anything. "It's always hard in the beginning," I persisted, trying to be encouraging.

George leaned over and turned on the radio instead of answering. The subject of school was now obviously closed for discussion.

I shrugged and sat back and listened to the music. If he didn't want to talk, it was fine with me.

"This is it," George said ten minutes later. He was pointing at a "No Trespassing" sign.

I squinted into the dark. At first I didn't see anything and then I did. The entrance to the access road was narrow and half-hidden by the scrub trees on either side. I must have passed by it hundreds of times and never given it any thought.

"Here we go," George said as we turned in.

Suddenly it was pitch-black. George switched on the high beams. Trees loomed on either side of us. The spindly trunks looked sickly white in the headlights' glare. Some had their tops broken off while others leaned against one another. Tires and abandoned plastic gallon jugs were scattered on the ground. The road itself was curved and rutted. We bounced along it faster than I thought wise.

"Don't you think you should slow down?" I finally asked.

"I'm afraid we'll get stuck in the mud if I do," George answered. Then he cursed and turned the wheel.

I slid against the door. "What the hell?"

George pointed to a boulder lying in the middle of the road as we went up on the side of the path. I hit my head on the roof as we jounced up and down over God knows what. A moment later we were back on the path.

"Fun, hunh?" George asked, grinning.

The grin was infectious, and I couldn't help smiling with him as I rubbed the top of my head. A minute later the trail widened.

"This must be it," George said as a chain link fence festooned with crime scene tape came into view.

He stopped the car and we both jumped out. The tape fluttered fitfully in the wind. Another storm was moving in. I could feel the rain in the air. The open gate groaned as it swung slightly. I shivered even though the wind was warm. Mud sucked at my shoes as I walked over to the metal chain hanging from the latch. I picked it up and felt the sharp edge of the broken link.

"It's been cut," I said.

"Probably by a kid," George said. "It wouldn't take much."

"Just a bolt cutter," I agreed as we ducked under the tape and went inside the enclosure.

Budweiser cans, paper cups, and fast food take-out bags dotted the ground. This place was perfect for keg parties, I thought as I kicked at a potato chip bag, but try as I might I couldn't imagine someone like Marsha coming up here. Just the drive up that narrow road would be enough to deter her. But if she hadn't come on her own, that meant that someone had brought her here. I stepped over the downed part of a second fence as I thought about who it could be, but nobody, except maybe Merlin, came to mind. Then there was the timing, I thought as I examined the fence. Constructed of wooden slats and bailing wire, it looked as if it couldn't have kept a chicken out. Marsha had come to see me on Friday, we'd made an appointment to talk on Monday, but she'd disappeared before we could meet, and now she was dead. The timing was a little too coincidental for my taste, I decided as I walked down to the water's edge.

"Be careful," George warned as I stepped over a log. "I don't want to have to go and fish you out of here."

I peered down. "Somehow I don't think you'd have much trouble."

George joined me. He clicked his tongue against the roof of his mouth as he surveyed the scene. "You're right," he allowed. "I wouldn't."

The water was deep, but it wasn't very wide. Reservoir was an optimistic name. Pond was better. As I watched a few pieces of wood, dark shapes on a darker surface, floating by, it occurred to me that unless you were an infant or a cripple it would be extremely difficult to drown in a place like this. Even if you couldn't swim, most people could manage to doggie paddle to a side and pull themselves up onto land. What would it take? Five, six strokes at the most? So why hadn't Marsha been able to do it? What had prevented her?

The more I thought about it the more I became convinced of one thing.

Marsha's death wasn't an accident. You didn't come to a

place like this accidentally. Even if she had though, even if she'd tripped and fallen in, she could still have reached the other side. So why hadn't she?

Because she wanted to kill herself? The problem was people don't usually drown themselves. It's too painful a way to go. When your lungs start craving air you can't help but put your head back up. And Marsha could. It wasn't as if she'd swum out into the ocean and then couldn't get back to land. But she hadn't. Why? Obviously because she couldn't.

I wound a lock of my hair around my finger. All the signs pointed to one thing.

Marsha had been murdered.

Chapter
5

The autopsy results were announced two days later.

"I don't believe it," I said when I read them. I threw the paper down on the counter in disgust.

"Believe what?" Tim looked up from the rawhide bones he was sorting through.

"This." I jabbed at the *Herald Journal*. "It says here the ME is ruling Marsha's death a suicide."

I picked the newspaper up again and reread the story. According to the reporter, the ME had found water in Marsha's lungs. There'd been no sign of a struggle. Still, that didn't mean that someone couldn't have held her face in the water till she'd drowned. I studied the picture of Merlin the paper had run with the story. He was covering his face with his hands. Someone I didn't know was holding him up. The caption read, "Husband overcome with grief."

I lit a cigarette and stared at the picture some more. Did the cops know that Marsha and Merlin were involved in a messy divorce? Did they know that Marsha was ready to drop the dime on Merlin? Did they know she'd taken what I'd guess to be important papers from his office? I drummed my fingers against my thigh while I thought about what to do.

Normally I like to steer clear of the police. Ever since I was the chief suspect in a homicide case our relations have been somewhat less than cordial. Which was why I hadn't called them up when I'd read about Marsha's death. But it looked as if I should have. The ME might have brought in a different verdict if the cops had known about my meeting with Marsha. I took a deep breath and phoned the Public Safety Building. I got put on hold. Then I waited. Then I got disconnected. It was nice to know their phone system was as loused up as everything else in that place.

"Aren't you going to try again?" Tim asked as I hung up the receiver. I reached for my keys.

"No. I'm going to run down there." What the hell. The way things were going it looked as if it would be quicker to drive over than to try and get reconnected.

"Hey, pick me up a Big Mac on your way back," Tim yelled when I was halfway to the door.

I told him I would and left. I spent ten minutes driving downtown and another five looking for a legal parking spot, but I couldn't find one. You'd think in a city this size there'd be parking spots all over the place, but there never are. What we've got instead are lots of indoor garages with lousy security systems, a fact I can personally attest to since I was mugged in one a couple of years ago. Finally I gave up circling the block, parked in front of a hydrant, and got out. What was another ticket? I never paid them anyway.

I crossed the street and headed toward the PSB. The building's style was institutional bland. The new jail going up next to it would probably be the same. Why shouldn't it be? I thought as I pulled the heavy glass door open and went inside. Most of the new buildings built in this town, with a few exceptions, range from the pedestrian to the downright ugly.

Except for the officer on duty sitting in back of the inquiry desk and a woman trying to make a phone call the lobby was empty. Come to think of it, I've rarely seen it full. It took about five minutes, but I finally got the desk officer to call upstairs and have the detective in charge of the Marsha Pennington case come down and talk to me. If I had known who it was, I would have saved myself the aggravation and gone and gotten myself a cup of coffee.

"Christ," Connelly snorted when he saw me. "I might have known."

Great. Just the man I didn't want to talk to. I'd run into Connelly on the last case I'd worked on and we hadn't exactly gotten along. He thought I was arrogant and impetuous while I thought he was fat, lazy, and stupid. To be fair we both had a point—only I had more of one than he did. As I stood there watching him glowering at me I thought of the Pillsbury Dough Boy—the Pillsbury Dough Boy with a bad hair cut and a stained, brown polyester suit.

I threw out my arms in a parody of a greeting. "What? No hello? No 'how are you doing?' "

Connelly didn't smile. His lips didn't even twitch. That was another thing I admired about the man: his sense of humor. Instead he jerked his head toward the guy sitting behind the desk. "Crew said you had some information for me." I could tell he was really anxious to hear what I had to say.

"I do. But first tell me, did Marsha Pennington leave a note?" The *Herald* had said she hadn't, but I wanted to make sure.

"You read the local paper?" Connelly asked.

"Yes."

"Then you got your answer." He flicked a piece of food off

of his front tooth with his thumbnail. "Now say what you came to say because I've got a desk load of work waiting for me upstairs."

While he acted bored I told him about my conversation with Marsha on Friday.

"So?" Connelly said when I was done. "What's your point?"

"My point, if you'd been listening, is that I don't think Marsha Pennington committed suicide."

He began scraping the dirt under his right thumbnail out with his left one. "The ME says she did. You telling me you know more than the ME?"

"I'm telling you, you guys should take the time to explore some other possibilities," I replied, picturing the expression on Marsha's face when she was talking about her Shih Tzus.

Connelly rolled his eyes, and I jammed my hands in my pockets so I wouldn't be tempted to slug him. The man definitely does not bring out the best in me.

"What I'm telling you," I continued, even though I knew it was useless, "is that she wouldn't have done something that left her dogs in her husband's care and that even if she did want to kill herself, she'd never have gone to a spot like the LeMoyne Reservoir."

"You know this for a fact?"

"Yes," I lied, not that it mattered since Connelly was so obviously uninterested in anything I had to say.

"Then put it in writing and send it to the District Attorney. As far as I am concerned the case is closed. The lady killed herself. The ME said it. The death certificate is filled out that way. That's all I have to know. Frankly I don't give a fart about her dogs or her conversation with you or the papers you never saw, but if it makes you feel better, by all means send a letter."

"So it can go in a file?"

"I don't have time for this," Connelly said. "I've got too much to do." He turned and went toward the elevator.

I watched him go. His response didn't surprise me. I'd expected it. Well screw him. I'd write that letter to the DA all right. But first I'd get some more facts to put in it, enough so that the investigation would have to be reopened. Then if that didn't work, I'd take the story to the newspaper.

I stepped outside and stopped to light a cigarette. While I searched around in my bag for my lighter I thought about the grieving widower. I wondered how long he'd be grieving and if he had a little cutie on the side. He probably did. For some reason ugly men always seem to get good-looking girls. No. Whichever way I looked at it Marsha's death was just too damned convenient. She'd come to me wanting to get out of a bad marriage; then two days after that she "kills herself" in a place I'd wager anything she didn't know existed, and surprise, surprise the husband winds up with everything including the dogs, the one thing Marsha hadn't wanted him to have.

I put my hand to my mouth. With everything that was happening I'd forgotten all about my promise to take care of them. I went back in the lobby and used the pay phone on the far wall to call Merlin. He wasn't home. As I left the PSB and crossed the street to my car I decided I'd try again later. From what Marsha had said I was sure Merlin would be glad to have them off his hands. The next question of course was what to do with them? I thought about that while I got in the cab. Then I remembered a customer of mine, Nancy Sharen. Her toy poodle had died a couple of months ago, and she'd been talking about getting another one. Maybe she'd like a couple of Shih Tzus instead. I glanced at my watch. It was a little after four. The beauty salon Nancy worked at wasn't that far away. Maybe I could catch her there and get the matter resolved.

But she wasn't in. She'd stepped out to do an errand and I'd missed her by five minutes. I left a message with the receptionist and got back in my cab. If Nancy wanted the dogs, she could call me, and if not, I'd find someone else. I was running through my list of possible people as I drove toward Wellington. Marsha's papers, the ones she'd wanted me to see, were probably long gone by now, but it wouldn't hurt to ask. Maybe Garriques could tell me. I took a left at the next intersection and headed toward the school.

As I turned into the entrance a sign proclaimed, "Welcome to Wellington." Except for a couple of cars scattered here and there the parking lot was empty. Eight girls were clustered on the far side of the grassy verge watching what I took to be the boys' track team running sprints. Even from the distance I could hear their coach yelling at them to go faster. Half hidden behind a stunted plane tree four scrubby-looking kids were huddled in a side doorway smoking. The jocks, the cheerleaders, and the punks. I shook my head. Some things never change.

The school building was a rambling one-story affair of yellow brick. I parked right out in front and went inside. The hallway I was standing in had that slightly shabby air that comes from too much use and too little money. Announcements of club meetings and the coming school play were taped over the tile walls. I walked over and read them, wondering as I did what it would feel like to be that young again and if I could be, what I would do differently. Then I followed the arrows over to the main office. The door was closed. No one was inside. It looked as if everyone was gone for the day.

I lit a cigarette and walked back toward the main entrance. On the way out I heard voices rising and falling. I turned and followed them into a large room that turned out to be the cafeteria. Six kids were sitting at one of the tables. They stopped talking when I came in.

"Any of the office staff around?" I asked.

"They went home," a skinny boy with bad skin and a nose ring answered. "Why? What you want? You got a kid in trouble?"

"No. Actually I wanted to talk to them about Mrs. Pennington."

"What you want to talk about her for?" his friend asked. "She's dead."

A real comedian. "I know. I was a friend of hers."

"Oh." He seemed momentarily taken back at the news.

"Did any of you know her?" I inquired.

"I was in her study hall," the one I was talking to said. "She was okay."

"Yeah," his friend agreed. "Her classroom is right down the hall."

"Could you show me where?"

"Sure." He got up and took me there.

Marsha's classroom wasn't very big. In fact, I'd seen closets that were larger. A window would have helped. So would a ventilation fan, I thought as I sniffed the stale air. The desks were pushed so close together there was barely space to walk between them. From the looks of things ESL students didn't rate real high in the priority scale. Of course to be fair, up until recently there hadn't been a lot of immigrants coming to Syracuse either.

I sighed and walked over to Marsha's desk. The top was bare just as I knew it would be. I sat down at her desk and pulled out the middle drawer. Except for a box of paper clips it was empty. I closed it and was just about to try one of the side drawers when I heard a noise. I looked up expecting to see the kids that had shown me the classroom.

But I didn't.

Instead the doorway was filled by a large, glowering man.

Chapter
6

"What the hell are you doing?" he demanded, shifting the mop and pail he was holding from one hand to the other.

"People ask me that a lot," I cracked, doing funny.

He didn't laugh. Obviously he didn't think I was very amusing. But then I've been told lots of people don't.

"I asked what you're doing here?" the man repeated doggedly. "I'm the custodian and I have the right to know."

No kidding. I didn't think I was dealing with the head of the English Department here. But I didn't say that. Instead I explained as I studied him that I was looking for some papers that Mrs. Pennington had said she was leaving for me. He looked as if he was in his early forties. He was balding and pasty skinned with a broken nose that had never healed properly and the look of an ex-high school football player whose athletic career now consisted of watching the games with a remote in one hand and a bag of chips in the other.

"You're too late," he informed me when I was done. His

voice was deep and he had a slight lisp. The combination was somehow disconcerting.

"Why's that?" I asked, even though I had a pretty good idea what the answer was going to be.

"Because her husband came and took her belongings home a while ago," the custodian replied impatiently. He rattled his pail as a sign I was keeping him from his work.

I sighed. "Are you sure?" I guess I was hoping he'd say no, even though I knew he was going to say yes.

" 'Course I'm sure. I was here. He got a carton and threw everything inside and left." Even though he hadn't said it, the tone of the custodian's voice gave the impression that he found something wrong with Merlin's actions. "You know you ain't supposed to be in the building without a pass," he told me, working his mouth into a moue of distaste at my offense. "You're supposed to sign in at the office. It says so by the main entrance."

"There was no one in the office."

"Then you shouldn't have come in. Rules is rules," he continued. "The problem these days is that nobody thinks they apply to them."

If this man ever killed someone, I decided he'd do it by boring them to death. I rose. It was definitely time to go. "That's why we got those signs posted," the custodian added as I went by him just in case I hadn't gotten the message the first three times around.

I glanced at the laminated ID clipped to the neck band of his T-shirt as I passed. Brandon Funk. Maybe that explained everything. I mean with a name like that you didn't even have a fighting chance. For a while as I walked down the hall I could hear the swish of his mop behind me; then I turned the corner and the sound was gone. I passed the posters and the trophy case and was almost at the door when someone called my name. I turned. It was Garriques. He smiled and came toward me.

"I thought you were gone," I said.

"I wish. No, I'm always here late. Just ask Enid. She'll tell you. At length."

"Because I knocked on the office." I pointed down the hall. "But no one answered."

"That's Attendance. I'm around the corner. In fact," he continued, "I just got off the phone with Tim. I left a message for you about Estrella. You could have saved yourself a trip."

I didn't bother correcting his misconception. "What about Estrella?" I said instead.

"I think I might know where she is. One of my afternoon school kids just told me he saw her at a house on Deal this morning." Deal was a not very good street on the outskirts of downtown. "I thought maybe you could run down and see if she's living there. I'd go myself, but I have a math committee meeting in about twenty minutes."

"I guess I can manage that," I said with more enthusiasm than I felt. "Do you have the number?"

"No. But it's a green house in the middle of the block. It shouldn't be too hard to find. I really appreciate this." He turned to go.

"No problem. I was wondering if you could answer a quick question for me."

Garriques turned back. "Of course."

I explained about the papers.

He shook his head. "Sorry. Her husband came and got all her things on Friday. I probably shouldn't say this," Garriques said slowly, "but Marsha was right. There really is something sleazy about him." He shook his head. "If I'd known she was that depressed . . ."

"You thought she was depressed?"

"Upset would be a better word."

Neither of us spoke for a moment.

"It's tough on the kids when something like this happens," Garriques continued. He loosened his tie. "We make counseling services available. I don't know how much it helps, but at least it gives me the illusion that we're doing something. God, this has been a long day." He rubbed the bridge of his nose as if he could rub away his fatigue. "It makes me feel as if I'm back on the force."

"Tell me," I asked, thinking of George, "was it hard for you to give up being a cop?"

Garriques gave a short bark of laughter. "Hell no. It was one of the easiest things I've ever done." He nodded toward the school hallway and made a sweeping gesture with his arm. "At least here I feel I'm doing something positive. Out on the street I used to feel like I wasn't doing anything at all. You see stuff, lots of bad stuff. The pictures stay in your mind, and you feel like crap because you know the same things are going to happen tomorrow and the day after and the day after that and there's not a goddamned thing you can do about it. I knew I had to get out before I lost control and hurt someone."

He gave an embarrassed shake of his head. "Sorry. I didn't mean to run on like that." He looked at his watch. "God, I've got to get ready for my meeting." But he didn't leave. "Did you know," he continued, "that thirty percent of our ninth graders failed their Course One Regents last year. Thirty percent!"

"That's high."

"You're damn right it is and I want to find out why."

"I'm sure you will."

"You can bet on it." He slapped the small table next to him

for emphasis. Then he turned and marched back down the corridor.

I sure as hell wouldn't want to be one of the teachers he was about to meet with, I decided as I watched him turn the corner. He didn't look like he was a whole lot of fun to be around when he got annoyed.

All the kids, jocks and punks alike, had left by the time I stepped out of the school. They'd probably gone home to dinner. It had gotten colder since I'd been inside and the wind had picked up. The magnolia tree in front of the school was raining petals down on the grass below. A couple of robins and a sparrow or two were pecking around the tree's base looking for worms while a crow sat on one of the higher branches. The weatherman on the radio had been predicting snow showers for tonight. It looked as if he might be right. Spring in Syracuse was definitely a sometimes thing.

As I walked toward the parking lot I started thinking about how fast Merlin had been to claim Marsha's things. But maybe Merlin was just one of those efficient types, the kind that likes to tie up all the loose ends quickly. Not that he'd ever impressed me that way when I'd been living next to him. Then he couldn't even be bothered to take his garbage can back in from one week to the next. But hey! Maybe the man had changed. I'm told that people do. Sometimes I even believe it.

I opened the cab door, slid inside, and rested my head against the back of the seat. Suddenly I felt very tired. I sat there feeling sorry for Marsha and sorry for myself, and then I pulled myself together and drove over to Deal.

I found the house I was looking for quick enough. It was

the most rundown on the block, the kind that gets visits from police and social services on a regular basis. I knocked. A moment later a skinny, drugged-up white kid with dreds answered. His face fell when he saw me. Clearly he'd been expecting someone else.

"What you want?" he demanded.

I had to strain to understand him because he was slurring his words so badly. In another situation he might have turned hostile, but now he was too blitzed to do anything but take sips from his Forty and cling to the door frame for support.

"I'd like to speak to Estrella," I told him.

"She's not here." He swayed slightly. Then he turned to go. Clearly all he wanted to do was go back inside and sit down.

"Do you know when she's planning to return?" I asked quickly.

He just stared at me. I wondered if he understood what I was saying.

"Do you know when she's planning to return?" I repeated.

"You wouldn't happen to have a fiver, would you?" he mumbled. "I'm flat broke."

I sighed and gave him my pocket change, two dollars and fifty cents. I know lots of people would disapprove. They would call giving money to someone like this "enabling," and maybe it is; but I always figure there but for the grace of God, etc. etc. etc.

"Thanks," he muttered.

"Anytime." And he reached over and closed the door.

I didn't knock again. There didn't seem much point in it. I'd try again after work. Maybe I'd have better luck then.

I got back in the cab and drove off. Two blocks later I was lighting a cigarette and thinking about the rough time I'd given my mother when I spotted two girls walking on the other side of the street. I slowed down to get a better look.

From what I could see the girls looked as if they were the right age and size to be Estrella. Unfortunately both of them were platinum blondes. Not that that meant anything. Hair color is one of the easiest things a person can change.

I rolled down the window and stuck my head out. "Hey, Estrella," I yelled.

The shorter of the two girls glanced at me, then quickly turned away. I repeated her name.

She faced me again. Her lower lip was quivering. "You got the wrong person."

"I don't think so." Despite the bleached hair, the face was the same one that had stared out at me from the yearbook.

"I don't know what you're talking about."

"Your aunt is very worried."

Estrella increased her pace.

"So is the school."

It was the wrong thing to say. The kid was gone before I got the last word out of my mouth.

I cursed and pulled the cab over to the side and went after her. "I'm not a truant officer," I yelled at her back.

But she and her friend were halfway across the vacant lot by that time, and I don't think she heard. One thing I did know. For a chubby girl she sure moved fast. Of course, having all those burn scars on my legs didn't exactly help my speed either. When I got to the other side I saw the girls were already climbing through a broken window on the ground floor of the Colony Center. I groaned.

The Colony Center is a five-story deserted office building on the outskirts of what is referred to as downtown Syracuse. A white elephant, complete with graffiti, peeling paint, and smashed windows, the place has now been empty for at least ten years and stands there only because it is cheaper to leave it than to tear it down. Over time the police have boarded up the windows in an attempt to keep people out, but they keep getting in anyway. Witness Estrella and her friend.

As I hopped through the window they'd just gone through, I was betting that the girls didn't think I'd follow them in there, but they were wrong. When someone runs away from me, I have a tendency to go after them—especially when I'm in a pissy mood to begin with. For a moment I just stood there listening for footsteps, letting my eyes grow accustomed to the gloom and studying the room I'd entered.

Shafts of light from the broken window formed jagged patterns on the wall and floor. A desk not unlike the one I'd seen in Marsha's classroom sat across the far wall, only this one was covered with graffiti. A chair with its bottom ripped out stood nearby. The carpet on the floor was littered with torn papers, broken telephones, unraveled typewriter ribbons, and beer and soda cans. Near me lay a handful of pretty-colored pills.

I bent down and picked them up and thought about when I'd been taking stuff like this. What had Murphy called them? Candy for the mind. The capsules felt smooth. I let them run through my fingers. They plinked as they rained on the cardboard box below my hand. "Try this," he'd urge, and I'd take whatever he offered. In those days I'd wanted to share everything with him. Sometimes we'd take 'ludes, other times we'd take uppers, lid poppers we used to call them. Murphy knew a Hell's Angel out in Yonkers who mixed the stuff up in his kitchen. Once a month we'd hop onto Murphy's Harley and go out and buy some. I liked the rush. As an added benefit for the next three or four days my apartment would be spotless. Mostly, though, Murphy and I stuck to the basics— grass and hash. We'd smoked before we ate, before we went out, before we went to bed together. We'd had some good times. It was when I decided we should go respectable that I think our troubles began. I'd started losing control and that scared me. I figured I'd taken the drug thing as far as it could go. It was time to move on. Too bad Murphy hadn't agreed. I sighed and took a deep breath.

The smell of mildew and trash filled my nostrils. I banished the past from my mind and concentrated on the present. It was so quiet that I could hear myself exhaling. I leaned forward and listened. For about thirty seconds I heard nothing; then I heard footsteps up ahead of me. A muffled giggle. And another one. It didn't sound as if Estrella and her friend were that far away.

I tiptoed toward the sounds trying to avoid the garbage on the floor, but it was impossible. There was too much of it. Styrofoam and newspaper crackled and rustled underneath my feet. I cursed and continued on. The entrance to the next room was partially blocked by a table. I slipped between it and the door frame and went inside. It was darker than the room I'd been in, and I realized that the farther I went into the building, the darker it was going to get since there weren't any windows and the electricity had been shut off years ago.

In the dim light I could see another desk against the far wall. A stained mattress was perched on top of it. Someone had spray painted a giant anarchy sign on the wall. The other wall was riddled with bullet holes. Seeing them made me wonder about the wisdom of continuing on. I couldn't hear the girls anymore, and by now I'd made enough noise so they had to know I was in the building. This place was like a warren. If they wanted to hide, there was no way I could find them—especially since I didn't have a flashlight—and I didn't want to go tromping around and accidentally stumble on one of the building's residents. Call it brilliance, call it intuition, but something told me this would be a bad thing to do.

I cupped my hands. "Estrella!" I yelled, hoping I could say

something that would make her come out. "Your aunt is frantic. She just wants to talk to you." I waited for a response. There was none. I tried again. "She wants to make sure you're all right. Why don't you come talk to me? Maybe we can work something out." Nothing. Not that I had really expected otherwise. Estrella didn't strike me as the kind of girl who put a lot of stock in conversation.

By now the Colony Plaza was beginning to get to me. It was too quiet, too big, too empty, and too dark. I decided to do one more room, then call it quits and go back to the store and phone Garriques. I had too many other things to do to spend the rest of the day playing hide-and-seek with a high school runaway.

The third room was even dimmer than the other two had been. I hesitated for a moment before I stepped inside. It was so dark the only thing I could see was a few blurry shapes along the wall. I reached in my pocket, took out my lighter, and flicked it on.

I gasped.

My heart began racing.

A man was standing over by the far wall.

Two seconds later I realized the man was a coat rack. I put my hand over my mouth to stifle my giggle. God, I was really losing it. When my heart rate returned to normal I took another step in, more to prove to myself that I could do it than for any other reason.

"Come on, Estrella," I called. "I just want to talk to you. That's all. I promise."

Silence.

By now the flame from my lighter was beginning to burn my fingers. I took my thumb off the lever. Even I had to admit this was dumb. This was more than dumb. Estrella obviously wasn't going to talk to me, and there was no way I was going to find her in this place. It was time to leave.

I was turning to go when I heard a noise to the left of me. A sharp pain knifed across the back of my skull. Lights exploded in front of my eyes and I caught a flash of white hair.

Oh shit, I thought as a black curtain descended, this really is turning out to be a lousy day.

Chapter
7

The first thing I heard was the scurrying. I opened my left eye. All I saw were carpet fibers. Then a small, blurry shape came into view. When my vision cleared I realized it was a gray rat. He was sitting about a foot away cleaning his whiskers with his paws. I opened my right eye. The rat didn't move. Neither did I. Actually I wasn't sure if I could. For a while we just looked at each other. Then I got bored and tried lifting my head off the ground. Bad idea. Everything started swimming. I put it back down. Well, one thing was for sure, I thought as I closed my eyes again and waited for the dizziness to subside: Estrella definitely did not want to be found. I was wondering why when the blackness descended again.

The next time I opened my eyes two rats were staring at me. Jesus, I was probably the event of their week. Pretty soon they'd start selling tickets. A moment later another large rat joined them. Enough was enough. I yelled at them and they scampered underneath a large, white cardboard carton.

"And stay there," I added as I lifted my hand and began gingerly exploring the back of my head.

I felt a lump, but nothing wet. That was good. At least Estrella hadn't split my skull open. I wouldn't need stitches. She'd probably just given me a concussion. Thank God for small mercies. I tried raising my head again. This time all I got for my troubles was a blinding pain behind my eyes. Things were improving. I slowly worked myself into a sitting position. Then I stood up. The room started spinning. I leaned against a wall while I waited for the spinning to stop and consoled myself by thinking about what I was going to do to Estrella.

The more I thought about what the kid had done, the more I couldn't understand why she'd done it. It didn't make sense. Why knock me out like this? It must have been obvious I couldn't get her if she didn't want me to. Then the pain came back and I couldn't think at all.

After a few minutes the throbbing subsided and I straightened up. Maybe I'd figure out why Estrella had done what she had later, maybe I wouldn't, but right now it was time to get out of here. I took a deep breath, said goodbye to the rats, and started walking. As long as I went slow and didn't move my head the throbbing wasn't as bad as I thought it was going to be. When I reached the window I'd climbed through I brought my watch up to my face and took a look. Eight o'clock. I'd left the shop a little before four. I'd told Tim I'd be back between five and six-thirty. He wasn't going to be pleased.

And he wasn't.

"It's about time," Tim said as I walked through the door. "Cats N' Things has been calling all evening. There's a question about your order. I didn't know what to tell them. They'll be there till about eleven."

"I'll call tomorrow," I said as I headed toward the bathroom. By now I was feeling nauseous.

"What happened to you?" Tim asked as I got closer.

"It's a long story." Zsa Zsa jumped up and licked my hand.

George walked out of the back room. "What's a long story?" he asked. He stopped when he saw me and whistled. "You don't look too good."

"I know."

I stumbled to the bathroom and promptly threw up. It didn't make me feel any better. I turned the cold water on and splashed some on my face. Then I turned it off and inspected myself in the mirror. I had a streak of some sort of black stuff running down my hair and a bump the size of a goose egg growing on my forehead. I guess I must have hit the floor forehead first when I went down.

"So what happened?" George asked me when I came back out. He was leaning against the wall opposite the bathroom.

I told him about Estrella.

George shook his head in disgust at my stupidity. "Come on," he said. "I'm taking you to the hospital to get checked out."

I didn't argue. I didn't have the strength.

After two hours in the ER I was advised I had a mild concussion and was told to go home and go to bed. No kidding. My head was still throbbing when I woke up the next day, but it didn't feel as bad as it had the night before. The resident who'd seen me in the ER had told me to stay in bed and rest for the next couple of days, but I got up anyway, took four aspirin, walked Zsa Zsa and went to work. Unless I'm really sick—as in dying—I don't enjoy lying around.

I opened the store, made myself some coffee, and fed Zsa Zsa and Pickles. Then around nine, after I'd disposed of

Pickles's latest kill, I called Wellington and told Garriques what had happened. He was in the middle of a meeting so he couldn't really talk, but he made it clear from the few words he got out that he wasn't too happy. But whether he was unhappy with me or Estrella I couldn't tell, and frankly I was still feeling too lousy to care. I called Merlin next. He wasn't in so I left a message on his machine regarding the dogs. He never called back. After I attended Marsha's funeral I realized why.

The service took place the next day. I would have missed it if I hadn't seen the notice in the morning paper Tim brought in.

"That's interesting," I mused as I read through Marsha's obit.

"What?" Tim looked up from the roll of nickels he was emptying into the cash drawer.

"That Marsha was Jewish." I folded the paper and put it back down. Then I realized I should have known that. After all, her maiden name was Wise.

Tim didn't answer. He was too busy counting out the bills. Zsa Zsa came up and scratched at my leg with her front paws. I picked her up and rubbed her belly. She groaned in delight and licked the inside of my wrist. Then she spied Pickles coming around the corner, leapt out of my arms, and took off after the cat. I leaned against the counter and began constructing a rectangle with the day's mail.

"Still thinking about Marsha being Jewish?" Tim asked.

"No. I'm trying to decide whether or not I should go to the service."

He closed the drawer. "I thought you didn't go to things like that."

I picked up a circular and tapped my chin with it. "I don't," I said slowly. "They upset me too much. But in this case I'm going to make an exception."

"Why's that?"

"Because I want to talk to Merlin, and I think that this is going to be a good time to do it."

The Gottlieb Funeral Home was one of two Jewish funeral homes in the city of Syracuse. Originally located on Ashworth, the owner had recently moved his establishment to a large Victorian house near Dewitt after a mourner had inadvertently interrupted a drug deal taking place on the pavement outside and gotten shot. Gottlieb, who also ran a meat packing business, had reasoned that this kind of activity was bad for business. As he said, he didn't need to make clients. He had enough of those already.

I looked at my watch as I pulled off of East Genesee and followed the blacktop driveway around to the back of the building. It was nine-forty-five. According to the announcement in the paper, the funeral was scheduled for ten o'clock. Good. I had fifteen minutes to spare. I'd been afraid I was going to be late because I'd had to drop off a fifty-pound bag of dog food on my way over. I stubbed out my cigarette, parked the cab, got out, and walked over to the entrance.

The door, all lead glass and wood, gave off an impression of substance; but when I pulled it open it felt light, and I decided it must be one of those new, cheap, hollow ones—the kind you get at a do-it-yourself store like Hechinger's. A draft of cold air hit me as I stepped inside. Even though it was warm outside it was frigid in here. I guess I should have worn a long-sleeved shirt.

I rubbed my arms as I looked around. The vestibule walls

were paneled in oak and dotted with a few floral prints. A large dried flower arrangement sat in a porcelain vase. My feet sunk into the blue carpet. The pile on it was at least an inch thick if not more. I felt as if I'd just stepped into an exclusive men's club and was waiting for the maitre d' to seat me. Clearly this was no place for sobbing, maybe a single, tasteful tear rolling down the cheek but that was about it. The atmosphere in the place felt as phony as Marsha's suicide, and while I was thinking about why that was, a thin, pale-faced young man materialized at my elbow and guided me to the chapel.

The first eight rows in the plain white room were already filled. It looked as if Marsha had gotten a good turnout. People were chatting in the subdued way they often do when someone their own age dies. I immediately spotted Garriques sitting in the middle of the second row. I nodded to him as I walked by. He returned my gesture while continuing to talk to the woman sitting next to him. A few rows in back of Garriques I spied Brandon Funk, the school custodian I'd had the run-in with when I'd been looking for Marsha's papers. He looked ill at ease in his frayed gray suit and yellowed shirt, and I got the feeling he'd have been happier among his mops and pails. The only other person I recognized was an old neighbor of mine from the housing complex Marsha and I had lived in. Her name was Shirley Hinkel, and she'd been Marsha's best friend. I tried to catch her attention, but she was staring out the window and didn't turn around. As I slipped into the ninth row I made a note to talk to her after the service was over.

The man I was sitting next to looked familiar. A moment later I placed him. Don Eddison. He was a psychologist who ran Improvement Associates, one of those New Age centers that supposedly help you overcome your bad habits. There'd been an article about him in the local papers, and I'd briefly, very briefly, considered going to him to stop smoking.

"It's a shame, isn't it?" Eddison said, pointing to the gleaming cherry casket in the front of the room. His receding hairline served to accentuate the vees his eyebrows formed.

"Yes it is," I agreed.

He looked down at the prayer book he was holding. "I never thought she'd do anything like this," he murmured to himself. "I really never did."

I was just about to ask him why when Merlin came in and took his place in the first row. For all the expression his face contained he could have been wearing a latex mask. He was dressed in a cheap, ill-fitting navy blue suit and a white shirt with a too tight collar. His skin was even pastier than I remembered it being. He'd gotten fatter, too, and his jacket couldn't hide his bulging paunch. He was accompanied by a woman who looked as if she was his sister. There didn't seem to be anyone who came from Marsha's side of the family, but then I remembered her obituary had said she was an only child and that her father was deceased and her mother was ill. A moment later the Rabbi entered and the service began.

As he started reciting the prayers I found myself thinking back to Murphy's funeral, but all I could conjure up was a scene here and a face there. I couldn't remember most of the people who had attended or what they had said. My sharpest memory was of shaking a seemingly endless succession of hands. It had been warm in the building. Too warm. And there had been flowers everywhere, banks of them. Their smell had sucked the air out of the room. I'd thought I was going to faint. I rubbed my forehead and made myself listen to the Rabbi. By now he was halfway through his eulogy. He was talking about how much Marsha's husband would miss her and what a wonderful marriage they'd had. I was busy watching Merlin's face when Eddison snorted. I turned toward him.

"Obviously," he whispered, "the Rabbi didn't know them very well."

"Obviously," I agreed, wondering how well Eddison did.

A couple of minutes later the service ended and we trooped outside and got into our cars. From there we followed the hearse to Hillcrest Cemetery. It was a flat, utilitarian place full of squared-off rows of tombstones and young trees struggling to provide a little shade. The service was brief. Merlin stood at the foot of the grave with his hands folded while he listened to the Rabbi recite the prayer for the dead. Again his face betrayed nothing. It probably wouldn't either, I decided as I studied the flowering crab on the other side of the macadam path. The tree's limbs were gravid with unopened pink blossoms.

A moment later I noticed a white Caddy Eldorado with tinted windows pulling up beneath it. The driver rolled down the window and looked at us. Merlin glanced up. The two men's eyes locked. The color drained out of Merlin's face leaving him as pale as his dead wife. The man behind the wheel curved his thin lips into a scimitar of a smile and wiggled his fingers in a parody of a wave. Then he rolled up the window and drove off.

Merlin's color returned, but he kept plucking at the edges of his shirt cuffs and shifting his weight from one foot to another as if he couldn't wait to get away. I spent the rest of the service watching Merlin, and the drive over to the house wondering who the man in the Eldorado was and why Merlin was so scared of him. I was still wondering as I parked the car on the corner of Reynolds Avenue and walked down the block to Marsha's house.

It was one of those standard, nondescript colonials, the kind builders had put up en masse in the fifties when it looked as if America would grow forever. A couple of low-growing yews served as foundation plantings. A line of white and yellow crocuses stood in front of them. The grass was full of last winter's debris and needed to be raked—as did mine, I reflected as I walked up the path to the house. The door was ajar and I pushed it open and went inside.

The living room and the entrance hall were packed with people. I shouldered my way through them and went looking for Merlin. But I couldn't find him. He wasn't in the dining room or the kitchen. I walked down the hall. The door on the left was open. I took two steps inside.

Then I stopped.

My stomach lurched.

I couldn't believe what I was seeing. Or maybe it was just that I didn't want to.

Chapter
8

P o and Pooh were sitting on the mantel of the fireplace facing each other. Two bizarre bookends with nothing but air in between them. Someone, and I was pretty sure I knew who that someone was, had killed and stuffed them. The tips of their little pink tongues protruded between their teeth. One of the dogs was wearing a blue bandana around his neck while the other one was wearing red. Their fur looked stiff, as if it had a coat of shellac on it. As I drew closer I could smell a faint rancid odor. Looking at them made me want to cry, and then it made me very, very angry. I was just about to reach up a hand and touch what was left of Po's fur—a penance for things left undone—when I became aware of a movement behind me. I turned. It was Merlin. He'd lost the serious expression he'd assumed at the funeral home and replaced it with a jittery smile.

"Did it myself," he said, pointing at the two dogs. "They look almost alive, don't they?"

"They'd look better if they were."

Merlin's smile faded slightly. He ran his finger around the edge of his collar. "Hey," he protested, fanning his hands out in a gesture of denial, "I admit this is a little weird, but Marsha asked me to do it. Really," he told me when I raised an eyebrow. "It was in her note. Her dying wish. You got to honor someone's last request," he whined. "She said that this way I'd always have something to remember her by."

I folded my arms across my chest so I wouldn't be tempted to put my hands around his neck and squeeze. "I didn't think she'd left a note."

Merlin's smile flickered and went out as if it had been a candle I'd blown on. His face looked puddinglike in the dim indoor light. "Are you calling me a liar?" he demanded.

"Among other things." You had to give it to the man. Not much got by him.

Merlin's eyes got as dark and opaque as the black marbles in Po and Pooh's eye sockets. "Who the hell are you to come into my house on the day of my wife's funeral and say something like that?"

"I'm Robin Light."

Merlin's face collapsed in confusion. "You've changed. I didn't recognize you."

"Well it has been a while."

"Is Murphy here, too?"

"He died a couple of years ago."

"Oh." I watched Merlin fumble around for something to say. He finally came up with, "I guess that gives us something in common."

"Something," I said dryly before pointing to the dogs on the mantel. "Didn't you get my message about them?"

"Well I . . ." Merlin's voice faded off. Then he rallied. "What do you have to do with them?" he demanded.

"Marsha asked me to take care of them if anything happened to her."

"She never told me that."

"Well, she told me."

"When?"

"On the Friday before she died. She came to see me at the store."

"Store?"

"Noah's Ark. It's a pet store."

"I see," Merlin replied even though he clearly didn't. He gestured to the mantel. "You know those dogs always hated me. Marsha made sure of that. One of them bit me last month. Right here." He showed me his wrist. "I had to get a tetanus shot. Check with the doctor if you want."

I pushed a hank of hair off my face. "Is that why you couldn't wait to kill them? Because they bit you?"

"I got your message too late," Merlin muttered.

"You sure didn't waste any time, did you?"

"They would have died anyway. They wouldn't eat for me. I bet they wouldn't have eaten for you either," he said sullenly. "She cooked for them, you know. She made them steak and meat loaf. She made me TV dinners." Merlin the aggrieved husband.

I pointed to Po and Pooh. "So you were really being charitable when you did this?"

"Yeah. Yeah I was." Merlin brightened slightly at the new excuse I'd given him. "I didn't want them to suffer."

"Because you're such a nice guy."

"I am. Ask anybody."

"I don't have to. I remember what you were like."

Merlin flushed. "You can think what you want, but there ain't nothing illegal in what I done, and you can't say that there is. I know. I checked."

And he was right. There wasn't. That was one of the things that made this so galling. "Tell me," I said, taking a deep breath and changing the subject. "If you disliked them so much, why were you suing Marsha for custody?"

"For God's sake I didn't really want them. It was a negotiating strategy. All I wanted her to do was be reasonable. She wanted everything."

"So that's why she took the papers?"

"What papers?"

"The ones she took from your office."

"My office?" he scoffed. "She never went near my office."

"She did this time."

Merlin shrugged. "She was always getting crazy ideas in her head."

"Like what?"

"Nothing worth talking about."

"I see." I leaned forward. "Divorces can be so messy. Such a drain on finances."

"So?"

"Well, now you don't have that problem, do you?"

A vein started throbbing on the left side of Merlin's temple. "I don't like what you're implying." He gestured toward the door. "Get out of my house."

I ignored him and pointed to the dogs on the mantel. "Does seeing them turn you on? Did you hate Marsha so much that you had to kill the things she loved and stuff them and put them up there to gloat over?"

Merlin balled up his fists. He was taking a step toward me when Shirley Hinkel appeared at his side. I guess I'd been too engrossed to notice her entrance.

"What's the matter?" she asked Merlin, patting his arm as if she were a mother calming down an unruly child. "Are you all right? I was getting worried."

"No, I'm not all right," Merlin snapped. "I'm not all right at all." He stormed out the door.

Interesting. I was wondering if those two were seeing each other and if so for how long when Shirley rounded on me.

"That man has high blood pressure. What did you say to him to upset him like that?" she demanded.

"Not nearly enough." I reached for a cigarette.

A red flush crept over Shirley's face. The mottling made her look even more unattractive. When I'd last seen her Shirley had had a tight body and a ready smile, but time hadn't been kind to her either. She'd aged into a short, frizzy-haired woman with enormous melon-shaped breasts, a stomach that stuck out, and match stick legs.

She looked me over. "I remember you," she said slowly. "You used to live next door to Marsha."

I nodded. "You know Merlin well?"

"We're friends," she answered, but the slight hesitation in her voice told me, if I'd had any doubt, that they were a lot more than that.

"You were Marsha's friend, too, weren't you?"

"Yes." Shirley avoided my eyes.

"Her good friend," I said, rubbing the words in. "You two used to go to the movies together."

"That was a long time ago." Shirley smoothed down the navy blouse she was wearing as if she wanted to smooth her guilt away. "I know what you're thinking, but Marsha wasn't the easiest person to deal with. A lot of what happened between her and Merlin was really her own doing."

"How's that?"

"She was always snipping at him. Whatever he did wasn't

good enough." Shirley pursed her lips. "If you ask me, I don't think she wanted Merlin to succeed. I think she wanted him to fail. I think she liked being the one in control."

Funny but Marsha hadn't sounded as if she'd been in control when she'd been sitting in my office asking me to help her. She'd sounded as if she had no one to turn to and no place to go, but before I could say that Shirley began talking again.

"She was never there for him when he needed her," Shirley continued, reciting a litany she obviously knew by heart.

"But you're going to be?"

Shirley blushed.

I sighed. It was the same old tired story. There was nothing wrong with Merlin. Marsha just hadn't understood him. She hadn't handled him properly. But Shirley would. And Merlin would be eternally grateful, sweet, kind, and loving. I pointed to the mantel. "Don't those dogs say something to you?"

Shirley looked away from me again. "If she hadn't made such a fuss about them, he wouldn't feel the way he does. He wouldn't have done it."

"Do you really believe that?"

Her eyes told me that she didn't, but that she wanted to. Desperately. She gave me an angry look and scurried off into the living room where she could play Merlin's hostess and not think about the things I was suggesting. Oh, well. I lit my Camel. No matter what I said Shirley would believe what Shirley wanted to. I could understand that. It wasn't as if I hadn't done the same thing myself with Murphy. When we were living together in New York I'd kept telling myself everytime I found another book of matches with the name of a restaurant we hadn't been to that Murphy had been there on business or that he'd been there with his friends. I didn't want to hear the truth—that he was out with someone else—because it was too scary. I didn't know what I'd do without him, so I was careful to look the other way.

The same thing was true the last couple of years we'd been together. There'd been the phone calls taken in the other room, the "I'm going out for a walk" when Murphy had never walked half a block in his life if he could drive, the coming to bed after I did. But whenever I'd asked him what was going on he'd tell me I was crazy. "Everything's fine," he'd say. If I persisted, he'd get angry and storm out of the house. In the end I pretended everything was all right because I didn't know what else to do. I was afraid that if I pushed I'd lose Murphy. As it turned out I lost him anyway to the White Lady. I should have done something. At least then I could say to myself I'd tried.

But I couldn't say that to Shirley. She wasn't ready to listen. Instead I stood there smoking my Camel and studying the room I was standing in. The furnishings consisted of a "traditional" tweed sofa, two matching chairs and a wood and glass coffee table on which copies of *TV Guide* and *Reader's Digest* were neatly arranged. A large, dark wood desk stood against the far wall. On impulse I walked over and quickly rifled through the papers sitting on top of it. Maybe I'd get lucky. Maybe the papers I was looking for were here.

But a two-second search revealed that they weren't. The papers were mostly bills and circulars. I opened another drawer. This one was full of pens and pencils, a couple of writing tablets, and a box of tissues. An old picture of Marsha and her dogs lay off to the side. I took it out of the drawer and studied it.

The picture had been taken in this room. Marsha was sitting on the sofa. The two dogs were in her lap. She was laughing. How long ago had this been taken? A month? A year? And now everyone in the picture was dead. Somehow that didn't seem right. It didn't seem right at all. I slipped the picture in my backpack and glanced at Po and Pooh. They shouldn't be sitting there. It was obscene. Something should be done. Definitely.

Then I saw the can of lighter fluid sitting on the bookshelf and I knew what that something was.

I grabbed the can, walked over to the fireplace and moved the screen aside. A couple of pieces of crossed-over charred wood, leftovers from the winter, sat on the firebox floor. Good. I opened the damper and lit a piece of paper and held it underneath it. The paper flared. The chimney was drawing. I looked around. Nobody was in the hallway. Everyone was still chitchatting in the living room. I took the dogs off the mantel and put them on the two sticks of wood. Then I uncapped the lighter fluid, doused the Shih Tzus with it, took out my lighter, flicked it on, and held it to the fur. It went up with a whosh. The smell of burning shellac and hair and flesh filled the air.

I turned and quickly walked out of the room. The odor was traveling down the hall and through the house ahead of me. By the time I reached the living room I could smell the stench I'd created. Merlin, followed by several other people, went running by me as I headed for the front door. It was definitely time to leave.

I heard Merlin curse as I stepped outside.

I walked a little faster. I didn't want to be around after Merlin put the fire out. He was stupid, but he wasn't that stupid. As I went down the front porch steps I smiled, thinking about how angry he was going to be. I'd almost reached the sidewalk when Garriques came out of nowhere and touched my shoulder.

"We have to talk," he said.

Chapter
9

"Yes we do," I agreed. A gust of damp wind tugged at the hems of my silk trousers and blew strands of hair over my eyes. I thought it brought a whiff of smoke from Merlin's house, but that was probably my imagination.

Garriques loosened his tie and unbuttoned the top button of his shirt. He looked exhausted in the late morning light. The funeral seemed to have taken his last bit of energy. "I'm sorry about what happened with Estrella. Are you feeling better?"

"Much."

"You sound better."

"It's lucky I have a hard head," I said. "Come walk me to my car." I turned and headed down the block. If Merlin wanted me, he'd have to come and get me.

Garriques nodded and fell in step.

For a moment we walked in silence. I watched the gray clouds floating in, covering up the blue. The temperature had dropped at least fifteen degrees in the half hour I'd been inside Merlin's house. We were in for a storm.

"You should have told me Estrella was dangerous." I skirted a bike some kid had left lying across the pavement. "I would have acted differently if I'd known."

"She's not."

"Really?" I pointed to the back of my skull. "Then what do you call someone who does this?"

"Scared. Angry."

"What is she scared and angry about?"

He shrugged. "The same thing most fifteen-year-olds are. Life."

I made a retching noise. "Please spare me the sociological crap. Most fifteen-year-olds don't hit someone over the head."

"She probably felt trapped. You were coming after her . . ."

"She could have just kept running. She didn't have to stop and ambush me."

Garriques bit his lower lip. "Maybe her friend hit you. Maybe it wasn't Estrella."

I stopped in front of my cab. "Why are you making excuses for her?"

"I'm not," he protested.

"Oh, but you are."

He sighed and adjusted the cuffs on his shirt. "You know, when I was a kid I got into a lot of trouble, serious trouble, the kind they put you away for. If it wasn't for my high school principal, I'd probably be in jail right now. Or dead. He went out on a limb to save me. He actually lied to the cops and told them I was in class when I wasn't. When I asked him why he did it, he said, 'because everyone deserves more than one chance.' I've never forgotten that."

I reached for a cigarette and lit it. "Well, I can appreciate the sentiment and I think what you're trying to do is very noble, but when you bring someone else into the picture and ask them to do you a favor, I think you owe it to them to tell them the truth."

"You're right. I made a mistake." A car drove by. Garriques watched it turn the corner before he spoke. "I'd like you to keep looking for her."

"I don't think I want to do that."

Garriques studied his shoes. They were highly polished. "I guess I can't blame you." I turned to go. "Maybe if you heard the whole story . . ."

I turned back. "You mean there's more?"

"Yes." Garriques glanced at his watch. It looked as if it was a Movado. I wondered if it was a knock off or the genuine article. "I have a meeting with the real estate agent in ten minutes, and then I have two meetings and three parent teacher conferences back at school. Why don't I drop by the store later? We can talk then. Maybe I can make you change your mind."

"I doubt it, but I'm willing to listen."

"That's all I can ask." Garriques scratched the bump on his nose. "Listen, I don't suppose you know anyone who wants to buy an old house out in the country?"

"If your real estate agent isn't doing a good job, maybe you should switch."

"I can't." Garriques smiled ruefully. "The agent's family." He started back to his car.

As I got into my cab and pulled out into the street I wondered what it was Garriques was going to tell me; but then after about five blocks my mind started drifting back toward Marsha and Merlin and Shirley, and I started thinking about how long Shirley had been seeing Merlin and whether or not

Marsha had known about it and if so had that been the impetus for everything that had followed. And then I thought about what Merlin had done to the Shih Tzus. The more I thought about it, the angrier I got. By the time I turned into the store parking lot, I'd decided that one way or another Merlin was going to pay for what he'd done to his wife.

Zsa Zsa came running toward me as I walked through the door. I bent down and scratched behind her ears. Then I picked her up and kissed her. "Nobody's going to stuff you," I crooned.

Tim looked up from the discus he was feeding. "What is with you?" he asked. "You're getting weirder by the second."

"You think?" I told him about my morning.

"Jesus," he said when I was done. "Jesus. I never heard of anything like that."

"Me either." Zsa Zsa started wiggling and I put her down. I suppose there's only so much affection anyone can take at once. "So how did we do this morning?" I asked, changing the subject. "Any sales?"

"A few." Tim capped the fish food and put it on the shelf underneath the aquarium. "Little Mike came in about ten. He bought the last two frilled lizards and a couple of anoles for his kids."

"Good." I made a mental note to order more. We'd really done well with them in the past couple of months.

"And Joe O'Malley called."

"God, what did he want?"

"He wanted to know if we could get him a thorny lizard."

"Did you explain why that wasn't a good idea?" I asked as I went over to the counter and began leafing through the day's mail. Trust Joe to pick a difficult keeper. The man had a positive genius for wanting species that were almost impossible to keep alive and well in captivity.

"Yeah, when I told him that thornies eat about a thousand ants per meal, he decided on a gecko instead. I said I'd save him the large tokay out in the back. He's going to come by this afternoon and pick it up."

"Fine." I opened up the telephone bill and scanned it. It was one hundred and fifty dollars. Which was par for the course. The only problem was that I couldn't pay all of it. I was standing there, staring at it, and trying to decide how much I could get away with writing the check for, when Tim came around behind me.

"We need some more pinkies; we're running low," he informed me. "And Carolyn dropped off ten dwarf Russian hamsters—I took the money out of the drawer to pay her, and there's something else. A Mrs. Breen called up and wanted to know if we could come over and get a bat out of her bedroom. I said we would."

"Did you now? And who is Mrs. Breen?"

"A friend of Mrs. Rodriguez."

"Great." I threw the circulars into the garbage can and picked up the bills. "Now we're getting requests from people who aren't even our customers! If this keeps up, we should start charging people."

"I told her we were," Tim said.

I smiled. "How much?"

"Thirty-five bucks. It's not a lot, but I figure every little bit counts."

"True. Especially these days."

Tim twirled one of his earrings. "Do you want to go or should I?"

"You. I have some catching up to do."

Tim saluted, gathered up the net and gloves and took off.

I spent the rest of the afternoon setting up a cage for the

two ball pythons we were getting in the next day, calling in my orders to my suppliers, and fending off a salesman who wanted to sell me sanitary napkins specifically designed for bitches in heat. I'd just hung up the phone when Rabbit, one of Manuel's more moronic friends, came in.

"Look what I just got," he said. Then before I could tell him I didn't want to see what it was he opened the brown paper bag he was carrying and dumped a diamondback rattler onto the counter.

I gasped and jumped back. For a second the snake just lay there. Then it slithered across the counter and fell off the edge onto the floor. It lay there furiously shaking its rattles.

"Keep away," I warned Rabbit as he came over to take a look.

"It ain't coiled," he said.

"So what?" I reached under the counter for my collecting stick. It wasn't there. I made a mental note to find out who had taken it and strangle him.

"I thought they couldn't bite if they ain't coiled."

"Rattlers can strike from any position," I informed him as I desperately rummaged for something I could use. One thing I did know was that this snake wasn't disappearing into a crack in the floor—at least not if I could help it. That had happened to me a couple of years ago and it wasn't going to happen again. Finally I grabbed a dust rag and a shovel I used for a pooper scooper. They weren't the best implements for this job, but they were better than nothing. "Open the bag," I ordered.

"Why? What you gonna do?"

"Watch." I threw the rag over the rattler's head, scooped him up with the shovel and plopped him into the bag he'd come in. I grabbed the sack and rolled down the top. Thank God he'd been small.

Rabbit wet his lips with the tip of his tongue. "That wasn't too bright of me, hunh?" he said, shuffling his feet from side to side.

My hands were shaking. I reached for a cigarette to steady my nerves and tried not to think about the last time something like this had happened. Someone had died then. "I suppose that's one way of putting it," I said as calmly as I could.

"T.J. said if it bit anyone, it wouldn't be so bad."

"And you believed him, a guy that sells uppers to his own sister?"

Rabbit hitched up his pants. "Yeah. Well, maybe you got a point," he conceded. He cleared his throat. "Ah . . . what would have happened if he'd snagged someone?"

"That person would have to go to the hospital."

"Would they get really sick?"

"They could."

"How about dying?"

I lit my Camel and took a puff. "If someone is young or old or sick, that's a distinct possibility." I pointed my cigarette at him. "You'd just better thank your lucky stars that Zsa Zsa and Pickles weren't around. Because if they had gotten bitten, I can tell you now you'd be real sorry."

Rabbit swallowed. "Listen, maybe you'd like to keep him."

"The rattler?"

Rabbit nodded.

"Yeah, I can do that." Actually I'd been going to suggest it.

Rabbit pulled on his ponytail. "I gave T.J. seventy bucks for him."

"You made a bad deal."

"See," Rabbit explained, anxious for me to understand, "I was gonna milk the rattler for the venom and sell it. T.J. said I could make a lot of money doing that."

I rolled my eyes. "Jesus. I don't know who's worse: you for believing him or him for telling you something like that."

Rabbit started shuffling his feet again. "I don't suppose there's a chance . . . you'd . . . you know . . . give me the seventy bucks for it?"

"Are you nuts? It's not as if I can sell it." Actually I could, but I wasn't going to. "I'm doing you a favor taking the snake off your hands." You and everyone you know, I added silently.

Rabbit sighed. "I guess maybe you're right. It's just that I needed that money for my rent."

"You live at home."

"I still pay my mom something."

I laughed. "Nice try. However I will give you twenty if . . ."

"If what?" Rabbit asked eagerly.

"You can get me some information."

"Okay."

"It's about a girl named Estrella Torres." I had Garriques's version of her. I wanted another view before I met with him again.

"What about her?"

"You know her?"

"Yeah I know her. She's a burnout."

"Burnout?"

"Yeah," Rabbit replied. "A burnout. You know. Someone who does too much dope."

"What else does she do?"

Rabbit shrugged. "A little dealing. Nothing big. Just enough to pay for herself."

"Do you know where she's staying?"

Rabbit shook his head. "I heard she ran away."

"She did. Do you know where she went?"

"Why? Is she in trouble?"

"No. Her aunt wants to speak to her. She's really worried."

"That's cool. Will you give me that twenty if I find out?"

I nodded.

"Then I can manage it." Rabbit indicated the bag. "So what you gonna do with my snake?"

"I'll see if the zoo wants it. If they don't, I'll probably take it out to the woods somewhere and let it go."

Rabbit leaned forward. "Can I come?" he asked eagerly, sounding like the eight-year-old boy in the sixteen-year-old body he really was. "I like the woods."

I was just about to answer when the front door opened and Garriques walked in. Rabbit took a look and his mouth dropped opened. If he could have disappeared, he would have.

"Ah, Mr. Randazzo," Garriques said to Rabbit in his most jovial voice, the kind of voice I remember my principal using when he'd caught me sneaking out of the building. "How's the leg?"

"The leg. The leg," Rabbit stuttered. "It's getting better." He turned and limped across the floor.

Funny, but he hadn't limped when he'd come in.

"I thought it was your right leg that got hurt," Garriques observed as Rabbit passed him.

"No. No, it was my left," Rabbit muttered as he hurried toward the door.

"Ah. I could have sworn your mother said you'd injured the right one in the note she wrote, but I could be wrong. So I'll see you in school tomorrow," Garriques said as Rabbit took hold of the door knob and pulled it open.

"Right," Rabbit assured him. "Absolutely." He practically bolted out the door.

Garriques shook his head as the door slammed shut. "God only knows where that one is going to end up."

"Maybe he'll surprise you."

"I don't think so." Garriques's eyes took on the bleak look that people get when they've been disappointed too many times.

I was about to remind him of what he'd said earlier about giving everyone more than one chance when I heard a rustling noise. The sides of the brown bag were moving. The snake was getting restless.

"What's in there?" Garriques asked.

"A rattler. Rabbit brought him in."

"Figures," Garriques said. "Can I see him?"

"Sure. Why not?" I leaned down brought up a cracked ten-gallon aquarium that Tim had taken in trade for a gerbil and dumped the rattler in it.

Garriques looked at him longingly as I secured the screen cover. "I'd love to have something like that, but Enid would never let me."

"I'd say she has a point."

"I'm not so sure. There's something to be said for living with death. It makes you appreciate life more."

"How philosophical." As I've gotten older my tolerance for platitudes has plummeted.

Garriques ignored my sarcasm and walked over to Monty's cage. "I think my wife's coming around on this one, though," he said, gazing down at the retic.

"Good." As far as I knew Enid was still buying him the salt water aquarium, but I didn't say that. It wasn't my place to.

He ran a finger along the top of the aquarium, then turned away. "I guess it's time we talked," he said.

"I think so." We went into my office and sat down.

Garriques began neatening the pile of circulars sitting on the edge of my desk. "The thing with Estrella—it's complicated," he said. Then he went back to playing with my mail.

Zsa Zsa ran in, jumped on my lap, stole a dog biscuit off the desk and ran away. A minute passed. And another.

"Look," I finally told him, "I have lots of things to do and I'm sure you do as well. If you want to talk to me fine, if you don't fine. But let's not waste each other's time."

"You're right." Garriques straightened up. "You're absolutely right."

"What does that mean?"

Garriques studied my ceiling. "The truth is," he said to a crack in the plaster, "I made up that story about Estrella. Everything I told you was a lie."

Chapter
10

I put my elbows on my desk, interlaced my fingers, and leaned my chin on the platform I'd created. "Let me see if I've got this straight," I said slowly. "First you were lying to me, but now you're going to tell me the truth?"

"That's right," Garriques muttered, a slight flush rising on his cheeks.

"Why should I believe you this time?"

Garriques reluctantly pulled his gaze away from the ceiling fan and fixed it on me. "No reason, really. You're going to have to take my word, and I know that's not very good at this moment." He stopped talking and looked at me as though he expected me to disagree with him, to tell him that I would believe anything he told me, but I didn't and I wasn't going to. "It's just," he finally went on when I didn't say anything, "that this mess with Estrella is . . . stupid. And I don't usually make stupid mistakes."

I unhooked my fingers and sat back. "I just bet you don't."

Garriques had had a fast rise from high school teacher to high school principal and was looking—and this I knew because he'd told me—to become a major player in the education game. To him, Syracuse was just a pit stop on his way to New York, Chicago, or maybe even D.C.

Garriques twisted his watch band around. "Of course, you know about Enid's illness?" he asked me.

"Yes. She has diabetes."

Again the twisting. At this rate he was going to wear a groove in his wrist. "Did you also know she has to give herself shots twice a day?"

"That's too bad." I extracted a cigarette from the pack on the desk and lit it with my lighter. "Forgive me. I don't mean to be nasty or anything, but what does Enid's illness have to do with what we're discussing?" I inquired after I'd taken a puff.

"It makes her depressed, really moody. Things that you and I might not take that seriously, she does."

I tapped my fingernails on my desk. "So what is this thing that you did that your wife is going to take seriously?"

Garriques ran his finger around the inside of his shirt collar. "God, do I feel like a jerk."

I asked the obvious question. "Did you go to bed with Estrella, is that what this is all about?"

Garriques's eyes widened in shock. "No, absolutely not. It's nothing like that at all. You have to believe that."

Looking at his face I did. The expressions of surprise and horror were genuine. Either that or he was turning in a stellar performance. "Then what is this all about?"

"It's simple, really. Estrella stole something from my house and I need to get it back."

"If it's so simple, why don't you go to the police?"

"Because then my wife would know."

"So then, Estrella's not really an illegal immigrant? That

part about coming to me so the police wouldn't find out was all bullshit?"

"It wasn't," Garriques protested. "She doesn't have papers. That part's true."

It was reassuring to know that something Garriques had said was. I sat back. "Okay. What did she take?"

"My wife's diamond brooch and earrings."

I raised an eyebrow.

"They're not that valuable in the monetary sense," Garriques said, quickly answering my unspoken question, "but the jewelry has enormous sentimental value to my wife. The pieces have been in the family for years. My wife is very attached to them. Now that her mother is selling the old family house they're all she has left of the past."

"And?" I prodded when Garriques didn't say anything else.

"Yes. Well." He cleared his throat. "Recently Enid and I have been having some . . . some problems . . . about different things." I could tell from the way one of his hands was kneading the other that he was upset, but I couldn't figure out whether he was upset about his marital difficulties or about having to talk about them. "I'm sure you know how that goes," he added.

"Yes, I do." I started thinking about how amazing it was Murphy and I had stayed married as long as we had. Looking back I realize that sex and drugs were the glue that bound us. We didn't have the same tastes. We didn't like each other's friends or families, and they, for the most part, returned the favor. We couldn't even agree on where we wanted to live. When we'd decided to leave New York I'd wanted to move to Boston, but Murphy had wanted to come to Syracuse. As per usual I'd let him sweet talk me into moving upstate, even though I knew I'd hate it. And I was right. I did. And that was my problem. I never said no. Then when something went wrong I'd blamed it on Murphy. He'd get pissed and we were off. The only time we were happy with each other was when we were in bed together. At least we'd done that well. I was thinking about how well when Garriques took a deep breath. I turned my attention back to him reluctantly.

"Anyway," he was saying, "one of the areas we've disagreed about is my students."

"Your students? I don't understand."

Garriques's face became more animated. "You see," he said, putting his hands on the edge of my desk and leaning forward, "I used to make it a policy to have some of the students, the ones I thought I could help, over to my house once in a while. We'd hang out, watch a movie, that kind of stuff, but my wife didn't like having them around. They bothered her. She kept on saying they were too loud, that they scared her, that she was afraid they were going to steal something. So finally I promised I wouldn't do it anymore. And I haven't."

"Except for Estrella," I guessed.

"Yes, except for Estrella." Garriques looked glum.

"Why her?" I'd asked before and hadn't gotten a very good answer. Maybe this time I would.

"I don't know." He started on his watch band again. "Maybe it was because she has so much potential. She's so bright that I just couldn't stand the thought of letting her fall away like everyone else." Garriques continued, "I thought if I got involved from the beginning before she dropped out of school and got pregnant, maybe I could stop the process. I went out of my way to take an interest in Estrella, to make sure that she came to class, to talk to her, to try and help her solve her problems. And it was working. She started coming around."

I interrupted. "Are you aware that she uses a lot of grass?"

Garriques made an exasperated noise. "Of course I'm aware. My job is to know things like that. But she'd cut back. She seemed more cheerful, less sullen. Recently she'd begun dropping in my office to talk. Have you seen the map I have mounted on my wall?"

I shook my head. "I've never been in your office."

"That's right." Garriques gave a deprecating laugh. "You haven't. I don't know where my mind is lately."

"The map," I reminded him.

"Yes, the map. It's a map of Transylvania done in the 1500s. Estrella found it fascinating. In fact, all the kids do. And when she learned that I have other old maps like that in my house she wanted to see them."

"So you took her home," I said, stating the inevitable.

Garriques corrected me. "Her and two other boys I've been trying to keep out of trouble." He leaned forward and began fiddling with the circulars on my desk again. "My wife was at work—she doesn't get home till after five—and I thought what the hell, what she doesn't know won't hurt her. I mean what was the harm? The kids just wanted to see the maps. I thought it would be a good thing to do . . ."

"Except . . ."

"Except that Estrella stole my wife's jewelry."

I interrupted before he could say anything else. "How do you know it was her? Why couldn't it have been the boys?"

"Because Estrella was the only one alone in the den. The two boys were with me the whole time. They'd gotten bored with the maps, so I took them into my office and showed them a computer game I'd just gotten; but Estrella wasn't interested. She wanted to stay and look at my books. So of course I said yes. I thought I could trust her. I guess I was wrong." Garriques smiled ruefully, picked up a price list, tapped his chin with it and threw it back down. "What can I say? I was an idiot. If Estrella had taken anything else, I don't think it would have mattered so much. Enid is never going to understand. Never. There's no way I can explain this to her." Garriques compressed his lips and gave my price lists his full attention.

I was surprised as I looked at him at how much Garriques seemed to care about what Enid thought—he hadn't struck me as the type of man who would. I stubbed out my cigarette and lit another one. "Exactly what happened?"

"I already told you. It's embarrassing to talk about it."

"Tell me again anyway," I commanded.

"It's simple. The four of us came into the house. We went into the den and looked at the maps. Then I took the two boys into the office and showed them Myst. They loved it. So do I. It's a great game." Garriques thought for a moment. "We must have been in there about twenty minutes. When we came back to the den Estrella was gone and so were the brooch and the earrings. Enid usually kept them in the vault, but that day I had them in my desk. I was about to take the pieces to the jeweler to get them cleaned and to get the clasp on the brooch fixed and a couple of the stones reset because they were coming loose." He hit my desk with the flat of his hand. "It's just bad luck they were there, but these days that seems to be the leitmotif of my life."

"So there's no way this could have been planned?" I asked.

"None at all."

"Now, I'm assuming your wife thinks the earrings and the brooch are at the jeweler."

He nodded. "I told her the jeweler said they'd be ready by the end of the week."

"That leaves four days to get them back."

"Believe me, I know."

"Has it occurred to you that Estrella might have sold them?"

Garriques blanched. "God, I hope not. Otherwise I'll be a divorced man." Garriques rubbed the bump on his nose with the tips of his fingers. "What a mess."

I pushed my chair away from my desk. "Now, this is it?" I asked him. "This is the whole story?"

Garriques nodded.

"No more surprises? No more things you forgot to tell me?"

Garriques put up his hand, palm facing outward as if he were in court. "I swear."

I spun the lighter around with the tip of my finger.

"So will you help?"

"All right," I finally said. "I'll see what I can do." I could sympathize with Garriques. He'd tried to do something good and things had just gotten worse and worse. It was a scenario I was not unfamiliar with.

"Great." Garriques's smile lit up the room.

"I'm not promising anything," I cautioned.

"I know." Garriques got up and we shook hands. I walked him to the door, and then I went into the back to look in on Rabbit's rattlesnake. He was coiled up under a sheet of newspaper. I was checking the latches on the top of the cage to make sure they were secure when the front door buzzer went off. Zsa Zsa woke up and started barking. I gave the latches one last shake to make sure they'd hold and went out to see who'd come in. It was Tim.

"Hi," he said. "Sorry I took so long, but Mrs. Breen insisted on feeding me."

Everyone insisted on feeding Tim. Despite the shaved head and the earrings and the cowboy boots, he looked like a boy who needed a mother. "And you just couldn't say no." Tim looked abashed. "How long did it take you to catch the bat?"

"About ten minutes," Tim mumbled.

"And you were eating the rest of the time?"

A hint of color crept across Tim's cheeks. "We talked, too."

"I see." It looked as if Mrs. Breen had definitely had a good afternoon. I only wish I could have said the same.

The grin Tim had been fighting burst across his face. "I figured you would." He then changed the subject. "You want me to go out to the airport and pick up the delivery now or do you want to do it?"

"You pick up the boas," I told him. "I have some phone calls to make."

He gave me a mock salute and swaggered out of the store. I wanted to slap him out of pure envy, but called the Purr-fect Litter Company instead. It seemed like the more productive thing to do. Ten minutes later I was on the line with the shipping clerk when Merlin walked in, took out a twenty-two and pointed it straight at me.

Chapter
11

Maybe setting the Shih Tzus on fire hadn't been such a good idea after all.

"Move away from the phone and out from the counter," Merlin ordered as he approached me.

Oh, good. The Pillsbury Dough Boy with a gun. Not that I wasn't going to comply. Hell, I would have complied if it had been Mr. Softee. A twenty-two may not be a .357, but it's big enough. If one of its slugs hits you in the chest or the stomach and does a Bouncing Betty routine, it can rip up everything inside.

"Why'd you have to do it?" demanded Merlin. We were now about five feet apart from each other.

"It?" I asked, playing dumb, which at the moment wasn't too far from the truth. "What's *it*?"

Merlin sauntered close enough for me to see the nick on his chin where he'd cut himself shaving. "I'm going to teach you a lesson," he hissed. "I'm going to teach you not to mess with other people's stuff."

"I don't know what you're talking about," I insisted, which made Merlin even madder.

"Don't lie to me," he snarled.

I studied him, wondering if a simple apology would do, but then I decided we were past that stage. Way past.

Merlin took a few more steps toward me. "You embarrassed me in front of my friends."

"I didn't know you had any," I couldn't keep myself from saying as I reflected that my mouth always has been and probably always will be my downfall.

Merlin's scowl deepened. His eyes grew darker, two raisins in a sea of barely baked dough. "You don't think I'm serious, do you? Let me show you." He took another step in my direction and Zsa Zsa started barking, a high-pitched yapping that filled the store and started the parrots off.

"Shut her up before I shoot her," Merlin snarled.

Instead I reached over and pushed his gun hand down with my left hand while I punched him with my right. I felt his flesh yield and then a satisfying thud as my knuckles connected with his jaw. His head jerked back. He stumbled. But he still managed to hold on to the twenty-two.

He was bringing it back up when I punched him again. A jolt of pain traveled up my arm. I heard a groan and realized it was me. Then I looked at Merlin. His teeth and lower lip had turned carmine. A thin red line of blood dribbled down his chin. His hand opened. The gun clattered to the floor next to Zsa Zsa. She danced around it. Merlin grunted and bent to get the twenty-two, but he was too slow and too fat. I dove to the ground and came up pointing it at his chest before he had taken two steps. Now it was my turn.

"Put your hands up," I ordered over Zsa Zsa's yipping. The noise was so piercing I wanted to kill her myself.

Merlin smirked. His hands stayed where they were. "The gun isn't loaded," he informed me.

"Yeah, right." How stupid did he think I was? Obviously stupid enough because I involuntarily glanced down at the gun before I caught myself and looked back up. Merlin had taken advantage of my momentary lack of attention to move two steps closer to the door.

"Stay right where you are," I said.

"Why should I?"

"Because I'm telling you to."

"What are you going to do if I don't?" he jeered. "Shoot me?"

"Now that's an interesting thought." I raised the gun slightly and fired over his head. For an instant the air around me smelled of cordite. Then a trickle of cedar shavings began falling out of the bag I'd hit. The noise was too much for Zsa Zsa, and she scampered into the back room.

"No bullets, hunh?" I said to Merlin.

He went slack-jawed. "Jesus," he stammered. "I didn't know. Marsha told me it wasn't loaded. I swear."

For a moment I almost felt sorry for the man. Almost but not quite. I lifted an eyebrow. "And how, pray tell, would she know something like that?"

"Because it was hers."

"You're lying." When I'd seen her, Marsha had had the air of a rabbit, someone who was ready to run whenever anyone said boo. People like that don't go out and buy themselves a gun.

"Look at the handle for Christ's sake," Merlin cried. "Do I look like someone who would buy pink mother-of-pearl?"

"No," I reluctantly conceded after thinking about it. "Probably not."

"I wouldn't have come in here like this if I'd known it was loaded," he continued earnestly. Like a lot of bullies he was all contrition now that I had the upper hand. "Honest. I just wanted to scare you, to teach you a lesson."

"And that's supposed to make things better?"

Merlin gently touched his split lip and looked at the blood on his fingertips. "You hurt me," he said reproachfully.

I nodded toward my bruised knuckles. "And you hurt me. I guess that makes us even."

"What are you going to do?" he asked, wiping the blood off on the back of his pants.

I shifted my weight from one leg to another. "Calling the cops is one possibility that comes to mind."

A simper of a smile flitted across Merlin's face. "I don't think that's a good idea."

"And I don't think you're in a position to think anything," I reminded him.

"If you do," Merlin informed me, "I'll tell them the gun is yours and that I came in here and you attacked me."

I smiled pleasantly. The man's gall was truly amazing. "Then maybe I'll just shoot you instead."

I didn't think it was possible for Merlin to get paler, but he did. "You're crazy," he whispered.

"So I've been told. Repeatedly." I leaned against the counter and watched Merlin's eyes dart back and forth as he assessed the distance to the door and tried to decide whether or not he should make a break for it.

"Don't try it," I warned. "You're not going to make it. You're too slow."

Merlin's eyes narrowed into two slits. His mouth twisted in a grimace. "This is all Marsha's fault," he spat out. "Even when she's dead she's still making trouble for me." The hate in his voice made the hairs on my arms rise. "I bet she pranced that fat body of hers in here and told you some bull-shit about me and you believed her." He leveled a finger at me. "You think she's the good guy. Everyone does. But she wasn't. Not by a long shot. Let me tell you that woman had problems of her own—big ones. Go ask Shirley. Just ask her. She'll tell you."

"I intend to," I said. "After I talk to you."

Merlin had just opened his mouth to say something else when I heard the front door open behind me. Fuck. Just what I didn't need. A customer.

"Hello," Tim said.

As I breathed a sigh of relief that it wasn't someone else Merlin spun around and ran for the door.

"Hey!" Tim yelled as Merlin bumped into him on the way out.

I cursed. Fluently.

Tim's eyes widened as he saw the gun in my hand. "What's going on?" he demanded.

I laid the twenty-two on the counter. "Nothing now."

"That doesn't look like nothing to me," he observed as he plunked the carton he'd been carrying down next to the register. "Somehow pink doesn't seem to be your color."

"It's not," I retorted and told him the story.

"You're really not going to call the police?" Tim said when I was finished.

I reached for the pack of cigarettes underneath the counter and took a Camel out. "Let me ask you a question." I paused to pull my lighter out from my black leather back-pack. "If it comes down to my word against Merlin's, who do you think they're going to believe?"

"Merlin," Tim replied immediately.

"Exactly." I lit my cigarette and indicated the twenty-two. "And with my luck I'd get Connelly, and I don't even want to think about what he'd do with this. Possession of an unlicensed firearm? He'd book me no questions asked. It would make his day."

Tim meditatively twirled his bottom earring around. "Why do you think it's unlicensed?"

"Because otherwise Merlin wouldn't have threatened to tell the cops it was mine."

"Good point." Tim took the bill of lading from the shipment he'd just picked up at the air freight office out of his shirt pocket and handed it to me. "So what are you going to do now?" he asked as I scanned the receipt. For once, Reptiles & Things had actually shipped everything I'd ordered.

"I don't know. I'll tell you one thing, though."

"What?" Tim asked as he took the box cutter from the utility drawer, slit the tape along the carton's flaps open, and bent the flaps back.

"This gun proves that Marsha didn't commit suicide."

Tim tossed the box cutter back in the drawer. "How do you figure that?"

"Why would she drag herself out to LeMoyne and drown herself when she could put a bullet through her head in the comfort of her home?"

Tim shrugged. "I dunno. Maybe she was a neat freak. Maybe she didn't want her husband to clean up after her."

I glared at him.

"Okay, okay. I'm sorry." Tim lifted a cloth bag out of the box and untied it. A corn snake slithered onto his wrist. "Let's suppose you're right."

I crossed my arms and waited.

"Let's suppose someone—possibly her husband—did kill her. That's too bad. Bad karma. But the lady's buried and the case is closed. Let it alone."

"She came to me for help."

"She asked you to help her keep her dogs, not to keep her from getting killed."

"I know that," I said irritably.

"Then why don't you leave this alone?"

"Because I'm pissed."

"About what?"

"About the fact that no one seems to care about what happened to her." I stubbed my cigarette out. "And anyway, I still have her money. I owe her."

"I guess you do." Tim conceded. Then he pointed to the gun. "What are you going to do with that?"

I put the twenty-two in the drawer and closed it. "The gun? Probably keep it."

"Why bother?"

I leaned forward. "Come again?"

"You heard me. You pull that on someone they're going to laugh."

"Not if I shoot them in the right place."

"And what are the odds of that happening?" Tim asked.

"Not high," I admitted. I wasn't a very good shot.

"Exactly. I rest my case." Tim went back to unpacking the carton.

Other than a few desultory comments Tim and I didn't talk for the rest of the evening. I spent until closing time housing the snakes we'd just received, cleaning out the bird room, waiting on customers, and wondering if Merlin had been telling me the truth about the gun being Marsha's and thinking about whether or not Marsha really did have some serious problems.

I closed up the store at nine. The wind tugged at my hair when Zsa Zsa and I stepped outside. An empty trash can was rolling around in the middle of the street. Zsa Zsa jumped. Then she began barking furiously. I guess she was still nervous about the gunshot. I quieted her down, put the trash can back on the curb and headed for home. As I drove Merlin's words kept ringing in my ears. I couldn't get them out of my mind, and before I knew it I found myself driving toward the apartments in which Shirley Hinkel lived.

As I turned onto Thurber I couldn't help thinking about the high hopes Murphy and I had had when we'd moved into the Crestville. We'd come up to Syracuse to make a new start. For a while it worked. We were busy finding a place to live, getting used to new jobs, driving around the countryside, but eventually the novelty had worn off and we'd gradually gone back to our old habits. Murphy would come home late smelling of other women. I'd smoke dope and take tranqs to dull the pain. I'd have a joint with my morning coffee, then have another when I walked through the door at night, a third before we went out. I'd rationalized my habit by telling myself I could take grass or leave it, but I realized that wasn't true when I went away for a working weekend in the country with my boss. Reality was too jagged, and I spent Saturday and Sunday counting the hours until I could light up and get back to the nice, warm cocoon I'd spun for myself. So I went back to smoking. I liked the feeling it gave me too much to quit.

A couple of months later I got my wake-up call. I'd been smoking some Maui Zowie with Murphy and one of his friends when I started getting paranoid. "No problem," I said to myself. "I'll just go to bed. I'll feel better in the morning." Only I didn't. I woke up feeling as if the walls were closing in on me. It began to dawn on me I wasn't riding the tiger anymore, the tiger was riding me. It was time, I decided, to cut back. And I did. I gradually tapered off. But Murphy hadn't.

Then somewhere down the line he'd turned to harder stuff. I sighed and pulled onto the road leading to the apartments.

Because the housing complex was up on a hill the wind was stronger, and the large white entrance sign was creaking under its onslaught. The houses looked the same now as they had when Murphy and I were living there, row after row of two-story attached town houses, all painted the same muddy brown. The parking lot was almost full—everyone was in for the night.

In the whitish glare of the street lights I could see the tree branches on the perimeter of the complex bending this way and that. Underneath one of the larger oaks a man was standing with a toy poodle waiting for him to do his business so they could both go in for the night. Years ago I'd stood there with my dog Elsie. Now she was dead and so was Murphy. Melancholy settled into my bones. It had been a mistake coming here. I'd underrated the power of memories. I should have called Shirley and met her in a coffee shop instead. But it was too late for that now. I parked the cab, told Zsa Zsa to stay put, and got out.

The sounds of televisions and radios drifted through the night air. I made my way across the parking lot and the grassy incline down to Shirley Hinkel's apartment. Even though the drapes in the front window were drawn, I could see lights and hear music playing. Someone was definitely home. I rang the bell, wondering as I did what she'd say when she saw me. Shirley answered almost immediately. She must have been sitting in the living room.

"Oh, it's you," she said, not looking particularly happy to see me. "What do you want?"

"A little chat," I replied.

Chapter
12

Shirley crossed her arms over her breasts and leaned against the door. "Well, given what you did at Merlin's house, I don't think I want to talk to you," she told me in a flat, hard voice. Then she proceeded to study a fold in the sleeve of the blue print dress she was wearing. It was obviously a home-sewn job. The puckered seams and collar were dead giveaways. She must have changed into it when she'd come home from the funeral.

I did contrite. "That was a mistake," I admitted. "I went too far."

Shirley's expression remained glacial. I tried again.

"It's just when I saw the dogs on the mantel like that . . . I don't know . . . something happened to me."

Despite herself Shirley made a little moue of distaste with her mouth. "I agree Merlin shouldn't have done that. I told him not to, but he just wouldn't listen. Sometimes he just goes too far."

"A lot of men do," I observed and flashed her a "we women are in this together" smile and was rewarded with one back. "I just wanted to find out more about Marsha," I said, taking advantage of the opening. "After all, she did hire me, and now I'm finding that everything she told me was a lie. It makes me feel like a jerk."

"I imagine it would," Shirley said dryly.

"And since you knew her . . ." I let the sentence hang.

"You did, too," Shirley said.

"I know. But that was a long time ago. I get the feeling she'd changed a lot since then."

"That's true." Shirley unfolded her arms. "She wasn't what people thought she was . . ."

"That's why I came to you. I was hoping you could help."

I watched anger and the desire to talk struggle on Shirley's face. The desire to talk won, and Shirley invited me in. I followed with alacrity, but the moment I stepped inside my stomach gave a funny little lurch and I began to wonder if this was such a good idea.

For the second time in less than five minutes I was transported back in time. I could have been standing in my old place, the one Murphy and I had nicknamed Silverfish Heaven in honor of the little insects that kept popping up around the drains. Shirley even had the same kind of sofa I'd owned, except my couch had been upholstered in green and hers was covered in blue. We'd both placed them the same way, too—facing the stairs leading up to the second floor—not that there was much choice considering the narrowness of the room.

"Bring back memories?" Shirley asked, fingering a strand of frizzy hair. It looked as if it had been badly permed.

"Too many," I ruefully replied and shook my head to clear them away.

"You were right to leave," Shirley informed me as I sat down in one of the armchairs. She picked the remote up from the coffee table and clicked off the TV. Then she plunked herself down on the sofa. "The management's letting this place go to hell. Things break and they don't fix them. They just let them get worse. All they want is the money. And now we've got these welfare families coming in." She twisted her mouth into an expression of disdain. "Loud parties. Kids running wild."

"So why don't you move?"

She gave a self-deprecating shrug. "I don't know. I guess after you've been in one place for so long it's easier to stay put." Then Shirley bent over and scratched a blemish below her knee. The skin on her legs was almost opaque in its whiteness. A network of fat, blue veins sketched spider webs below its surface. The area began to bleed, and she wet the tip of her finger with her tongue and rubbed away the blood. "Merlin's a good man," she said when she was done. She set her mouth in a stubborn line. "He's had to put up with a lot."

"I take it you mean from Marsha?"

Shirley nodded.

I suppressed a groan. I hoped I wasn't going to hear one of those "his wife doesn't understand him" routines. I'd heard it too many times from friends who were sleeping with the husbands of other friends. But Shirley surprised me. She said something else entirely.

"You see," she told me, "Marsha gambled."

I leaned forward. "You mean like buying a ticket for the lottery?"

"No. I mean as in going to the casinos, going to the race track, betting on football games."

I sat back a little. This was going to be a case of making a big deal over nothing. "So she dropped twenty, a hundred dollars once in a while. Lots of people do."

"This was different. She was into the loan sharks."

"For how much?"

"Thousands."

"I don't believe it."

"It's true. A couple of years ago Merlin took her to Atlantic City for a weekend. One session at the blackjack table and that was that. She was hooked." Shirley grinned, obviously pleased to be the bearer of such tidings. "Merlin told me he begged her to stop, but she wouldn't. That's why they were getting a divorce. He couldn't stand it anymore. People were making threatening phone calls. They were coming up to the house and demanding payment. It was horrible."

I suddenly remembered Merlin's reaction at the cemetery to the man in the white caddy. This would certainly explain it, but like Shirley's line of chatter the explanation was a little too pat to suit me. I kept that thought to myself, though, and asked Shirley another question instead. "Did you ever see Marsha gamble?"

"No, but she was always taking trips."

"To the casinos?"

"Yes."

"Did you ever go with her?"

"No."

"Then how do you know where she went? Did you ask her?"

Shirley tugged at her hair. "Merlin told me," she said reluctantly. "We weren't talking."

"Because she found out about you and her husband?"

"She overheard us on the phone," Shirley whispered. "I felt really bad."

But obviously not bad enough to stop, I thought uncharitably. "So what you're telling me is that your sole source of information on Marsha is Merlin. Not very reliable, I'd say."

Shirley flushed. "He wouldn't lie."

I raised an eyebrow. "Don't you think that killing Marsha's dogs and stuffing them indicates a man whose statements about his wife might be a little biased?"

Shirley's face turned beet red. "I should never have let you in. Merlin said you were an asshole."

I laughed. "Well, it's good to know he's right about something."

"Get out," she ordered. "Get out before I call the police."

"Fine. I'm going." I stood up. "Just tell me one thing: Is Merlin worth the price?"

"You're a fine one to talk about prices," Shirley sneered. "Don't think I don't remember you and Murphy and all the women he used to 'entertain' when you were at work."

Now it was my turn to flush. "That's not true!" I cried.

"Maybe it is and maybe it isn't." Shirley leered at me. "But you don't know which, do you?"

She was still smiling when I slammed the door. The moment I hit the fresh air I took a few deep breaths. Jesus, I thought as I tried to get myself under control, thinking about Murphy could still do this to me. It was amazing. I had to get a life. I mean even if what Shirley said was true. So what? Who cared? The man was dead. It didn't matter. By the time I got to the cab I almost believed it.

When I opened the cab door Zsa Zsa jumped out and made straight for the grassy verge. I lit a cigarette and smoked it while Zsa Zsa ran around chasing God knows what, and I watched the lightning off in the distance. The storm was definitely heading our way. It was time to go. I picked up Zsa Zsa and put her in the car and headed off to Pete's. After my scene with Shirley I needed a Scotch.

By the time I got to the bar the storm had arrived. The rain was coming down in sheets. Branches of lightning filled the sky. I parked as close to Pete's as I could, grabbed the dog, and ran for it, but even so we were both soaked by the time I got inside.

Except for George, Connie, and a small bunch of college kids down at the other end of the bar, the place was deserted.

"You guys look like drowned rats," Connie informed me. "Here, take these." She reached under the counter, took out a couple of towels, and threw them in my direction.

I caught them with my free hand, wrapped Zsa Zsa in one, and began rubbing her down as I walked toward George.

"She smells like a wet dog," he said to me as I put her on the stool next to mine.

"That's because she is." I began blotting the water out of my hair. "You look very prep this evening."

George fingered the collar on his blue oxford shirt. "That's the idea," he said. "You know you just missed Tim."

"Really?"

"Yes. We had an interesting conversation about a twenty-two."

Trust Tim not to be able to keep his mouth shut, I thought as I hopped up on the stool between Zsa Zsa and George. "You'd like it. It has a pretty pink mother-of-pearl handle and everything."

"Well, that's a relief," George said as Connie sent a double shot of Black Label down my way and set a small saucer of beer in front of Zsa Zsa. She began lapping up her Molson. "I'd be worried if the gun were ugly."

I took a sip of Scotch. It warmed by mouth and throat when I swallowed.

"Don't you think this Merlin thing is getting out of hand?" George asked.

"Well, *he* certainly is."

"Exactly my point." George took a swallow of his beer. The bottle looked small in his hand. "That's why you should drop it."

"That's what Tim said, too. The only problem is I don't think I can."

"No," George corrected. "You can, you just don't want to." He took a potato chip out of the bowl in front of him, fed one to Zsa Zsa and put another in his mouth. "So where have you been?"

I told him about my conversation with Shirley, taking care to leave out her comments about Murphy. It was too painful, and anyway I didn't want to discuss the subject with George. He'd been Murphy's best friend. I mean what was he going to say? That the man was an asshole? He was too loyal to do that. It was one of George's more admirable but annoying traits. I finished my Scotch and was just about to signal to Connie when she drifted back up from the other end of the bar. I ordered another Scotch and on a hunch described Merlin and Shirley and asked Connie if they'd ever come in.

"Not when I've been on," she told me as she set my glass down in front of me.

"But Marsha has been, right?"

"Like I said before, every Friday with the Wellington crowd."

"What did she talk about?"

Connie flicked a strand of hair off her forehead with a wave of a finger. "The usual."

"Which was?"

"Her classes. The weather. Her latest diet."

"Did Marsha ever talk about her husband?"

"Not to me."

"Did she ever talk about gambling?"

"I heard she's a player," Connie said cautiously.

"How big a player?"

She gave me an angelic smile. "Now that will cost you twenty."

My eyes widened. I knew Connie cared about money, but this was ridiculous. "You're kidding."

"Do I look like I am?"

"I thought I was your friend."

"You are. Anyone else I'd charge forty."

"Jesus," I grumbled.

Connie shrugged. "Hey, I'm sorry but I got expenses. I'm just trying to get along same as anyone else."

"All right," I grudgingly agreed. "But this had better be good."

"Oh, it is," Connie assured me.

I turned to George and said, "Do me a favor and give her twenty."

He choked on his beer. "What?" he asked when he could talk again.

"You heard me. I asked you to give her twenty."

"What's wrong with your money?"

"Nothing. I just don't have any." I pointed to my glass. "I spent it all on my drinks."

"You're really unbelievable. You have more chutzpah than anyone else I know."

"Thank you." I smiled sweetly. "I try. It's taken a lot of work and training to reach this advanced state, but despite unbelievable odds I've managed to persevere."

George snorted. "I want this back," he said, reluctantly pulling out his billfold and extracting a twenty.

"Don't worry," I told him as I took it and handed it to Connie. "I'm good for it."

"Yeah, right," George muttered.

"Don't I always pay you back?"

"In a word—no."

Before I could reply Connie leaned over the bar and plucked the twenty out of my hand. "Do you want to hear what I have to say or not?" she demanded.

"Yes," George and I said simultaneously.

"Fast Eddie Marino."

"Who the hell is Fast Eddie Marino?" I asked.

George took another gulp of beer. "He's a bookie over on the North Side. He's connected. He handles big stuff. Moves a lot of cash."

"That's right." Connie nodded her head vigorously.

Zsa Zsa jumped onto the bar and headed for the potato chips. I pulled her down and put her on my lap. "And?" I said to Connie.

"Marsha owed him."

"How much?"

"I heard four or five figures."

I choked on the sip of Scotch I'd just taken.

Chapter
13

George became absorbed in peeling the label off his bottle of Molson. When he looked back up he had on his cop face. I half expected him to reach into his pocket and take out a pad and a pen and start taking notes. I guess once you're a cop you're always one even if you quit the force. You just can't help it. Or maybe he wanted to make sure I got good value for his twenty bucks. Zsa Zsa reached over and licked the edge of his hand. George gave her an absentminded pat and began drumming his fingers on the bar.

"So Connie," he rasped, "where'd you get this information from? Did Marsha tell you?"

"Not exactly," Connie hedged.

"Then who did?" I demanded.

"My ex-brother-in-law."

George rolled his eyes. "Je-SUS."

I put out my hand. "Give me back his money."

Connie took a couple of steps to the left. "Hey, lighten up. The information's good. Reggie used to work for Fast Eddie."

"Doing what?" I demanded.

"Reclaiming Eddie's lost assets."

George raised an eyebrow. "You mean he was an enforcer?"

Connie nervously rubbed her top lip with a knuckle. "What can I say? My sister has lousy taste in men. Put her in a room full of good ones and she'll come out with the loser every time."

George clicked his tongue against the roof of his mouth. "Can we talk to this guy?"

"You can if you can find him."

George's eyes narrowed. "Why? Where'd he go?"

"Good question." Connie scratched her cheek. "I don't know. Nobody does. My sister came home from work last week and he was gone. He'd taken her Trans Am, cleaned out her checking account and split."

"She file a report?" George asked.

"Of course. But nothing's turned up."

I used one of my fingernails to make a "t" on the counter with George's potato chip crumbs. "So how come Reggie told you this stuff about Marsha?"

"Because he was here when she walked in. She took one look, turned sheet white, and ran out the door. When I asked him what was going on he told me she owed Fast Eddie some serious money."

"I guess we can assume he'd already spoken to her," I said.

"I think we can," George agreed. He turned back to Connie. "Your brother-in-law say anything else?"

"Not about Marsha," Connie replied. A couple of the college kids down at the other end of the bar started yelling for Connie. She turned and waved at them. "Gotta go," she told George and me. "My fans want me."

I fed Zsa Zsa a potato chip. "What do you think?" I asked George after Connie left.

"I think your friend had a serious problem."

"Besides that."

He cracked a knuckle. "Are you asking me if I think Marsha was killed for a gambling debt?"

"Yes."

"I don't. These guys don't kill people. They scare them, maybe mess them up, but that's about it."

I restrained Zsa Zsa from getting on the bar. "Yeah, but sometimes things get out of hand. Sometimes things don't always go as planned."

"True. Except if I remember the newspaper article about Marsha's death correctly, it stated that no marks of violence were found on her body. Believe me, if Reggie or one of his friends had had a session with her, she would have had bruises all over."

"You're probably right." I took a cigarette out of the pack in my backpack and lit it.

George scowled and waved the smoke away with his hand. "There's no probably about it. I've seen these guys work. Owing that much money however does give her a good reason for suicide."

"Or her husband a reason for murder," I mused. "I know if I had a wife like that I'd want her out of the way. She'd be a real liability." I thought again about the limo I'd seen at the funeral and Merlin's reaction to it. "I wonder if Fast Eddie considers Merlin responsible for Marsha's debts?"

"Interesting question," George observed.

"Think about it. Here you are putting in fifty hours a week on the floor of a furniture store working your ass off selling sofas to ladies who can't decide between chintz and plaid, and your partner goes out and not only spends everything you bring in but runs up an enormous debt as well. It would sure piss me off. Maybe it pissed Merlin off, too. Maybe that's why he killed her. He just couldn't stand it anymore."

"You're conjecturing."

"I know, but it makes sense," I argued.

"So would a lot of other reasons. The fact is, you want to kill someone, one reason is as good as another." George twisted his voice into a savage whine. "Officer, he beat me. Officer, she cheated on me. He owed me money. I loved her. I was drunk. She was stoned. It was an accident." He stopped and took a couple of breaths. "It all comes down to the same shit in the end."

"That's a pretty bleak view."

"Most murders are pretty bleak affairs."

I flicked my cigarette ash into one of George's empty Molson bottles. "Well, Marsha's certainly was." Zsa Zsa woofed and I scratched her back. "Merlin must have really hated her to do what he did to those dogs."

"I'd say so," George agreed. He took another drink of beer. "One thing you might want to bear in mind," he continued. "That stuff about Marsha and her gambling problems . . ."

"What about it?"

"It's all hearsay."

"I know." I took a moment and rubbed the front of my calf with my toe. My burn scar was itching, a sign I was tired. "Maybe I should just go to Fast Eddie and ask him."

He stared at me. "You really are crazy."

"Why?"

"What you gonna do, wear a short skirt, tight sweater and high heels and waltz in there?"

"Why? Will that help?"

"No."

"Good, because I was planning on wearing jeans and a T-shirt and sneakers."

"That's a relief."

"I'm glad you approve. Anyway, I thought I'd go in and tell him I was a friend of Marsha's and that I understand they did business together and that I'm very interested in getting in on the action."

"And you expect him to tell you—what?"

"At the very least I'll find out whether or not Marsha was a customer of his. As for anything else, I guess that'll depend on how chatty he is."

"He's not."

I stubbed out my cigarette and tossed it in the Molson bottle. "Maybe he'll talk to me."

"Why should he do that?"

"Because I'm good at getting people to talk. When I worked for the paper I used to make my living coaxing people to tell me things."

George leaned back and laced his fingers together and put them behind his head. "Gentleman's bet he won't say a word."

"You're on."

George grinned. Looking at the width of his smile I had a strong feeling there was something he wasn't telling me. Oh, well. I guess I'd find out what it was soon enough. "Now, you said this guy has ties to the mob."

"That's what I'm told. All these guys do. Central New York is like their summer camp."

"So where does he live?"

"On Pond. He shares an apartment over a sleazoid bar called Outlaw with his mother."

"His mother? You're kidding."

"No. I'm serious. She takes care of him. He's got emphysema or some sort of lung thing really bad. He can't get around much."

"Why do they call him Fast Eddie, then?"

"Because he's got this souped-up electric wheelchair he speeds around in. Except of course when you want to arrest him. Then the damn thing won't move. The prick," George said with feeling. "Last time I brought him in I had to call two other guys to help me pick Eddie up and put him in the van."

"I didn't think wheelchairs were that heavy."

"They are when you have someone weighing over three hundred pounds sitting in one."

I stifled a giggle.

George glared at me and took a pull of his beer. Then he started smiling, too. "It was pretty funny," he admitted. "The DA doesn't even want to prosecute him anymore."

"Why's that?"

"What the hell are you going to do with him? Put him in Jamesville? It'll cost an arm and a leg. They're not set up for that kind of thing. Put him under house arrest? He already is. And doesn't that sonofabitch know it, too. He's got a leer on his face I'd love to wipe off."

"He really gets to you."

"Yes, he does." George took another gulp of his Molson. "I'll tell you one thing, though."

"What's that?"

"You know who you should really be careful of?"

"His enforcers?"

"His mother."

"You've got to be kidding."

"I'm not."

"Why? What could she possibly do?"

George chuckled dryly. "I think I'll let you find out for yourself. I wouldn't want to deny you the pleasure."

"Thanks a whole bunch."

He gave a little bow. "I shall eagerly await your story."

"You know, sometimes you really are a creep."

"No. I just want my twenty dollars' worth of entertainment."

"Hey," I protested. "I told you I'd give you the money tomorrow."

George stood up. "Fine. I'll drop by the store to collect it."

"You do that."

He leaned toward me and twirled an imaginary mustache. "And if you don't have it, you're all mine."

Chapter
14

"He's interested," Connie said to me after George had left. She'd drifted back from the other end of the bar in time to catch the tail end of our conversation. "I can tell."

"You're nuts," I retorted.

"Trust Mother Connie." She patted her chest. "I know about this kind of thing."

I snorted. "Maybe you do, but you're sure as hell wrong this time. First of all I'm not his type. My boobs are too small and my IQ is too high."

Connie tsked. "Nasty, nasty."

I leaned forward. "But true—as you well know by some of the bimbos he's dragged in here. Remember Myra?"

"Be that as it may," Connie told me, "you think he's hot. Admit it, the guy turns you on."

I ran my finger around the edge of my glass. "I admit I like him, but that's as far as it goes."

"You do more than that," Connie declared as she cleared

away George's beer bottles and began wiping down the counter. "Really, you're such a chicken shit."

I could feel myself redden.

"I mean," Connie continued, "I know you've gotten shot at and all the rest of that junk, but the reality is you're chicken about what counts." She pointed a finger at me. "Ever since Murphy died I've watched you wall yourself off in your own little world. You're scared to get involved with anyone you could feel anything about."

"I didn't know you were getting a degree in psychology," I sneered.

Connie shrugged. "Fine. Have it your way."

"I will." I drained my Scotch, grabbed Zsa Zsa and left.

Okay, so maybe Connie was on to something, I admitted to myself as I zoomed out of the parking lot. She still didn't have to say what she did. I wasn't being a chicken shit; I was just being cautious. Given my relationship with Murphy it made sense. One of my friends had said that being with us was like being on a roller coaster. Either we couldn't keep our hands off one another or we were ready to slit each other's throats. I don't think we were ever really in love; we were in lust and when we started to cool off we had nowhere else to go. Now I think I didn't really know Murphy at all; all I knew was the fantasy of him I'd created in my mind. And that scares me. I don't want to do that with George. I also don't want to start something and have George go away. I like him too much. Which means what? That I should only go to bed with guys I don't like? God, how did I manage to get so screwed up? The question depressed me, and I pressed my foot on the gas and went flying down Meadowbrook at sixty miles an hour. I knew I'd have to deal with this stuff soon, but I wasn't ready to deal with it tonight.

I could hear my answering machine beeping as soon as I walked into the house. I went into the kitchen and played the tape back. There were three calls, all of them from the folks at Visa and MasterCard wanting to know when they were going to get paid. I deleted the messages and went into the kitchen. James was sitting on the counter waiting to be fed. I opened a can of tuna for him and grabbed a handful of Oreo cookies for myself. "Well," I said to him. "It looks as if we're going to be strictly cash-and-carry for a while."

James ignored me and went on eating. I sighed and went up the stairs.

That night I dreamt about George. I woke at five with a sense of dread I didn't understand and couldn't shake. I tossed and turned trying to get back to sleep, until finally I gave up, went downstairs, turned on the TV, and lay down on the sofa. I was just dozing off when Zsa Zsa woke me. She wanted to go out.

I was wide awake when I came back in, so I spent the rest of the time before I had to go to work alternating between writing advertising copy for the store and coming up with a plan to find Estrella.

Tim and I hit the parking lot at the same time—he with his container of yogurt and I with the three doughnuts I'd picked up at Nice N' Easy. Pickles was right by the door when I opened it. The moment I stepped inside she meowed and twined herself around my legs while Zsa Zsa danced around us. I petted the cat for a while, then got down to work. It was an annoying morning. Two customers returned fish which had died of ich. Then I signed for a case of flea powder only to find upon opening the carton that the company had sent me defoggers instead—which we didn't need.

It took me half an hour to get the distributor on the phone and another fifteen minutes to convince the secretary that a mistake had been made. Then on top of everything someone kept calling and hanging up. Finally around eleven I took a break and called Rabbit. There wouldn't have been any point in calling earlier because he's never up before eleven. I was hoping he'd come up with some information on Estrella, but he wasn't home. His brother told me he was with Manuel. Manuel's mother said the boys were with Will. Will's mother told me the three of them hadn't come home last night.

"If you see 'em, you tell 'em to get their butts over here," she growled.

I said I would, but privately I doubted they'd listen. If I had that waiting for me, I wouldn't be in a big hurry to go home either. I twisted a lock of hair around my finger. So much for that idea. The guys could be back in a half hour or two days from now, and I couldn't afford to wait and find out which one it was going to be. After a couple of minutes of consideration I decided to visit the house on Deal on my way to the bank. Who knew? Maybe I'd get lucky.

This time a girl answered the door. With her pale, scrubbed skin and waiflike body she looked eleven at the most. I wondered if the baby she was cradling in her arms was hers.

"What do you want?" she whispered. Her voice was so soft I had to strain to hear it.

"I'm looking for Estrella Torres," I told her.

"She's gone."

I guess I wasn't going to be lucky after all. "Do you know where she went?"

"No." The baby the girl was cradling let out an anemic mewl. The girl looked down. "Excuse me but I got to go feed her."

"She yours?"

The girl nodded. "She's three months old. She was born a month early, but she's doing all right now." She offered her up for my inspection. The baby had circles under her eyes.

She looked tired, as if she'd already seen more of life than she wanted to. "She's got to have an operation, though."

"That's too bad."

"Next month." The baby cried again. "The doctors said she's going to be fine." The girl leaned forward. "But I don't think she's going to be," she confided. "You believe in angels?"

I told her I did because I didn't have the heart to say anything else.

"Me, too." The girl was going to say something else, but another girl, an older one, appeared behind her.

"I was wondering where you went off to," the second one said. Her blond hair was streaked with blue. Her dark eyes were wary.

The younger girl pointed at me. "She was asking for Estrella."

"Well, she ain't here," the older girl said.

"I know." I tried again. "Do you know where she went?"

"I think she's living at the Colony or maybe at her mother's. She said something about going to see her mother."

"And where is her mother?"

"I don't know. Toronto maybe. I'm not sure."

I thanked her and turned to go.

"Hey," the older girl said to me, "you catch up with her tell her I want my shirt back."

I told her I would and left. Seeing the girl and her baby depressed me and I almost wished I hadn't come. Their vision stayed with me while I stood in line at the bank. It seemed as if we, as a country, were slipping back to an earlier, harsher time and place. It also seemed to me as if Estrella wasn't too far away from a similar fate. It made me want to look harder. I hadn't been able to help Marsha; maybe I could help her.

The first thing I did when I got back to the store was call Garriques and ask him for Estrella's mother's phone number. He didn't have it, but he gave me the aunt's. I could hear the school PA system announcing club meetings in the background while he talked. The sounds made me long for school's simplicity.

I called Ana Torres next. I wanted to tell her what I'd found out, but she wasn't home. A youngish-sounding child answered and told me that her mother had gone to the store and would be back in a couple of minutes. I decided to go over and talk to her in person. I didn't know how good her English was, but I knew that my Spanish was lousy. Communication would go better if we were face to face.

I was reaching for my keys when a man I'd never seen pushed the door open and walked in. He was wearing a gray suit and tie. The jacket pulled around the shoulders and the waist and looked as if it had been made for someone smaller. He had a round face, made even rounder-looking by a receding hairline, and a soft body; but his eyes were hard, and the scar running from his lip to his chin had fixed the left side of his mouth in a permanent sneer. But sneer or not the man was a customer, so I smiled and asked if I could help him.

"I'll take one of those," he said, pointing to the box of rubber mice sitting on the counter.

"That'll be $2.99 plus tax," I told him.

He reached in his pocket and handed me a five-dollar bill.

"So what kind of cat do you have?" I asked, trying to get a conversation going.

"I don't," he informed me. His voice was hoarse and low and I had to strain to hear him.

I tried again. "Dogs like these, too. Especially terriers."

"I don't have one of those either," he said as I handed him his change.

Strike two. "Well, is there anything else I can help you with?" I figured what was the harm in asking.

"No."

I tried one last time. "Are you sure you don't need anything else for your pet?"

"I don't have any pets." He threw the mouse back down on the counter.

"I don't understand." I was definitely missing something here.

"It's simple really. I just came in to get a good look at you."

I felt a chill going down my spine as he turned and walked out the door.

Chapter
15

"What was that all about?" Tim asked from behind me.

"You got me." I picked up the mouse and stared at it for a moment before I tossed it back in the box. "But I'll tell you one thing—I'd sure like to find out."

Tim made a dismissive gesture with his hand. "The guy's just a nut case from Hutchings."

Pickles jumped up on the counter, rubbed her head against my hand, then lifted it up so I could scratch under her chin. "I hope so." But I wasn't entirely convinced. There had been something very controlled about the guy, very purposeful. I had the feeling this was the opening shot in a game I didn't know I was playing. I shook my head to clear it. I was getting jumpy in my old age. Tim was right. The guy was a nut case. He'd probably just forgotten to take his morning Thorazine.

Tim twirled one of his earrings around. "Mrs. Garriques called earlier," he told me, changing the subject. "She wants us to deliver and set up the tank next week. I told her I'd check with you."

"That's fine."

"I guess she's really not going to get the retic."

"It certainly looks that way."

I took out a cigarette and was searching for my lighter when the door opened and Rabbit and Manuel came in. "Find Estrella yet?" Rabbit asked.

I shook my head. "Have you?" Maybe I wouldn't have to run over to Estrella's aunt after all.

"No." So much for that hope. "But I just heard she burned some dealer," Rabbit said.

"Great. It's nice to know she's doing well."

Manuel interrupted. "Did you get rid of Rabbit's rattler yet?"

I turned toward him. "No," I replied. "Why?"

"I think I got a buyer."

I left Tim to deal with the two of them and took off.

Ana Torres lived on Clifford Street. It was almost impossible to see the house from the street. The view was obscured by overgrown clumps of yew and cedars. If it wasn't for an old rusted-out Chevy Chevette parked in the buckling driveway I would have missed the place altogether. It had started raining, and the drizzle increased the house's sense of desolation, although in truth I don't think sunlight would have helped. The house was too far gone for that. I parked my car and followed the indentation of what had once been a brick path through the weed-clogged lawn to the door. Except for the tarnished brass knocker, the door was that grayish color wood acquires when it's stripped and left unfinished.

As I stood on the cracked concrete stoop I could hear the faint sounds of a TV inside. I used the knocker. The rapping scared a stray cat that had been peeking out of the shrubbery back into its hiding place. No one came. I sighed and wished I'd brought an umbrella. I don't like being damp. Of course, it was always possible that Ana Torres hadn't come back from the store yet. Or maybe she had come, taken the kid with her, and gone. Maybe that was somebody else's car in the driveway, but even if it was, I still wanted to talk to them. I knocked again. No response. Except for the TV I couldn't hear any activity inside at all. Shit. I took a step back, and as I did I happened to look up. I sucked in my breath. A face was staring down at me from the corner of the window. A second later the curtain dropped.

Well, one thing was for certain. Someone knew I was here.

And it wasn't the kid I'd spoken to on the phone either.

It was an adult, a woman. I was positive of it.

Whether or not it was Ana Torres was a different matter.

I cupped my hands. "My name is Robin Light," I yelled. "Gregory Garriques sent me. He asked me to help find your niece."

The curtain remained down. No one peeked out. I didn't hear footsteps coming down the stairs.

I tried again. "Listen, Mrs. Torres, if you're there, I really need to speak to you about Estrella. I'm not from Immigration. Call Garriques and check if you don't believe me."

Still nothing.

I repeated myself in fractured Spanish and got the same response.

Nada.

I turned and walked back to the car. There was no point in standing in the rain and getting even wetter than I already was. As I was getting into the cab I glanced up at the curtain covering the window on the second floor. There was no movement, the curtain didn't even flutter; but I couldn't help feeling that someone was watching me just the same. I waved, got in the cab and drove off. Then I circled the block and parked in back of a large red truck which was sitting about thirty feet down from Ana Torres's house and waited for her to come out. One way or another I was determined to talk to her. It didn't take long. I was just finishing my second cigarette when Ana Torres emerged. I flicked the butt into the street and ran over.

She gasped when she saw me and hugged the child standing next to her tightly to her side. "I don't want no trouble," she said. She was short. Her face was round. Her features were Indian.

I tried to reassure her, but the tremors in her hands told me she clearly didn't believe me.

"I didn't do nothing wrong," she protested.

"I know. I just want to talk to you about Estrella."

Ana Torres clutched the child next to her even more tightly. "I don't got nothing to do with her. Nothing."

"But she lived with you."

"Not no more."

I sighed. "Her friends said she may have gone to visit her mother. Do you have her address?"

"I clean house for Mr. and Mrs. Garriques," Ana Torres said, pretending she hadn't heard my question. "I do a good job. You ask them."

"I'm sure you do," I said soothingly.

"I even clean for that crazy brother of hers, the one with all the dead animals in his place." After saying those words Ana Torres made the sign of the cross.

I tried to steer the conversation back to the subject at hand. "So you don't know where your niece is?"

"No." She opened the door of the Chevette. The child scrambled in. "I must go now."

I played my last card. "Then she's not at the Colony Plaza?"

Ana Torres's eyelids fluttered in alarm. She'd told me what I needed to know. "She's in Liverpool," she lied.

I thanked her for the information, but from the expression on her face I could tell she knew that I knew that she was lying. As she backed out of the driveway it suddenly occurred to me that she might be going to warn Estrella that I was coming to find her. I cursed and hurried back to my car.

But it turned out I was wrong and I needn't have bothered following her. When I spotted the Chevette a couple of minutes later it was parked in front of Burger King, and Ana Torres and her child were inside eating lunch. Watching them made me realize I was hungry, too.

I stopped at the first Nice N' Easy I came to and bought myself two chili dogs and a cup of hot chocolate and consumed it all in the cab while I listened to the radio play Golden Oldies and watched a fine mist form on my car windshield. On the way to the Colony Plaza I stopped again and bought a flashlight and batteries at Fay's, then continued on. I parked the cab under the metal overhang in the vacant lot next door—after all I didn't have to advertise my presence; I was trespassing—and went inside through the window I'd used earlier.

The first thing I saw was a rat. It was sitting in the middle of the floor next to a white crumpled up paper bag. When I took a step in its direction it scurried halfway under an upturned chair, then stopped. It watched me as I walked over to where it had been sitting. The remains of somebody's hamburger and fries were spread out on the floor. The question was, was it Estrella's hamburger and fries or someone else's?

I entered the next room carefully. Nothing had changed from the last time I'd been here. I took a cursory look, turned on the flashlight, and cautiously moved on to the third room. This time no one was there waiting for me. The only living things I saw were two more rats. Caught in the beam, they froze for a few seconds, then scampered under a desk. I walked by them quickly, went through a fourth and fifth room and landed in the main hallway.

Light streaming in from the windows that weren't boarded up illuminated the blue tiles that lined the walls and floor. A fountain, a monument to better times, stood in the middle of the entrance way. Its basin was filled with paper cups and beer cans. I walked around it to the stairway. Portions of carpet covering the steps had rotted or been ripped away, and I could see the concrete underneath.

It took me twenty minutes to go through the second floor. The rooms looked the same as the ones on the first floor. No one seemed to be living in any of them. Whoever had been here had just trashed the place and left. When I was done making the circuit I went back to the hallway and lit a cigarette. At least if I smoked I wouldn't be able to smell the urine and the garbage. I started up to the third floor. I'd climbed five steps when I heard the music. I stopped dead and listened. It was coming from somewhere above me. It looked as if someone was here after all. I wondered if it was Estrella. And then I wondered what whoever was up there would do when they saw me.

I gripped my flashlight tighter and tiptoed up the rest of the stairs to the third floor.

The sounds were louder.

They were even louder on the fourth floor.

Now I could almost make out the words to the song that was being played—and I heard a cry that I couldn't quite place.

I moved up the next flight of stairs as quietly as I could.

I shouldn't have bothered.

Because when I got to the top someone was waiting for me.

Chapter
16

The first thing I noticed about the guy was his hair. It was blond and dreaded, and since he was bean pole tall and skinny it made him look like a human string mop. The second thing I noticed—which should have been the first thing—was the hunting knife he was carrying in his right hand.

"What are you doing here?" he demanded and scowled, but the squeak he ended his question with counterbalanced the effect of menace he was trying to create.

"I'm looking for someone," I explained, doing reasonable and inoffensive, although if I were a reasonable sort of person, I wouldn't be in the Colony in the first place.

His eyes narrowed and he looked me up and down. "You a Five-oh?"

"Do I look like a cop?"

"They come in all shapes and sizes, man," he observed. He had enough sincerity in his voice to make me think he'd had a sufficient number of run-ins with the law to know something about the subject.

"Look," I told him. "I'm not from the police and I'm not interested in anything you've done or could do. All I want to do is find this girl." I started to tell him about Estrella, but he interrupted before I got ten words out of my mouth.

"I've never seen her." He shifted his weight from foot to foot. His dreads bobbed to the rhythm of his movements. "She ain't been in here."

I didn't believe him, he'd cut me off too fast, but I didn't say that—never insult a man with a knife is my motto. Instead I asked if he could give her a message for me.

"I just told you I haven't seen her." His tone was querulous. I decided he was in his late teens, early twenties at the most.

"I know, but *if* you do, could you give her my card and tell her to get in touch with me. Tell her Garriques isn't going to have her arrested. Tell her he just wants his stuff back."

"And I'm telling you she ain't here," the kid repeated. "She ain't gonna be either."

"Well, she was here last week," I retorted. "I know because I followed her in."

"She never made it up the stairs." The kid's voice was flat, admitting no debate.

"Okay." I raised my hands and did placating.

"You're damn right okay."

I didn't reply immediately. I was thinking of some way to jump start the conversation when the mewling I'd heard earlier started up again. Then it changed into an odd bark. The kid muttered something under his breath. I thought he said "damn bird," but I couldn't be sure and I wasn't interested enough to find out. Even though I didn't think this guy was dangerous, I still didn't like having someone standing there pointing a knife at me. I just wanted to wrap up the Estrella thing and get out. I was about to ask him if I could at least leave him my card when a woman's voice floated down from the top floor.

"Mike, is that Jennie?"

"No," Mike called back.

"Then who's there? Who are you talking to?"

"My name is Robin Light," I yelled up. "I'm looking for Estrella Torres."

The guy called Mike groaned. "Why'd you have to tell her that?" he asked.

"Why shouldn't I have?"

Before he could answer the woman started coming down the stairs. She was as pale as her boyfriend and about as young, but she had the hectoring tone of a long put-upon wife. She shook her finger at Mike. "I told you she was trouble, but did you listen? Oh, no."

"Aw come on, Traci," Mike whined. "What the hell was I supposed to say? She was scared. She needed a place to crash for a couple of days."

"She was crazy," Traci retorted. "She was loony tunes. People like that only bring trouble."

"How was she nuts?" I quickly asked before Mike could say anything.

Traci cocked her head and regarded me carefully. I guess she must have liked what she saw because she answered me a few seconds later. "She did stuff."

"You mean like drug stuff."

"Among other things." And she threw a meaningful look in Mike's direction. He flushed and looked down at the floor.

"Come on. Stop it," he mumbled. "We went through this already. She was doing some dope—so what?"

Traci ran her hand through her cropped blond hair. It was clean, as was her face. Her clothes, jeans and a T-shirt, looked washed and pressed. I was wondering how she managed to do that in a place with no running water when she started talking again. "Hey, Mr. Wiseguy," Traci snapped. "What about the bad acid she popped? She thought she had roaches all over her body. She was gonna jump out the window. I had to knock her out to stop her."

"Hey, I'm sorry I wasn't here to help. Excuse me for going out and collecting bottles so we could get something to eat." Mike jabbed his knife in the air for emphasis.

"Why don't you just put that thing away," Traci said, pointing to the blade. "It makes me nervous."

"I was just trying to protect you."

"From what? Her?" Traci asked contemptuously. I felt oddly insulted that my appearance didn't evoke more fear. "What's she gonna do?"

"She could be a cop," Mike said.

Traci curled her lips in derision and put both hands on her hips. "You think they're gonna send someone special to look for you? You ain't that important to them."

I decided not to ask what Mike was wanted for. It seemed better that way.

Mike snorted. "KE-RIST," he muttered as he sheathed the hunting knife. "I try and do the right thing and this is what I get."

"Excuse me," I said, trying to work the conversation back to Estrella.

"Yeah?" Traci said.

"How long was Estrella here for?"

Traci ran her hand through her hair again. "You know I was readin' in some magazine that information is becoming the new currency."

"So you want me to pay you?"

"It's not that I don't want to help you," she explained, "but we're a little short right now and you look like you got a few bucks extra."

"Fair enough." I took my wallet out and extracted two twenties. I'd just ask Garriques for it the next time I spoke to him.

Mike's eyes gleamed as he took the money. "Two days," he said. "She was here for two days."

"Three," Traci corrected, taking the bills out of his hand and stuffing them in the side pocket of her jeans. "She was here for three." Mike glared at her. "Well, she was," she said to me. "She kept making eyes at him, wanting to sit next him."

"You're nuts," he said.

Traci's jaw set. "Don't think I didn't see her rubbing up against you, mister."

I interrupted again. "Did she have a friend with her?"

"No," both Mike and Traci said simultaneously.

"Did you see anyone else around?"

"No," the two repeated again. Well, at least they agreed on something.

"Are you sure?"

"Yeah." Traci rubbed the corner of her eye with one of her knuckles. "Absolutely. See, people can run around downstairs and we don't hear 'em, but once they get up to the third and fourth floor we know they're coming."

Interesting—I wondered what had happened to Estrella's friend.

"What did Estrella talk about?"

"Nothing really," Traci replied. "The first night she was like hungry, you know? So we gave her the rest of our pizza. Then we gave her some of our newspapers to use as a blanket and she curled up and went to sleep. She was gone before I got up. The second day she showed up, she wasn't hungry or anything. Mike was out and she just went and sat in a corner, and then all of a sudden she went nuts. She started ranting and raving and carrying on."

"What did she say?"

"Just shit about her face melting and people were gonna come and put her away and everything kept disappearing on her—you know, stuff like that."

"And then what happened?"

"I told you. She screamed she had roaches crawling all over her and she tried to throw herself out the window. I had to knock her over the head to stop her."

"Did you hurt her?"

Traci grinned. "Naw, she was fine. The next day she got up and walked out."

"Did she tell you where she was going?"

"She said she had to go see a friend."

"Any names?"

"No."

"And then she came back?"

"For a little while. Then she left again. She said she had some sort of appointment and we ain't seen her since."

"Did she say anything about any jewelry?"

"You mean like gold chains?"

"No, I mean like diamond pins and earrings."

"Wow." Mike's eyes widened. "I wouldn't have figured her for big-time stuff."

"Neither did the person she took them from," I said dryly. "So," I continued, "she never mentioned anything about the diamonds?"

Mike shook his head.

"You sure?"

"Yeah, I'm sure."

"I don't suppose you happened to get a chance to glance in her backpack?"

"I don't do things like that," Mike told me in a tone that indicated that he had.

"And she didn't talk about selling any jewelry?"

"The only thing she was selling," Traci said, "was a couple of nickel bags of weed, and we weren't buying."

I tried one last question. "I don't suppose Estrella mentioned the names of any friends?"

Traci shook her head. "Sorry."

I sighed. Well, I'd found where Estrella had stayed all right, only it hadn't done any good. I was now forty dollars poorer and no closer to finding the girl than I was when I walked in. Oh, well. Who knew? Maybe she'd come back here. The problem was I couldn't wait around to find out. I had too many other things to do. The best I could do was give Traci my business card and ask her to call me if Estrella showed up. I was just reaching in my backpack for one when a loud shriek cut through the air.

Mike's eyes narrowed. "Can't you shut that goddamned bird up?" he snapped at Traci.

"She's bored," Traci growled. "What the hell do you want me to do?"

"Get rid of it. You complain about me letting Estrella stay here, but then you have that goddamned bird. You can hear her through the entire building."

"No, you can't."

"You sure as hell can."

"What kind is it?" I asked, hoping to head off another spat.

"A raven," Traci said.

Well, that explained all the sounds I'd heard. Ravens were excellent mimics. "That's an unusual bird," I told her. Which was true. "You don't see many of those around."

Traci's eyes brightened. "You know something about them?"

"A little. I run a pet store called Noah's Ark."

"Hey, I heard of that," Traci said to me. Then she turned to Mike. "She sold that lizard to Angelo."

"Maybe you could sell her the bird."

Traci balled her hands into fists. "I told you. I ain't selling it. She's been with me longer than you have."

"Yeah, but it ain't looking so good."

I volunteered to take a quick peek. Traci hesitated for a moment, then said yes. We trotted up the stairs and I followed them into the second room on the left side of the hall. It was not what I expected. For one thing there was no garbage on the floor or graffiti on the walls. A stack of newspapers sat between two beige sofas.

"We use those to keep warm at night," Traci explained.

The room smelled pleasantly of oranges.

"We scatter orange peel around the baseboards 'cause mice and rats don't like them," Traci told me when I asked. "My grannie taught me that."

"I bet they don't like the raven either," I commented.

Traci laughed. "Yeah, Annette does her part."

"We put boric acid down, too," Mike added. "For the roaches. It collects in their joints and freezes them so they can't move. It's not bad, is it?" he went on.

"Not at all," I agreed.

"It took us two days to clean this room out. The only problem is the water—we gotta bring it in from outside—but the guy that owns the Mobil station across the street lets us use his bathrooms to wash up and do our business."

Traci looked around. "And we ain't gonna be here for that long. We're gonna get out of here real soon."

"Before the end of the summer," Mike agreed, reciting what was obviously a familiar mantra. "We just got to put together some cash and we'll be on our feet."

"That's right," Traci said and moved toward the bird. "Annette, meet Robin," she introduced.

"Hello, Annette," I said.

Annette cocked her head, regarded me, and gave out with a deep *corronk*.

"She looks okay to me," I told Traci. The bird's feathers were glossy, her eyes bright.

Traci stuck out her tongue at Mike. For a few seconds they were both twelve years old again.

"How did she make it through the winter?"

"Oh, we've just been here since the end of March," Traci told me. "That's when Mike got kicked out of his house."

Mike muttered something under his breath and turned to the wall.

"But we're gonna be going someplace soon," Traci told me, an anxious expression on her face as she watched Mike. "And things are gonna be fine. Isn't that right?"

"Yeah," Mike said softly and faced us again, having put his private demons back in their boxes. "Yeah. Everything is gonna be fine. We're going to head down to Austin. I hear they got lots of jobs down there."

I hoped for his sake he was right. He certainly needed some luck.

"She, Estrella, left a jacket here," Traci volunteered. "You want it?"

I told her I did.

"What did you have to do that for?" Mike demanded when she handed it to me.

"Because I want it out of here," Traci snapped. "It stinks of tobacco."

Mike extended his neck and raised his chin. "What happens if she comes back to get it? What do we say then?"

I pointed to the card I'd just put in his hand. "Just tell her to come see me and I'll give it to her."

They were still arguing when I left, and somehow I didn't think it was about what happened to Estrella's jacket.

As I walked down the steps I looked at the denim jacket Traci had handed me. It was indistinguishable from any of the others out there. The question was, why had she left it behind? This was April, not July. There were still plenty of cold nights ahead. By the time I got down the stairs and had climbed out the window I thought of two possible explanations.

One: she intended to come back and get it and something had stopped her. Or two: she didn't need it anymore because she had money to buy something else. For Garriques's sake I hoped the first possibility was the correct one. Of course, there was a third possibility—that she'd come in and hadn't come out. But as much as I tried I couldn't picture Mike and Traci killing someone: stealing from them, yes; murdering them, no.

Once I got outside I just stood for a minute and enjoyed the fresh air. It had stopped drizzling and the sun was trying to come out. I started walking to the cab. While I did I couldn't help thinking about Mike and Traci and wondering if they'd ever make it to Austin, and if they did how things would go for them down there. As I turned the corner I heard a shout and looked up. Traci was waving to me from a broken window. I waved back. Then she disappeared and I kept going.

Once I reached the cab I got in and lit a cigarette. Then I went through Estrella's jacket pockets. I found a stick of Chapstick in the first, a package of breath mints and a condom—ribbed—in the second, and in the third I found an appointment card for Don Eddison, the psychologist I'd sat next to at Marsha's funeral. I flipped the gray card over. Someone had written a date from last week and Estrella's name in green ink.

Maybe the afternoon hadn't been such a waste after all.

Chapter
17

I called up Eddison the moment I got back to the store. His receptionist picked up after the second ring. When I asked for an appointment she told me in a way too cheerful voice that I was in luck. Due to a last minute cancellation, there was a slot available at eight o'clock that evening. I said I'd be there, hung up, and went back to work.

I spent the first part of the afternoon removing another bat from a house and the second part of the afternoon helping a customer chose a bird for her boyfriend. Tim left at seven. At seven-thirty I closed up the shop, dropped Zsa Zsa back at the house, and took off for Eddison's. I got there with five minutes to spare. His office was located in a rectangular, three-story brick building located in Wide Water's Plaza. I'd been told the building had been constructed for an ad agency, but the agency head had been arrested for embezzling funds and was serving two-to-five somewhere out in the Midwest. The building was now home to a multitude of therapists and one- and two-man white collar operations. The turnover rate was high.

As I climbed the stairs to Eddison's office I wondered what Estrella was doing with him and how she'd gotten here. From the little I knew of the girl I would have expected her to be seeing the school psychologist or a probation officer instead of a New Age therapist who specialized in phobias, stress reduction, and finding your center—whatever that was. Eddison's operation, Improvement Associates, was the last door at the end of a long, narrow corridor. A series of chimes sounded when I walked in.

"I'll be right out," Eddison called out from the back room.

I stood there for a moment and studied the room. The waiting area was small. The furnishings, a receptionist's desk, a small sofa, and a coffee table, left just enough room to walk around. The pieces were all wicker, the type of thing a college graduate might buy when decorating his first apartment. Well, one thing was for sure. Either Eddison's business was on the skimpy side or he didn't like to spend money. The sofa squeaked when I sat down on it. I looked around for an ashtray, but naturally there wasn't one so I occupied myself by scanning a brochure on building self-esteem. I had just turned it over and was reading the testimonials printed on the back, one from a Brandon F. and the other from Elise R., when Eddison appeared. When he saw me he got an I've-seen-this-person-before-but-I-can't-place-them expression on his face.

I helped him out. "We met at Marsha Pennington's funeral," I told him as I stood up.

His smile flashed and died. It was all teeth. "That's right, we did." He came over and pumped my hand as if he was running for office. "Poor Marsha," he murmured. "She must have felt she had nowhere to turn. And Merlin . . ." He sighed and shook his head.

"What about him?"

"Well, you know how they got along. I don't think that's any secret. But still . . . when someone kills themselves like that . . . sometimes the guilt is overwhelming . . ." Eddison's voice trailed off. "I just hope Merlin has a good support system."

"I don't think you have to worry about that," I said dryly, thinking of Shirley.

"Was Marsha a friend of yours?" Eddison asked. "Is that how you got my name?" Then he went on before I could answer. "She was very nice about that kind of thing. I got a lot of referrals from her."

"She must have thought highly of you," I observed.

"She did." Eddison fiddled with the top button of his maroon shirt. He looked lost and ineffectual. I couldn't imagine him helping anyone. "We were making wonderful progress. That's why I don't understand . . . what she did."

"Neither do I."

"There was something I must have missed." I wanted to say that there was a lot he'd probably missed, but I didn't have the heart. Eddison's shoulders sagged. For a moment he seemed to be conducting an internal dialogue with himself. Then he straightened up. "But enough of that," he said briskly. "Let's talk about you. How can I help?"

"Actually I'm hoping you might be able to assist me in locating this girl." I gave him the card I'd taken out of Estrella's jacket.

He stared at it for a moment and handed it back. "Estrella Torres." His voice was flat. His face was hard. "I can't say I'm surprised."

"You're assuming she's done something bad. Why?"

"She has, hasn't she?"

"Yes," I allowed.

"I don't think it would be breaching confidentiality if I said that she is a very disturbed, hostile young woman."

"Somehow she doesn't seem like your type of client."

"She's not." Eddison clasped his hands in front of him. "She's not at all. Usually my clients are more . . . more . . ."

"Middle class," I suggested. "More verbal."

"Exactly." The smile came and went again.

"Do you mind if I ask how she wound up here?"

"No. I don't mind at all. It's no secret. Actually the *Herald* wrote an article about this several months ago." He assumed a lecturing stance. "I'm taking part in a pilot program with the city high schools. Several people, including myself, thought it would be nice to offer an alternative experience to troubled young men and women of different cultural backgrounds, to open them up to new, more growth enhancing experiences."

"That was generous of you."

"Oh, don't misunderstand. I am getting a small stipend. Nothing much. Really just enough to cover my expenses." He paused and shook his head regretfully. "But I'm afraid it hasn't worked out as well as I hoped. The program is being discontinued at the end of June. It's really too bad. I was beginning to make progress with some of the young men. I'm afraid they'll be losing a wonderful opportunity for spiritual growth."

Not to mention the money you'll be losing, I thought uncharitably.

"Of course," he continued, "to be honest Estrella wasn't one of my successes. I kept trying to get her to visualize a more," he hesitated, "positive lifestyle for herself. But I failed completely. I simply couldn't reach the girl."

"How many times did you see her?"

"Five, and every one was a waste."

"Did you and she ever talk about her friends or activities?"

"No." Eddison smoothed over the collar of his shirt. "We didn't talk at all, at least not in any meaningful sense. Mostly she'd sit in the chair in my office and tell me how stupid everyone was. She didn't want to try meditation. She didn't want to try visualizations. She didn't want to talk. Usually after fifteen minutes she'd get up and leave. By then her boyfriend would be downstairs waiting for her. She'd hop in his truck and off they'd go."

"Then why did she come?"

"She had to. It was part of the deal she and the principal in her school worked out. Otherwise she'd have been expelled."

Another thing Garriques hadn't told me about, I thought. "Did you tell the school that she was leaving early?"

"No, I didn't." Eddison started fiddling with his tie. "Maybe I should have, but I wanted to gain her trust. Unfortunately I never did." His shoulders sagged again.

"Did her boyfriend ever come up to the office?"

"No, but I could see him from the window in my office. He was tall and skinny. He had spiked platinum hair. And the three times I saw him he was always dressed in black."

"I don't suppose you know his name."

Eddison pursed his lips. "Ray . . . Ray Diamond. Estrella mentioned it in one of her rare conversational outbursts."

"Thanks a lot," I told him. "You've been very helpful."

He reached over and put his hand on my shoulder. I hate when people do that. "Now that we've solved that problem, is there anything I can help you with?"

"I'm fine, thanks."

"Visualization, smoking cessation, relaxation techniques?"

I held up my hands. "Maybe another time."

"Because if you don't mind my saying so, you're looking a little tense. Maybe Marsha told you about my special?"

"No, she didn't," I said, backing away.

"Basically you get three sessions for the price of two."

"I'll think about it," I promised and I turned and fled out the door.

He looked so woebegone when I left that I felt guilty.

Which was ridiculous.

But maybe that's how he got his business. He guilted people into becoming his clients.

The first thing I did when I got outside was light a cigarette. Then I got in the cab and drove over to a Chinese take-out place on Erie Boulevard called the Golden Coin and ordered an egg roll and a small orange beef, extra hot. While I was waiting for my order I looked up Ray Diamond in the telephone book. I was in luck. There were thirty-one Diamonds listed, but only one of them was a Ray.

Unfortunately when I rang him up no one answered. I retrieved my quarter, copied down Diamond's number and address and picked up my food. I was so hungry I ended up wolfing down everything in the car. Maybe it was because I'd eaten too much too fast, but I was just finishing my last spoonful of rice when a wave of exhaustion hit me. All I wanted to do was go home and lie down; but then I thought about Garriques and the fight he was going to have with Enid if I didn't get those jewels back and how she'd probably be mad enough to cancel her order for the fish tank, which meant I'd be out hundreds of dollars, and I decided to run by Diamond's house after all. Lotus Avenue wasn't that far away and who knew? Maybe Estrella was hiding out there. Maybe Ray wasn't answering the phone. At the very least he should be able to give me the names of some of Estrella's friends.

There weren't many cars on the road and I made the drive over in less than twenty minutes. Five-thirty-two was a small, tired-looking house in the middle of the block. I parked the cab, got out, and rang the bell. Somebody yelled out they'd be there in just a minute. It was good I'd taken the time to come after all. A few seconds later a man fitting the description Eddison had given me came to the door. As he stood there I realized I'd seen him before. And then I knew where. He was the guy who'd gotten out of the M & M Exterminators truck when I'd been talking to Manuel.

"If you're looking for Tony, he's cleared out," he told me.

"Actually I'm looking for Estrella Torres."

"Well, she ain't here either."

He started to close the door, but I'd already put my foot in it. "I thought she was your girlfriend."

Ray looked disgusted. "Whoever told you that don't know fuck-all."

"They saw you picking her up."

"We hang together once in a while—not that it's any of your business. You a cop or something . . ."

"Or something."

"Well, if you ain't a cop, I don't have to talk to you."

"Listen," I told him. "I really don't want to get you in trouble and I don't want to get Estrella in trouble. All I want to do is recover the jewelry that she stole from someone's house."

Ray snorted. "Good luck, lady. She probably sold it on the street by now. It's gone."

"Do you know that for a fact?"

"No, but she's been talkin' about goin' to New Jersey, and I ain't seen her lately."

"Any idea of who she was gonna stay with?"

"Frankly I don't know and I don't care. Estrella, she just

dropped too much acid. She isn't all there no more if you get my meaning. Always carrying on about how everyone was out to get her. That kind of stuff gets old real fast."

"I don't suppose you know the names of her other friends."

"No," he said, but somehow I didn't believe him.

I handed him my card. "If she turns up, give me a call."

He grunted and slammed the door.

As I drove home I thought about the fact that I was not much closer to finding Estrella now than I was when I started this morning. Ordinarily that fact would have depressed me, but I was too tired to care. All I wanted to do was go home and go to bed. Which is what I did.

I was in a deep sleep when the phone rang. It took me a minute to wake up and another minute to find the damn thing among the pile of newspapers I keep meaning to throw out.

"Yes," I mumbled.

"Robin? Robin Light?"

I groaned as Zsa Zsa walked across my stomach. "Who is this?"

"Traci."

"Traci who?" My head felt as if it were filled with cotton wool.

"Traci from the Colony Plaza."

"Okay. Right." My mind was beginning to clear.

"You'd better come down here." Her voice sounded far away.

"Where are calling from?"

"The Mobil station across the way. Please come now," Traci pleaded.

"Why? What's the problem?"

"We've found Estrella."

Chapter
18

I sat straight up in bed. Now I was awake. "Where is she?"

"She's on the third floor. She's not moving. I think she's dead." Traci started to sob. "I know I shouldn't be calling you, but I'm afraid to call the police. I'm afraid they'll think we did it. I don't know what to do."

"Where's Mike?"

"He's with me." I could hear Traci gulping for air.

"Okay. Both of you stay put. I'll be there in ten minutes."

I was there in five. On the way over a voice in the recesses of my mind kept telling me I should stop at the nearest phone and call the police. I ignored it and kept on going.

Traci and Mike were waiting for me by the window I used to slip in and out of the building. I took an extra moment to stow the car under the overhang. Then I grabbed my flashlight from the glove compartment and ran to join them.

"Jesus, Jesus," Mike kept muttering over and over again while Traci hovered around him.

"Okay, tell me what happened?" I ordered.

"We heard this noise," Mike stammered.

"Like this crash, like things were falling," Traci said. Even in the dim light I could see her face was streaked with tears. Mike's face was slick with sweat. "It woke us up."

"And then we didn't hear anything."

"I thought it was a cat," Traci said.

"But then we heard this car backfiring."

"Only I knew that it wasn't. I knew it was a gun going off."

"So what did you do?" I asked.

Traci pointed at Mike. "He wanted to go down and see what was going on, but I didn't want him to," Traci said. "I wanted him to stay upstairs with me. But he wouldn't listen."

"See," Mike explained. "I didn't want no one comin' up here and messin' with Traci. So I took out my knife and my can of mace and kind of crept down the stairs." Mike pulled on one of his dreads. "Jesus. Estrella was just laying there staring up at nothing at all. There was all this black stuff underneath her. At first I thought I was looking at a doll, man. She didn't look real."

"And then what?"

Mike looked abashed. "I was really freaked. I just ran back up the stairs. I was almost at the top when I heard something below." Mike shuddered. "I saw this black shape running down the stairs." His face looked yellow under the street light. "I coulda been dead, man. I coulda been dead just like Estrella. My heart was beatin' so fast I couldn't hardly breathe."

"And then we were afraid to come down," Traci said. "We hid under a desk 'cause we thought that this guy was gonna come up and get us. And we waited and waited. But then I couldn't stand it no more and we ran down as fast as we could and called you." Traci pulled at her T-shirt. "I hope he ain't still in the building."

I looked at the Colony. "I'd give you ten-to-one odds that he's gone. There'd be no reason for him to stay."

"Man oh man." Mike swung his head from side to side. "What we gonna do now? Nobody's gonna believe that we didn't have nuthin' to do with this."

I took a deep breath. "I think the first thing we'd better do is take a look at Estrella."

"I don't wanna go back in there," Mike whispered. "I don't wanna see her eyes no more."

"You don't have to look at her, but I need someone to show me where she is. I have to make sure she's dead."

Mike let out a strangled sob.

"I'll show you," Traci volunteered.

"No." Mike squared his shoulders. "I'll go. It's only right. If it weren't for me, we wouldn't be in this mess right now."

"We'll all go," I said. "It's better than being out on the street if a patrol car comes around."

The dark in the building was like a blanket. It wrapped us in blackness. The only sources of illumination were the beams from our three flashlights bobbing along the walls and the floor. Traci and Mike moved along on sure feet, but I kept on tripping over furniture and boxes. I heard scurrying and rustling all around us. Occasionally small yellow eyes peered out at us and I had to repress a shudder.

"They won't bother you unless you're eating," Traci said.

"Or unless you get too near a nest," Mike added. Then he fell silent.

The only noises were the rodents and the echo of our feet walking up the stairs. The climb seemed interminable. I kept thinking I heard someone coming up after us, but it was only my imagination. No one was there. Finally we reached Estrella. She was sprawled out on the hall floor. She must have been backing away from her killer. Her eyes were staring straight up, and for a moment I thought about the old belief that her murderer's image was burned in her pupils for everyone to see.

Then I put that thought away and studied the rest of her face. Her mouth was gaping open. A thin line of blood ran down her chin and onto her throat. Her chest was all blood. In the flashlight's glare it showed up as a black pool fouling her shirt and the floor underneath her. I swallowed to keep myself from throwing up and played the light over her body. Her shirt was rucked up and one of her sneakers had fallen off. I pulled her shirt down and put her sneaker back on. Then I went through her jean pockets. Except for a couple of coins they were empty. If she'd had the jewelry, she didn't have it now. Poor kid. All she'd wanted to do was get out of town. Now the only place she was going was the ME's.

I straightened up and looked around for her belongings. There weren't any. Whoever had killed her must have taken whatever she'd had. They'd followed her in, robbed and shot her.

"The cops are gonna think I did this," Mike cried. His voice cut through the silence.

"Why should they do that?" I asked, even though I pretty much knew what he was going to say.

"Because I'm here, man. Because they know me."

Traci started to sob.

The sound ricocheted through my head. I rubbed my temples. I knew what I should do. I knew what the right thing to do was. I also knew what I was going to do.

"How much money have you got?" I asked abruptly.

"Maybe fifty bucks," Mike said. "Why?"

"Because you have to get out of here."

But fifty dollars wasn't going to get them very far, that was for sure. I rubbed my temples while I thought. I had about two hundred and fifty dollars in petty cash at the store. I guess my creditors could wait another month if they had to.

"But what about Estrella?" Mike's voice was quavering. "We can't leave her here."

"Don't worry. I won't." I turned and led them up the stairs.

It didn't take them long to gather their possessions. Between the two of them they had two backpacks, a couple of shopping bags, and the bird.

"Where are we going?" Traci asked once we were out on the street.

"To the store and then to the bus terminal."

"But what am I going to do about Annette?" she wailed, indicating the covered cage I was carrying with a nod of her head.

"If the driver won't let you take her on the bus, I'll keep her at the store until you get settled," I promised. "You can give me a call and I'll ship her down when you're ready."

"Thanks," Traci whispered.

"Forget about it," I told her as we hurried toward the cab.

No one said anything on the ride over to Noah's Ark. As I cleaned out the petty cash drawer and gave the money to Traci I tried not to think about the next round of bills coming due.

"We can't take this," Traci said as I pressed the money into her hand. "It just ain't right."

"I don't think you have a choice," I told her. Then I bundled them back in the car and drove them to the bus station.

A Trailways bus was idling next to the north exit. A line of tired-looking people were straggling onto it. I pulled up and asked the bus driver where he was headed.

"Atlanta. In five minutes."

Mike, Traci, and I looked at each other.

"I never been out of Syracuse," Mike said. There was a quaver in his voice.

"You'll do fine," I told him.

"Atlanta *is* pretty near Austin." Traci's voice was quavering, too.

I didn't dispute her. This wasn't the time for a geography lesson.

Mike ran in and got the tickets.

I pulled the driver aside, pointed to the raven, and gave him thirty dollars. He shrugged and palmed it.

Mike, Traci, and I hugged in the chill spring air.

The driver tapped her on the shoulder and told her it was time to go. As they were climbing up the stairs Traci ran back. "I don't know if this is important or not," she told me, "but right before she left Estrella said something about getting Ray to take her out to her mother's."

"Did she say anything else?"

Traci shook her head.

"You have my card. Call me if you remember anything else, anything at all."

"I will," Traci promised.

"Come on," the bus driver said. "We're leaving."

Traci and I hugged again and she climbed on board.

A moment later the bus roared off. I wished I was on it. Then I smoked a cigarette and went inside the depot and did what I had to do.

First I called Garriques and told him about Estrella, then I called my lawyer, and then I called the police.

They were not pleased. Or pleasant.

I met them at the Colony and took them up the stairs.

Then they took me to the PSB for questioning.

I told them about Estrella and Garriques and about how she'd taken his wife's jewels and that I'd been hired to find them. Then they asked me why I was in there at four o'clock in the morning, and I told them I hadn't been able to sleep so I decided to check the building again because I figured Estrella might still be crashing there. And I explained about having followed her in and getting hit over the head. It was obvious they didn't like my explanation, but since Garriques had verified that he'd hired me there wasn't much they could do. Four hours later, at eight in the morning, they finally threw in the towel and let me go.

I met Connelly as I was going out the door. He must have been coming in for roll call. "What they get you for?" he sneered, looking me up and down. "Vagrancy?"

Joe, my lawyer, dragged me off before I could reply. "I don't even want to hear about this," he told me when we got outside. His Italian silk shirt was wrinkled and he had pouches the size of laundry bags under his eyes, but then I probably didn't look too good either.

"Fine," I said as we walked toward his BMW.

He dropped me off at my cab and bid me a rather surly goodbye. He didn't like losing sleep. Well, neither did I, but at least he was being paid for it. Handsomely. As he sped off I turned and stared at the Colony.

The building was quiet. The police cars and the crime scene van and the ambulance had all left. Everyone had packed up their equipment and gone home. The Colony once again belonged to the rats and the mice and the dispossessed. Yellow crime scene tape fluttered across the windows, a memento of the last few hours' activities. Soon someone from the city would come and board up all the windows. Then a few months later the boards would be wrenched off and another version of Traci and Mike would be living there. The place should be torn down and made into a park.

I was reaching for a cigarette and trying to decide whether or not I should go up to the fifth floor and see if Estrella had written her mother's address anywhere when a cop in a patrol car cruised by. He slowed as he passed me; then when he was about thirty feet away he made a U-turn, came back, stopped in front of me and demanded to know what I was doing.

"Leaving," I said and I got in my cab and drove off. I could see him watching me in the rearview mirror. I briefly thought about waiting him out, but I didn't. I'd had enough aggravation for one night.

Instead I stopped at the Dunkin' Donuts on the corner of South Salina and got two peanut-covered chocolate doughnuts and a cup of coffee and headed off to the store. I knew I should go to sleep, I'd been up for twenty-four hours now, but I couldn't. I was too wired. I kept thinking about Estrella and Traci and Mike and wondering if I'd done the right thing, and then I started thinking about Ray Diamond and wondering if he had in fact driven Estrella out to her mother's house. And then I wondered if she'd left Enid's jewelry there. Even though I really didn't want to, it seemed as if I should get Estrella's mother's number off of Ray and talk to her.

I used the phone in front of the Mobil Mini Mart at Teall and Erie to call him. He wasn't home. He'd probably left for work. I looked up M & M Exterminators. Nobody answered, but according to the recording the business was supposed to be open. I went back to the phone book and read the address. It wasn't that far away. I decided to stop by on my way to work. Maybe I'd get lucky. Maybe Ray was in and he just wasn't answering the phone.

M & M Exterminators turned out to be a one-story wood structure located between a vacant lot and a burnt-out house. When I got out I could see two vans were still parked in the driveway. I walked over and rang the bell.

Merlin answered the door.

Chapter 19

Merlin's face, never a thing of beauty under any circumstances, turned even uglier when he saw me. "What the hell are you doing here?" he growled. "Don't you have anything better to do with your time than bother me?"

"I could ask the same of you."

"I own this place."

"You own M & M Exterminators?" This was news to me.

"That's right."

"Since when? I thought you were a furniture salesman."

"I am. I do that at night."

"You have two jobs?"

"That bother you?"

"It just seems quite a switch from the old Merlin."

"People do change," he said shortly. "Now get out of here before I call the cops." He slammed the door in my face.

Sleazy business, sleazy owner. It figured. For a moment I thought about knocking again and demanding to know how much he was making off his bat removal service, but then I thought why bother? It would be quicker to report him to the Better Business Bureau. Let them deal with his little scam— only the problem was that they probably wouldn't. They'd just tell him he'd been a bad boy, and he'd say he was sorry, and then he'd go on charging people who couldn't afford it a thousand dollars to lay down bat repellent in their attics which not only didn't work, but could poison them.

As I walked back to my cab I began wondering if maybe Merlin hadn't used some of his products on Marsha. After all, the stuff they used on bats could kill a person, too. Maybe Merlin had poisoned Marsha, then dumped her body in the LeMoyne Reservoir. The problem was that without a tox screen there was no way to prove that, and the ME sure wasn't going to dig her up again to do one without an awful lot of evidence—which I couldn't provide.

I sighed and got back in the cab and lit a cigarette. As I took a puff of my Camel I thought about Estrella. How did she fit into the picture? She had known Ray. Ray worked with Merlin. The connections were provocative. I began wondering if Estrella had been killed for the jewels after all. Maybe she'd been killed because she'd seen something she shouldn't have. Maybe she'd wanted to go to New Jersey to talk to Marsha's mother—Marsha had been there right before she'd been killed. Maybe acid hadn't fried Estrella's brain. Maybe she wasn't paranoid. Maybe someone really was after her. Maybe she'd stolen Enid's jewelry because she was hoping to sell the pieces to pay for a ticket out of town. I twirled a lock of hair around my finger and thought about how there were just too many maybes.

I spent the next half hour turning various scenarios over in my head while I waited for Ray to emerge from the store. I'd just about given up when he finally walked out the door, jumped in his truck, and took off. I caught up with him two blocks later when he stopped at Rocky's, a mom-and-pop grocery store. He was already in the store when I pulled up behind the van. I got out of the cab and waited. He came out a couple of moments later.

"Jesus," he said when he saw me standing by the front fender. "You again. What the hell do you want?"

"To ask you something."

"I already told you I don't have anything to say about Estrella." He unwrapped the Danish he was carrying and took a bite. "You have any questions go find her and ask her them yourself."

"I can't."

"Why the hell not?" His mouth was full of food when he spoke.

"Because she's dead. Someone killed her."

Ray swallowed. His eyes widened. "You're kidding, right?"

"Do I look as if I am?"

"Wow, this is heavy shit," Ray murmured.

"That's one way of putting it."

"Do the police know?"

"Yes, they do."

He shook his head. The blond spikes he'd sprayed his hair into quivered as if they were porcupine quills. "I gotta go get me a smoke. This is too much."

I put my hand on his arm. "One thing."

"What?"

"Did you take Estrella to see her mother?"

A wary look crept across Ray's face. "Yeah, but she wasn't home. Why?"

"You drove all the way to Toronto and she wasn't there?"

"Toronto?" He looked as if he found the suggestion ludicrous. "Where'd you get that from?"

"Then where did you take her?"

"Estrella told me not to tell anyone."

"I think you should tell me."

"Why's that?"

I lit a cigarette. "You want to go home and get mellow, right?"

"Right." Ray narrowed his eyes.

"Well, if you don't tell me what I want to know, you're going to be down at the PSB."

"How do you figure that?"

"Because I'll call the police and tell them about your relationship with Estrella. They'll turn up at your door and drag you downtown for questioning. You'll be sitting there for a couple of hours at least—maybe even more."

In reality the police were going to drag him downtown anyway—if I had found Ray, so could they—but from the expression on Ray's face I could tell he didn't realize that.

I watched as conflicting emotions warred across his face. "Okay," he finally allowed. "I don't suppose it makes no difference now anyway, Estrella being dead and all. I took Estrella to this house near Manlius."

"Do you remember the address?"

"No, but it's on Route Ninety-two."

"Route Ninety-two is an awfully long road," I pointed out.

"You turn off right after this big yellow house with a 'Jews for Jesus' sign in the window."

"And then what?"

"And then you go down this road and there it is." A girl walked past us. Ray Diamond followed her with his eyes. "You know, the last time Estrella and I saw each other we had this big fight—I don't even remember what it was about. We was always fighting." He shook his head regretfully. Then he got in his van and drove off.

I finished my cigarette and went home. Zsa Zsa was waiting for me. She was not pleased with me for leaving her alone the entire night—as the condition of the floor demonstrated. I petted her, fed her, mopped up the pee, and drove over to the store.

Tim was waiting for me when I got in. "I can't make change," he informed me.

"I know."

"What happened to the petty cash?"

I stifled a yawn. "It's a long story." I wrote Tim a seventy-five-dollar check on my personal account. "Take this down to the bank and cash it," I told him. Suddenly every bone and muscle in my body ached. Last night had finally caught up with me.

"So, are you going to tell me the story?"

"Later," I promised. "I don't think I could put a straight sentence together now."

I could hardly keep my eyes open. When Tim came back I headed for my office, closed the door, and lay down on the sofa. Zsa Zsa woke me two hours later. She was sitting on my chest and licking my chin. I pushed her off and closed my eyes again. She got back up and nipped the tip of my nose. I groaned, sat up, and put my head in my hands. All I wanted to do was go back to sleep. But I couldn't, I had a store to run. Finally I forced myself up, went into the bathroom and washed my face, combed my hair and brushed my teeth. Then I made myself a cup of coffee and changed into the spare jeans and T-shirt I keep at the store for emergencies. By the time I was done with the coffee I felt semi-human.

"Ah, sleeping beauty emerges," Tim cracked as I walked into the front.

I grunted and got to work. I was in the middle of cleaning out gerbil cages when Garriques called.

"Are you all right?" he asked.

"I'm fine. I just feel bad about Estrella."

"I know. It's terrible." I could hear a student laughing in the background. "Did you know this is the second sixteen-year-old to be shot this month in the city?"

"No. I didn't know." I lit a cigarette and pulled the Coke can I was using for an ashtray closer.

"He was a runaway, too." Garriques coughed. "Bad things happen to kids on the street."

The sentiment seemed too obvious to comment on, and I asked him instead if he still wanted me to keep looking for his wife's jewelry.

"Why? Do you have an idea where the pieces might be?"

"I might."

"Good, because I checked the Torres house. Nothing. I'm beginning to think that whoever killed her took them."

"They probably did," I conceded. "But I just heard Estrella went up to visit her mother right before she died. I'm thinking maybe she gave the pieces to her." Although now that I thought about it, it seemed an unlikely possibility.

"Her mother?" Garriques's voice went up. "Is she back in town?"

"Actually she's somewhere out in Manlius."

"How'd you find that out."

"Estrella's boyfriend told me. I figured I'd take a ride out and see if I could find the house."

"That sounds . . ." The rest of Garriques's reply was drowned out by a loud clanging. "Damn," he said when the noise stopped. "I forgot about the fire drill."

"So you want me to go or not?"

"I do, but I don't."

"Do you mind explaining?"

"Well, of course I want the jewelry back. I just don't want you to get hurt again. Some of those bosses on the migrant labor gangs aren't very nice to people who come snooping around."

"I'll be careful," I said, thinking of the money I was going to lose if I didn't find his stuff. Then I went out back and raided my chocolate cache, after which I went into the bird room and told Tim I was going to be out for a little while.

"Well, I hope it's something important." He locked the door on the lovebirds' cage. "Because you seem to be forgetting that you have a store to run."

"I know what I have to do," I replied testily.

"Sometimes I wonder," Tim muttered.

There was no sense in prolonging the conversation. I whistled for Zsa Zsa and went out the door. Surprisingly I didn't have as much trouble finding the place as I thought I would. Ray's directions turned out to be accurate. I found both the house and the turn off on the first try. The road I turned into was narrow. My tires kicked up gravel as I wound through a stand of birch, honey locust and sumac. A short time later the trees ended and the open ground began. It was warm in the cab, and when I rolled down the window the soft smells of spring flooded in. A little while later the road dipped, and I caught sight of five gravestones standing about ninety feet away from the road in an open meadow. The graves looked abandoned as did the cluster of old farm equipment in back of them. The people buried in the small graveyard must be the original owners. They'd built the land up, worked it, and been buried on it. It was something you didn't see anymore.

The road went by what must have once been grass but was now rapidly becoming meadow and stopped in front of an old farmhouse. I parked the car and Zsa Zsa and I got out. Aside from the chittering of squirrels and the gentle whosh of traffic back on Ninety-two the silence was absolute. No one was here. The farmhouse looked as if it had been empty for a long time. It was listing over to the left as if it was tired and wanted to lie down. Its disheveled appearance was increased by the white splotches on the blue clapboard. Someone must have scraped off the loose paint, primed the spots and then grown bored with the job and walked away.

When I walked up to the door the steps groaned beneath my feet. I tried the bell. When it didn't work I knocked. No one answered. I waited a minute, then walked back down. A hawk circled overhead, drifting on the currents, waiting for the opportunity to strike.

I called to Zsa Zsa and headed toward the barn. A For Sale sign lay on the grass next to a old, broken chair. A rusted car with four flat tires sat in the feeding pen, replacing the cows that must have congregated there in better days. The barn itself was missing pieces of siding here and there. There was nothing here. If Estrella's mother had ever been here, she was gone now. It looked as if I'd reached a dead end. When I got back to the store I'd have to call Garriques and tell him the news. I picked up a pebble and tossed it. It plinked as it landed on the rim of an old tire. On the way out I stopped and took a look at the gravestones, more out of curiosity's sake than for any other reason.

The graves hadn't been tended to in a long time. The markers leaned this way and that. The earth around them was overrun with weeds. I squatted down and looked at the writing on the headstones while Zsa Zsa sniffed around. The names had been shallowly etched and the weather had scoured the stone, making the letters difficult to read. I made out a first name on one. Louisa. The first letter of her last name looked to be an "m." Then there was an "i" or maybe it was an "r" and an "a." I couldn't make out the rest. I got up, wiped my hands on the back of my jeans, and looked at the machinery rusting in the sun. All that effort and for what? The thought raised questions I didn't want to think about, and even watching Zsa Zsa chase a pheasant she'd spooked didn't cheer me up. I drove back to Syracuse and spent the rest of the day working.

At nine o'clock I closed up the shop and went over to Pete's. It had been a long day and I wanted a Scotch and someone to talk to. George was already there and Zsa Zsa and I sat down next to him.

"I think I lost a seven-hundred-dollar sale," I told George after I'd ordered a Black Label and given Zsa Zsa her saucer of beer. I proceeded to tell him about Estrella and Garriques and his wife's jewelry and that not recovering it probably meant Enid would reconsider her birthday present.

"I know I would if I were her," I said glumly.

George drained his Rolling Rock and signaled Connie to bring him another one. "Maybe she's not you."

I grunted a response.

"Sounds as if you've had a lousy day," George commented as he fed a handful of peanuts to Zsa Zsa one at a time.

"It was a frustrating day."

"Mine was, too." He threw a handful of peanuts into his mouth. "I'm thinking of quitting the program."

I looked at him with consternation. "You can't do that. You just started."

George glared at me. "I can do whatever the hell I want. The truth is I don't belong in grad school. I was stupid to think I would."

I ran my finger around the rim of my glass. "You know, stuff like research is difficult in the beginning."

"Oh, I can do the research fine," George said bitterly. "It's the writing I'm having problems with. I think one thing and it comes out on the paper another way."

"I told you I'd be glad to help."

"I don't want anyone's help," George snapped.

"If you just—"

"I mean it."

"Fine." I finished my drink and moved down to talk to Connie. Zsa Zsa followed. When George got pissy it was better to stay away from him.

Connie looked up from the book she was reading. It was entitled, *How to Make 100,000 Dollars In Six Months*.

"Learn anything useful?" I asked.

"Not yet," she replied and went back to her reading.

I looked around for someone else to talk to, but the only other people there were a couple who obviously didn't want to be disturbed. Great. I shredded part of my napkin, and then when I got tired of doing that I went into the kitchen to talk to Sal, the bar's resident cook and back-room bookie. I'd wanted to ask him some questions about Marsha and now seemed as good a time as any, but he didn't turn out to be too communicative.

"Yeah, I knew Marsha," he said, looking up briefly from the hamburger he was cooking on the grill. He was a small walnut-colored man who'd lost his four front teeth somewhere along the way. It gave his speech a whistling sound. "What of it?"

"Nothing." I leaned against the sink. "I just wondered if she ever placed any bets with you."

He didn't say anything. I could hear the meat sizzling on the grill.

"I heard she was a big player."

He snorted. "Who told you that?"

"Connie."

He lifted an eyebrow. "There you have it, then." He reached for a hamburger bun and set it on a plate. Then he put a couple of handfuls of potato chips next to it.

"You're saying Connie lied?"

"I'm saying she tends to exaggerate."

"Then Marsha didn't place big bets with you?"

Sal's eyes narrowed slightly. "Listen, I don't place bets for people. I do favors for them."

"My mistake." I guess that was one way of putting it. I shifted my weight from one leg to another. "Does Fast Eddie just do favors for people, too?"

Sal flipped the hamburger and pressed it down with his spatula. The juices oozed out. "I wouldn't know. I've never talked to him."

"I see."

"I'm glad you do." Sal put the burger onto the bun, added a limp slice of tomato, slid the plate through the serving window, and pushed the bell down with his hand. Then he began scraping the grease off the griddle with his spatula. His moves were slow and deliberate.

"You're not going to tell me anything, then?" I asked.

Sal didn't look up. "There's nothing to tell."

"Could you call me if you do hear anything about Marsha?"

"Sure." Sal put the spatula on the counter and wiped his hands on his apron. Somehow I had the distinct feeling he was wiping his hands of me. The gesture didn't improve my mood. "I got no problem with that." But I didn't believe him.

"Do you think you could tear yourself away from that book long enough to get me another Scotch," I snapped at Connie when I came back out.

"I guess." She unenthusiastically put the book down and poured me a Black Label.

"So what have you learned?" I asked as she slid the drink along the bar.

"That it takes money to make money."

"Well, that lets me out."

"Me, too," Connie said sadly.

"Then why are you reading it?"

"I got to do something." Connie looked around. "I'm sure not going to make any cash here. This place gets any deader we'll have to hold a memorial service. Speaking of which, how was Marsha's funeral? I was thinking of going but . . . I don't know . . . I just didn't."

"What do you mean how was it? It was depressing. How else could it be?"

Connie shrugged. "I don't know. I just figured if her boyfriend showed up things might get a little interesting."

"Her boyfriend?"

"I told you about him."

"No you didn't."

"Well, I thought I had," Connie said.

"So who is it?" I asked impatiently.

"You know. The guy with the funny last name."

"What guy?" I realized I was talking through gritted teeth.

"The one that works at Wellington as a janitor."

I thought for a minute. "You mean Brandon Funk?"

Connie smiled. "Yeah. That's who I mean."

Chapter
20

"So how do you know this?" I asked.

Connie ran her fingers through her hair. "How do you think I know? They used to come in together."

"Did they act like that?" I pointed to the couple necking at the far end of the bar.

"No. But I could tell anyway."

"How?"

"I could just tell, that's all."

Knowing Connie I was sure that she could. God knows she'd had enough experience in this particular field. I tapped my fingers against my teeth.

No wonder Brandon had been so touchy when I'd been in Marsha's room at Wellington.

No wonder he'd seemed so lost at her funeral.

Who would have thought it?

Maybe that's why Marsha had been so anxious to get a divorce.

Maybe that's why Merlin had been so vindicative to the dogs.

Things were beginning to make a little more sense. I was just about to go and tell George my latest discovery when a blonde came through the door and made a beeline for him. It was obvious from the way George was smiling he wasn't sorry to see her.

"Who's that?" I hissed at Connie.

"Nadine. She works at the video store down the street."

"Why didn't you tell me about her?"

"There's nothing to tell. Go over there and introduce yourself."

"I can't. I have to leave," I lied. Suddenly the only thing I wanted to do was get out of there. I called for Zsa Zsa and headed for the door.

George glanced up as I passed. A puzzled expression crossed his face, but he didn't say anything. Neither did I.

I wanted to kick myself when I got outside. I'd acted as if I was fourteen. I should have stayed, but I hadn't and it was too late to go back in now. So I went home, but I was fidgety. I couldn't sit still. Even walking Zsa Zsa didn't help. I had to do something and that something, I decided, was going to see Brandon Funk.

I looked up his number and called. Funk must have been sitting by the phone because he picked up right away. When I told him I wanted to talk about Marsha he told me to come right over. I said I would and hung up. The wind was picking up when I stepped outside. Zsa Zsa's nose started twitching and she gave an alarmed little bark. Nights like this make her uneasy. As I drove down Colvin the swaying branches of the trees looked ghostly under the street lamps. We were in for another storm.

Brandon Funk lived on Ruth Street in the smallest house I'd ever seen. It was square, built of cinder blocks, and looked for all the world as if a giant toddler had been playing with Legos and then just wandered off and left his creation sitting in the middle of a building lot. As I walked up the path to the front door two pink flamingos and a small ceramic bear marked my progress. Before I could ring the bell the door flew open.

"You're here," Funk said and he motioned me inside.

When I crossed the threshold I stopped in amazement. Every available inch that wasn't taken up with furniture or clothes or photographs was covered with stuffed animals, and I don't mean the toy kind either. There were deer and moose heads, bats set in picture frames hanging on the walls, and a family of raccoons standing on the top of the bureau. The faint odors of rotting flesh, formaldehyde, and varnish mixed with a floral air freshener hung in the air. I was glad I'd left Zsa Zsa in the car. Somehow I didn't think she'd do well with this stuff. I know I didn't.

"Did you shoot these?" I asked.

Funk shook his head. "People just give them to me. Taxidermy is my hobby. Marsha and I . . ." He clenched his fists. A spurt of anger flashed across his face. "Sit down," he said when it passed. "You want a beer?"

"That would be nice."

As he went to the refrigerator to get it I looked around. The house seemed to consist of one large room, maybe fifteen by twenty feet at the most, that functioned as a combination living room, dining room, and kitchen. From where I was sitting I could see a small sleeping alcove off to the right and what I assumed to be a bathroom off to the left. The furniture was dark-wooded, carved Victorian and there was

enough of it to furnish three rooms. A variety of framed photographs sat on one of the chests. I walked over and took a
look. Most of the pictures were of bats flying in and out of a
barn at dusk. Only one was of a person, a man. His hair was
unkempt and so was his beard. His clothes looked as if they'd
been slept in. He was the kind of person you'd go out of your
way to avoid if you saw him on the street.

Funk came back with the beer. "That's Porter," he said as
he handed me the can. "He was my best friend. He taught
me how to do this." Brandon gestured toward the stuffed animals. "We started on bats 'cause they were easy and there
were always lots of them in the barn. Then we went on to
snakes. He was gonna show me how to do a raccoon, but he
went away. He didn't even say goodbye or nuthing."

"Bats." Something rang a bell. "Did Porter ever write a
book about bats?"

Funk's eyes widened. "How did you know that?"

"One of the curators at the zoo mentioned it. I don't suppose you happen to have a copy?"

Funk nodded.

"Can I see it?"

"All right." His tone was reluctant, but he went over to his
bookcase, got it out, and handed it to me.

I turned the book over in my hand. It looked as if it were
a vanity press job. Whoever had printed it had done it as
cheaply as possible. I was about to open it when Funk took it
out of my hands.

"I don't like people handling it," he explained. "It rips too
easy."

So much for looking at it, I thought. "Whatever happened
to Porter?"

Funk shook his head. "I already told you. He went away."

"Do you know where?"

His eyes turned mournful. "No," he said. "And I don't want to talk about it no more either."

"All right." As far as I could see there was nothing more about Porter to discuss anyway.

Funk pointed to the can of beer he'd given me. "Are you going to drink that?"

"Absolutely." I popped the tab off my Schlitz and took a sip. It was terrible. I tried not to make a face.

"My mother owns this place," Brandon confided to me. "She owns lots of places. My uncle gave them to her." He went rambling on the way a person will when they're lonely and have no one to talk to. "She lets me live here. She lives next door with my grandmother. They don't like all my animals." Brandon gestured around the room. "Or the chemicals. That's why I stay here. Only it's warmer over there." His face clouded over. "I don't like being cold. That's why I don't like the country. It's cold out there." He took another sip of his beer, then put it down on the coffee table. "You know, I'm glad you did what you did with the dogs," he confided.

"How do you know it was me?"

"I heard Merlin talking to somebody. He mentioned your name."

I repressed a smile.

Brandon glanced away. "What he did, that was wrong." For a minute I thought he was going to cry.

"I agree."

"He had no call to do that. None. You know, Marsha and me were going to open up a little shop." Brandon stared down at his hands. Like everything else about him they were big and pink. "We had the place all picked out. We even had a name—Porter." Brandon pointed to the man in the picture. "I was gonna name the place after him, but now I guess that ain't going to happen, 'cause there ain't gonna be no place."

"What kind of store were you planning on opening?" I asked gently. I realized I was talking to him the way I would a child.

He gave me an incredulous look. "Taxidermy of course. You can make lots of money doing that. I sent for this book that tells you how." He got up. "Here, let me show you." The next thing I knew I had a pamphlet entitled *Taxidermy For Fun And Profit* sitting in my lap. "Do you know how many people hunt each year?"

I shook my head.

"Thousands. See, that's what Marsha and I were going to do."

"Maybe you can do it with someone else?" I suggested.

"It wouldn't be the same." His face grew hard. I took another sip of my beer to be polite and put the can down on the table.

"Did Merlin know about you two?"

"I don't care if he did."

"That's not what I'm asking."

Brandon scratched the side of his cheek. "He didn't say anything to me at the funeral."

"Would he have cared if he had known?"

"Why should he?" Brandon drained his beer can and squeezed it till it collapsed.

"Some men might object," I observed dryly.

"He has Shirley," he added, giving the name an ugly twist. "You ask me, she was the one that put him up to the stuff with the dogs. If you ask me, she probably killed them herself."

"I don't know." I thought back to what Shirley had told me. "She seemed pretty upset to me."

"Yeah, right." Brandon got up, walked over to the refrigerator and took another beer. "She likes killing things. Don't let her tell you no different. Ask her what she did to the cat that was peeing on her front door."

"I will," I said. "You seem to know a lot about her."

"I should. We lived together for a while. Mom said I shouldn't, but I wouldn't pay her no mind. Well, she was right. Let me tell you the only reason Shirley took up with Merlin was to get back at me." He opened his second beer and downed it. "You ask me those two make a good pair. She says it and he does it. You know, Merlin didn't even preserve them right. Porter woulda whopped him one with a strap for doin' that kind of job. The first rainy day those dogs would have started stinkin'." Brandon balled up his hands into fists again. "It's a good thing I didn't see Po and Pooh till after you left. Otherwise I would have done something real bad to Merlin. Real bad," he repeated.

For a moment I almost felt sorry for Merlin. Almost, but not quite. I put the taxidermy pamphlet down on the table.

"But I don't do stuff like that no more," Brandon told me.

"What kind of stuff?"

He looked down at his hands. "I used to have a bad temper." He began chewing on the inside of his lip.

Somehow I had the feeling that he still did—but I didn't say that. "Do you mind if I smoke?" I asked instead.

"Can't. Too many chemicals in here. That's another reason my mother don't like this place. She smokes like a chimney."

Brandon ran his tongue over his lips. They were so chapped they were almost bright red. "You know, Marsha and me were going to get married after she got divorced. We were gonna open a store together, too," Brandon murmured.

"I know. You already told me."

"Did I tell you I was gonna paint it red and white. And then we were gonna rent a house. We had it all picked out. It was on Fellows Avenue."

"All of that would cost a lot," I observed, thinking of the money Marsha owed.

"Yeah. Well." Brandon picked at his fingernail. "Marsha said not to worry about it. She said she'd get the money when she got divorced. She was gonna make Merlin sell the business. She said she could do it because she owned most of it." Interesting, I thought as I watched Brandon grin. "Boy, Shirley got mad when she heard about it. She went over to Marsha's and she was yelling and screaming and carrying on."

I took a deep breath. "I was told Marsha owed a great deal of money to bookies."

Funk flushed. "Who told you that?"

"I forget." The last thing I was going to do was give him Connie's name.

Funk's face turned redder. "I bet it was Shirley, wasn't it? Wasn't it? She was always saying bad things like that."

"Why would she want to do something like that?"

"I told you. Because she hated Marsha and me. She was jealous. She wanted me back. She told me so."

"Then why was she going out with Merlin?"

"To get back at me. And because he has money. Shirley likes money." Brandon jutted his chin out, balled his hands into fists, and slammed them down on the coffee table. Everything on it bounced up and down. Then he started to cry. "It's all my fault," he got out between sobs. "My fault. Everything is my fault." A low, keening moan escaped from his lips. He began plucking at his clothes.

"Brandon," I said.

He didn't pay any attention.

"Brandon," I repeated. He didn't respond. His eyes seemed to be focused on something far away. He'd gone into his own world. I reached over and shook him. He moaned louder and began pulling at the buttons on his shirt. I heard the fabric rip as they flew off. Then Brandon moved his hands up to his face and began scratching at himself. A small drop of blood ran down his cheek.

"Stop it," I yelled, and then when that didn't work I did the only other thing I could think of: I slapped him across the face.

He paused for a second, then went back to what he'd been doing before. By now there were large welts across his nose and cheeks.

I ran to get his mother.

Chapter
21

Brandon Funk's mother turned out to be a small, weak-chinned woman tucked up in a salmon-colored chenille bathrobe.

"What do you want?" she snapped.

"I think your son needs your help." I told her what was happening.

She crossed herself and hurried over to his house. I followed behind.

Brandon's wailing marked our path.

When we reached the doorway his mother gave me a furious glance and stepped inside. "I'll take it from here," she spat out. "You've done enough damage." She slammed the door in my face.

I stayed outside for a minute listening to Brandon's moans and his mother's urgent voice rising and falling, strands intertwined in some symphony I couldn't understand or participate in. Finally when the sounds abated somewhat I left.

Zsa Zsa was scratching on the window with her front paws as I walked up to the cab. I let her out and we went for a walk. For the next two blocks I did nothing but think about Brandon. I wondered what sort of bad things he had done in the past, and then I wondered how mad he'd gotten at Marsha when he found out she owed all that money, because no matter what he said I couldn't believe that he didn't know. It seemed to me he'd be very mad indeed. The question was, what would he do? I thought about it some more as Zsa Zsa raced ahead of me, dodging in and out of the laurel hedges as she chased the shadows the nearby trees were casting.

Brandon had kept on insisting everything was his fault. What was everything? The affair? The murder? After a few more minutes of turning the problem over in my mind I decided that like Zsa Zsa I was chasing shadows. I didn't know Brandon well enough to be able to answer the question. Then I wondered what Shirley would say and whether or not Brandon was right about her feelings toward Marsha. Brandon and Shirley. Marsha and Merlin. Two swinging couples. No reason everyone shouldn't be happy. Only they didn't swing and they weren't happy. I whistled for Zsa Zsa and turned around and started back toward the car. On the way a few rain drops fell on my cheek.

By the time I got back to the car the rain was falling in earnest. I was just getting in the car when the door to Brandon's house opened. His mother stood there framed in the light. Then she closed the door and headed back to her house. As she walked I suddenly knew who she had reminded me of—Enid. And then I remembered what Ana Torres had said about not liking to clean house for Enid's crazy brother, the one with all the dead animals in his house. Oh, my God. I put my hand to my mouth. Enid and Brandon were brother and sister. Amazing. For a moment I just stood there thinking about how I hadn't realized that they were and wondering about what else I didn't know. Then Zsa Zsa barked and I became aware that we were both standing out in the rain. I opened the cab door. Zsa Zsa jumped in and I followed. As I drove away I couldn't help contemplating what a small town Syracuse really is and how everyone is always related to everyone else in unexpected ways.

Zsa Zsa rested her head in my lap as I drove us home. She didn't like this weather and neither did I. It was raining so hard I was having difficulty making out the turns in the road. Then to make matters worse as I turned onto Comstock a car began tailgating me. He was so close his headlights were reflecting in my rearview mirror, making it even more difficult to see. I cursed and sped up and he did the same. Finally I pulled over to the side of the road to let him go. He waved as he went by. I gave him the finger and pulled out after him. For the next block I took a great deal of pleasure in making him as uncomfortable as he had made me. Then I turned onto Colvin and drove home.

It was a little after eleven when I walked into my house. James was waiting for me. The fur on his back was slick with rainwater, and his tail twitched impatiently as I opened the door. I let everyone in, fed the cat, dried off Zsa Zsa, and made myself a hot milk and Scotch and honey. Then I settled down in front of the TV. Of course, there was nothing I wanted to see. I ended up surfing the channels with the remote and thinking about Brandon. I couldn't keep myself from wondering how bad the things he used to do really were and whether or not he'd ever been arrested, when the phone rang. For a moment I thought about letting the answering machine get it, but curiosity won out and I got up and answered it. George was on the other end.

"I was just wondering if you were okay," he said.

"Why shouldn't I be?"

"You left Pete's kind of quickly."

"I had things to do."

"I see." George paused for a minute. "Are you mad at me?"

"No. Why should I be?" I mean, what was I going to say: I was upset because he'd been talking to another woman?

"Because you sound that way."

"I'm just preoccupied."

"With what?"

Grateful for a chance to change the subject, I told him about where I'd been and what I'd found out.

"This guy Brandon Funk sounds a little off center," George observed when I was through.

"I know." I reached over for the chocolate bar sitting on the kitchen counter and broke off a piece. "I was wondering if you could find out how off center?"

"And how would I do that?"

I put the piece in my mouth and let it dissolve on my tongue. "See if he has a record."

"In case you forgot I'm not on the force anymore," he reminded me. "I don't have access to that kind of information."

"I know, but you have friends that do." I ate another piece of chocolate. "All I'm asking is for someone to get on the computer and see if this guy has any priors. It'll take all of two seconds."

"I know how long it will take," George told me.

"So will you?"

"What's in it for me?"

"I'll help you with your paper."

George snorted. "Jesus, you just don't take no for an answer, do you?"

"Not if I can help it." I hung up before George could change his mind. Then I had another Scotch and milk and went to bed. Maybe it was the combination, but I had a bad night. I kept waking up thinking I was hearing things, then drifting back off to sleep to dream of invisible bats twisting themselves up in my hair. Every time I got them out they came right back. No matter how I tried I couldn't get rid of them. Finally at five o'clock I went downstairs, stretched out on the sofa and read yesterday's paper. It wasn't very interesting.

Zsa Zsa woke me up at eight o'clock to let me know she needed to go out. I got to the store at nine to find a Mrs. Sullivan anxiously waiting for me by the front door. Her hair was barely combed and she didn't have any makeup on. She started telling me her story while I still had the key in the lock. It seemed that this morning she'd gone down to the basement to do a load of laundry, and as she was leaning over the washing machine a bat popped out.

"I tell you I almost fainted on the spot." She crossed her hands and placed them on her chest to show how upset she'd been.

When I asked her why she was telling me this she uncrossed her hands, dug a flier out of her jacket pocket and waved it in my face. It was from M & M Exterminators.

"I called them and they said I had a colony living in my house."

"That's very possible," I replied cautiously.

"They said they'd get rid of all of them for two thousand dollars." It looked as if Merlin had raised his price. "I don't have two thousand dollars," Mrs. Sullivan wailed. She began cracking her knuckles. "I didn't know what to do. Then I called one of my neighbors and she said to call you." She peered at me through thick-lensed glasses. "Do you think you could help?"

I suppressed a sigh, took her phone number and address and told her either Tim or I would be there before twelve.

When I went inside, I called the Better Business Bureau to lodge a complaint against Merlin, after which I called George. He informed me his friend was on the one o'clock shift and he'd get back to me later in the day.

"When do you want to start on your paper?" I asked.

"I don't want to discuss it," George replied and hung up.

"Asshole," I said to the telephone.

"Who's an asshole?" Tim asked as he opened a container of yogurt and started eating his breakfast.

"George."

"What else is new?"

Pickles jumped up on the counter, and Tim spooned some of his yogurt onto the container's lid and pushed it toward the cat. She sat down and began lapping it up.

"So what's on the agenda for today?" Tim asked when he was done eating.

I told him about Mrs. Sullivan.

"Who goes?" Tim asked. "I have a lot of stuff to do."

"So do I."

We flipped for it. I lost. Cursing under my breath I picked up my gloves, my net, and a bath towel and headed out to the cab. It took me five minutes to get to the house. Since I'd last seen her, Mrs. Sullivan had put on some lipstick, blusher, and eyeliner. She said hello, then hustled me through a spotless kitchen to a gleaming back hall.

"It's down there," she said, pointing to the door that led to the basement.

It took me a while to find the bat. He'd gone to sleep in a crevice in the wall behind the dryer. He'd probably come out for a drink of water. Bats tend to get thirsty this time of year. They get dehydrated when they hibernate.

"You know," I told Mrs. Sullivan as I released him outside, "M & M Exterminators were right about one thing. Most bats live in colonies. This one might have brothers and sisters hibernating between the inner and outer walls."

Mrs. Sullivan clicked her tongue. "I don't see how. My brother-in-law insulated last year. He caulked everything up good and tight. Then he put on aluminum siding."

"Let's check the attic anyway," I suggested. As long as I was here it seemed silly not to finish the job.

Amazingly the only thing up there were four cartons of clothes.

"I try to get rid of things as I go," Mrs. Sullivan explained. "I don't like to leave messes sitting around."

I checked the cardboard boxes just to make sure. Nothing. "The bat had to come from somewhere," I said as we went down the stairs.

"But where?" Mrs. Sullivan asked.

I couldn't answer because I didn't know. As a last resort I suggested we walk around the house and see if we could spot anything. Sometimes you can see where bats have come and gone by their collection of droppings. We didn't see any of those, but we did find something else—a broken basement window in the rear of the house.

I knelt down to study it, then straightened up. "I bet that's how the bat got in."

Mrs. Sullivan looked perplexed. "Now, how did that happen? That wasn't there yesterday."

"Probably some kid with a baseball," I suggested, even though I could come up with another explanation with no trouble at all.

"Maybe."

I left her standing in her backyard wondering who the guilty party had been. Actually I had a pretty good idea, but I didn't say anything because I couldn't prove it.

I spent the rest of the day waiting on customers, housing

a shipment of hissing cockroaches that I picked up out at the airport, and negotiating with the telephone company about partial payment of my current bill. I was not in a good mood when Tim left the store at eight-thirty. I locked the door at nine and settled in to do my bookkeeping—a depressing operation these days—but around nine-fifteen my stomach started hurting, and I decided I'd better put something in it.

I told Zsa Zsa to guard the store and ran out to get a hamburger at McDonald's. The street was quiet when I stepped out. A cat meowed from somewhere nearby. It had started to drizzle again—but I didn't pay much attention. I was too busy thinking about other things, such as whether I should get two orders of fries or one order of fries and an apple pie, when someone grabbed me from behind and began dragging me to the curb.

Chapter
22

It all happened so fast I didn't have time to react, let alone to think. Before I knew it a man had thrown me in the back of a car and climbed in after me.

"That's for giving me a hard time the other night," he informed me as he clipped me in the jaw.

"Lay off," the guy in front told him.

"I just wanna teach her a little respect," the man who'd hit me whined. "She shouldn't have rode on my ass like that."

"Do what I say," the driver snapped.

"Who appointed you God?" the other man snarled.

I made for the door, but before I even got my hand on the handle the guy beside me grabbed my hair and yanked me back. He smelled of sweat and licorice. "Where the hell do you think you're going?"

"Nowhere now."

"You're goddamned right you're not."

"Do you mind if I ask what's going on?" I said as the car

pulled away from the curb. I moved my jaw from side to side. Nothing seemed broken.

"Shut the fuck up," the guy sitting next to me ordered. "You'll find out soon enough." He opened his jacket, took a .357 out of a shoulder holster, and pointed it in my direction.

"Fine." I certainly wasn't going to argue with that. I sank back in the maroon upholstered seat and studied the guy with the gun. He had watery eyes, a receding hairline he'd compensated for with a ponytail, and teeth that hadn't seen a dentist in a number of years.

"What are you staring at?" he demanded.

"Nothing." I turned my gaze to the Baby On Board sign tacked to my window and tried to figure out who these lowlifes were and what they wanted from me. Obviously they didn't want to rob me. Obviously this operation had been planned. But by whom?

Suddenly I thought of Merlin and the dogs and the scene in the store with his gun, and things began to make more sense. While I was trying to put it all together the man with the gun leaned forward and nudged the driver with his elbow.

"What do you think?" he asked. "You wanna stop for a little something extra?"

"We're too late," he answered. "Maybe on the way back." He turned and grinned at me in case I hadn't gotten the message.

It was the guy who'd come into the store a couple of days ago.

"You!" I cried.

"I told you to be careful." He smirked before turning his attention back to the road.

I wanted to kick myself. I was still berating myself when a police car sped by us.

"Don't even think about doing anything," the guy next to me warned before I could move. And he jammed the muzzle of his gun into my ribs.

"I got the message," I said and looked out the window.

We were passing Forman Avenue. Then we took a right on Waters. No one was on either street. No one would be on the surrounding blocks either. This was a business district. Everyone had gone home for the night. If I made a break for it, the guy with the gun would be able to pick me off with no trouble at all. Maybe they were going to do that anyway. Then I thought, No, even Merlin wouldn't go that far. What they were going to do was take me somewhere and beat the shit out of me. That thought didn't make me any happier than the first one had. The more I considered the possibilities, the more it seemed as if I didn't have much to lose by trying to escape. I sat back and waited for an opportunity to jump.

It came when we hit DePew. We were slowing down for a stop sign. I glanced at the guy beside me. He was busy studying a mole on his wrist.

"The doctor said I should have this taken off," he was telling the driver. "What do you think?" he asked him as I took a deep breath, said a silent prayer, and jumped.

I landed on my feet, fell, scrambled up again and started running.

Brakes squealed behind me.

Then I heard someone screaming, "You dumb fuck, she's getting away."

I didn't turn around. I just kept going.

I heard a pop to my right. Shit. They were shooting at me. I veered left and picked up my pace. Then I saw an alley and ducked into it. There was a Dumpster halfway down. I skirted the piles of debris and headed for it. It was small but big enough for me to hide in. Or it would have been if it hadn't been padlocked. I cursed and looked around for something to smash the lock with. I'd just picked up a brick when I heard a car approaching.

"There she is," the driver yelled.

The guy with the gun got out. He was about thirty pounds overweight and probably hadn't seen the inside of a gym in years, but with the gun he was carrying he didn't have to. I took off again. When I came to the end of the alley I made a left and went down Orange Avenue. I heard the man's footsteps pounding after me. They formed a counterbeat to my own. I had to get off the street and I had to get off now. But there was nowhere to hide. All the buildings on either side were shut tight, locked up for the night.

And then I thought about the Colony.

It was three blocks away. If I could make it there, I'd be okay. The operative word was *if*.

I kept going down the street, cut across a vacant parking lot, and went up the next block. By now I had a stitch in my side and my lungs were starting to ache. A garbage can to the right of me pinged as another bullet tore into it. Thank God the guy chasing me was a lousy shot. I put on a last burst of speed and tore down the pavement. Then I rounded the corner. The Colony was right there. As I made for the broken window I could hear the car coming up behind me. Dear God, let me do this, I prayed as I summoned up every last bit of reserve that I had and jumped through the window the police had taped up. I bumped into a chair and fell over. I kept going. I was in the third room by the time the two men came in. My heart was pounding; my side hurt so bad it had made me forget about my jaw. I couldn't move if I wanted to. I just leaned against the wall sucking air and listening to their voices floating in the dark.

"I'm gonna kill her," the man who had been chasing me gasped out.

"You know, you look like a tub of lard when you run," the driver said. "You should go to the gym and lose that gut."

"Shut up! Shut the fuck up!" the man with the gun screamed.

"Hey, lighten up. I was only kidding." There was a brief pause. Then the driver said, "Jesus, will you look at this dump. They ought to knock it down." His partner said something, but I couldn't hear what. "Come on," the driver went on, "let's find the bitch and get out of here. I don't want to be any later than I have to."

The papers and boxes and pills on the floor crackled and crunched as the men walked through the first room into the second. I crept into the fourth room as quietly as possible. I was halfway through it when I tripped over something.

"She's up ahead," the guy with the gun cried.

I ran into the next room. By now my eyes were beginning to get accustomed to the dark and I was able to make out shapes. If I remembered correctly, there were three or four more interconnecting rooms before there was an open door out into the hall. The suite must have been a doctor's office, a doctor's office with a big practice, I thought irrelevantly.

"Come out, come out wherever you are," the man with the gun sang.

"Maybe we should call the boss," the driver said.

"Let him wait. It'll do him good."

"No. He'll be pissed. You call and tell him we got held up, then come back here."

"Whatever you say." I could hear the guy start to walk away.

"Hey, Tony, leave the .357 with me." There was a pause, and then the driver said, "And see if we got a flashlight or something in the car. I don't wanna be here all night."

"You got it," Tony replied.

"And hurry up."

His footsteps moved away. A little later I heard a scream.

"Jesus, what's happening?" the driver cried.

"A rat bit me. A goddamned rat came up and bit my ankle. Just like that," Tony cried. I began to feel more warmly toward the rodent population. "I gotta get to a hospital and get a rabies shot."

"You're gonna get to a hospital if you don't do what I tell you to," the driver growled, and I heard the unmistakable click of a gun being cocked.

I guess Tony heard it, too, because he started back toward the window. A moment later the footsteps fell silent. Tony must have climbed out.

I stood there scarcely breathing, wondering what I should do. My heart was hammering in my chest so loudly it was amazing the driver didn't hear it. The building creaked in the wind. Spots of color danced in front of my eyes. I closed them. A picture of Estrella sprawled out on the third-floor landing rose unbidden. I tried pushing it away, but it didn't want to go. I kept seeing her vacant eyes staring into the blackness. A chill worked its way up my spine. If I wasn't careful I'd end up that way, too. Only there'd be no one to find me. Except for the rats. I had to get out of here. I had to get out of here now. I took a step and tripped over a chair.

"You're mine," the driver cried from what sounded like two rooms away. Then he started toward me.

Not if I can help it, I thought as my hand closed on the leg of the chair I'd just fallen over. I could hear him coming as I yanked on the chair leg. It gave slightly. I yanked some more. It began wobbling. Thank God the chair wasn't well made. The leg came free just as the driver crashed through the doorway of the room I was in. I scrambled up and hit him with it. He went down on his knees, and I turned and groped my way out the door. I was three rooms down when I heard Tony climbing back in.

"Hey, Richie," he yelled. "I called Angie. He's coming right over. He's gonna bring us some flashlights. The batteries in the ones in your car are dead."

Richie groaned.

"What's the matter?" Tony demanded. "Why aren't you answering me?"

Richie groaned again. "The bitch hit me in the gut."

I cursed silently. I should have hit him in the head. Now I was boxed in. I couldn't go forward and I couldn't go back.

"Be careful," Richie went on between moans. "I think she doubled back. She's in one of these rooms."

"Don't worry," Tony yelled. "I'll get her."

"No," Richie ordered. "Wait for Angie." He started to retch.

"I got the SIG," Tony said, and I heard the sound of a clip being shoved into the nine millimeter. "She's mine." He started my way.

I could hear desks and chairs being kicked aside as he came through the rooms.

I got behind the door and waited. For some reason I'd grown very calm. My mind was detached, floating free. I was aware of every sound.

Tony was in the second room.

Then he was in the third.

We were playing Blind Man's Bluff for keeps.

He halted in front of the fourth room. I could hear him breathing. I could smell the licorice.

Finally he came inside.

He'd taken two step when I hit him with the chair leg. He went sideways. I swung again. This time I got the side of his jaw. The gun went flying. He staggered and fell. I threw the chair leg down and ran like hell. I bumped into chairs and desks and boxes in my flight toward the window. Then suddenly it was there—my portal to freedom. I clambered through. I was three-quarters of the way out when I felt something hard and cold in the small of my back.

"You really are a pain in the ass," a man's voice said.

I remembered George had just said something similar to me. Then everything went black.

Chapter
23

I didn't know where I was when I came to.

At first I just lay on my side listening to someone moaning and wishing they'd shut the hell up.

Then I realized that someone was me.

A little while later the pain arrived, waves of it radiating from the back of my skull to my temples.

It pulled me back from the brink of unconsciousness. I opened my eyes. All I saw was blackness. My heart began to pound. I put my hands up and touched something hard a couple of inches away from my face. I kept going. Whatever I was feeling was all around me. And then it hit me.

Oh, my God, I thought. I'm in a coffin.

I've been buried alive.

A scream started building in my throat. It had just reached my mouth when I felt a lurch and smelled a whiff of gasoline. I giggled. Talk about losing it. Jesus. I was locked in the trunk of a car. Not that that was great, but it was a damned sight better than being six feet under. I sighed in relief and did a quick personal inventory. I ran my tongue over my teeth. They were all there. I moved my arms and legs and wiggled my fingers and toes. Aside from the throbbing in my head everything seemed to be in working order.

I groaned again as the car went around a turn and tried to figure out what had happened. Someone—probably the guy called Angie—must have been waiting for me. When I appeared he'd knocked me over the head and thrown me in here. What I wanted to know was how he'd gotten to the Colony as fast as he had. Who was this guy anyway? Batman? When the next spasm of pain passed I put my hands up and pushed on the trunk lid. It didn't budge. I pushed harder. Nothing. I began pounding on it. Then, despite my resolution not to, I began yelling. Nobody came. Finally I put my head back down and closed my eyes. I was too exhausted to do anything else. The next thing I knew someone was shaking me.

"Get out," a deep, raspy voice ordered.

A shaft of pain shot through my skull. I gritted my teeth to keep from crying out.

Someone shook me again. I wanted to tell him to leave me alone, but my lips didn't want to form the words. When he shook me for the third time I tried moving my legs, but I couldn't. They'd stiffened up. Then I felt someone tugging at me. A moment later I was standing. Everything started to spin. My legs buckled, and I stumbled onto my hands and knees, and threw up.

"Jesus," the raspy voice cried. "She almost got my new shoes."

"I told you you shouldn't have hit her so hard," another voice said.

I looked up. Two men were standing over me. I didn't recognize either one.

"That's the trouble with you," the man near me snapped. "You're always big on advice and short on action."

"Don't start with me," the other man warned.

The two men glared at each other. For the moment they'd forgotten about me. If I felt better, it would have been the perfect time to make a break for it; but I couldn't even walk much less run, and somehow I didn't think that crawling was going to get me too far.

"Come on," the first guy finally said to the second, "let's get going. We're late enough as it is."

"Yeah." With that the second man grabbed me by my collar and yanked me up. I had trouble standing. My knees started buckling again. "No you don't," the man said and he pulled me back up.

We got to a door and stopped. Strains of Metallica came pouring out from the bar next to it. Every beat reverberated through my head. I groaned as one of the men opened the door and pushed me through.

"Shut up and climb," he ordered.

I looked up. It was one flight. It could have been Mount Everest. "I don't think I can make it," I told him.

"You'll make it if I have to pull you up by your hair." He gave me a push.

Something told me he was telling the truth. I stumbled over the first step and righted myself. He shoved me again. The climb took forever. I tried to distract myself from the pounding in my head by counting the eyelets in my sneakers and the paint chips on the risers. It didn't work. When we got to the top the man in front of me opened another door and we went through. The hallway we walked into was covered with cut red velvet wallpaper. It was hot and stuffy. The air smelled of floor wax, onions, Mr. Clean, and something vaguely medicinal that I couldn't identify. The man standing next to me was just opening his mouth to say something when a small, prune-faced woman dressed in black came bustling out. She took one look at me and whirled on the two men.

"Look at her," she cried. "She can't come in here. She's filthy. She smells."

"Eddie wants to see her," the one who was holding me up replied. His voice disclaimed all responsibility for what he had in his hand.

Eddie. The name sounded familiar, but I couldn't place it. The pain in my head made it hard to think. Then I heard Connie's voice. I saw her leaning over the bar. I heard her telling me about Marsha and the money she owed, and all of a sudden I knew where I was. I was at Fast Eddie Marino's. God. Why? What could he possibly want with me? But I decided not to waste time worrying about it. I had an idea I was going to find out soon enough.

The woman glared at us. "I don't care what Eddie wants. This is my house and you don't bring nobody who looks like that up here."

One of the men groaned. "Come on, Ma, give us a break. It's been a rough night."

The woman folded her arms across her chest and stuck out her chin. The gesture made me aware of the fact that it receded slightly, and I felt the urge to giggle. Then I realized there was something familiar about her face. She reminded me of someone. The name was on the tip of my tongue, but then she spoke and the thought vanished.

"Before she takes one more step in my house she gets

washed and changes her clothes," she told the two men. "I'm not having my floors and my furniture messed up by the likes of her." She turned and shook a finger at me. "What did you do? Drink too much? A woman your age. You should be ashamed."

"I'm not drunk," I protested, feeling some unfathomable urge to set the record straight. "These two guys hit me over the head and dumped me in the trunk of the car."

The woman turned a basilisk stare on the two men. "Which car?" she demanded.

"The Acura," one of them mumbled, looking down at the floor.

"Vinnie, you took Teresa's car?"

Vinnie muttered something I couldn't catch.

The woman poked a finger in his chest. "You better make sure you clean it good, you understand. I don't want nothing stinking in there."

"Yes," he muttered.

"What did you say?" she demanded.

"I said I understand," he repeated in a loud voice.

"Ma, who is it?" a wheezie voice called from inside one of the rooms.

"Angie and Vinnie. They got a woman with them."

"Robin Light?"

"Yeah," Angie answered.

"It's about time. Bring her in."

"She's gotta get washed first," the mother called out. "And I'm gonna give her some clothes to change into. I don't want her tracking her filth all over the house."

"Whatever you say." He sounded as if he didn't have enough energy to argue—but then neither did I.

"How's he doing?" Vinnie mouthed.

The woman shook her head. "He's having a bad night," she whispered. "He's gotta sit straight up all the time or he can't breathe. That's why we're going to Arizona in a couple of weeks. I hear the air is better down there. At least that's what my cousins tell me. They've been down there for ten years." Then she turned and left. A moment later she was back with a towel and some neatly folded clothes. "Here," she said, thrusting everything in my face. "Take them and go get washed." And she pushed me in the direction of the bathroom. I felt as if I were five again.

Once she closed the bathroom door I sat down on the toilet seat and rested my forehead on the edge of the sink. It was an old-fashioned washbasin with a wide rim. The porcelain felt cool against my skin.

Someone pounded on the door. "Hurry up," he yelled. "We ain't gonna wait for you all night."

"Fuck you," I mouthed. Then I straightened up and glanced at myself in the mirror.

I looked even worse than I felt. My skin was dead white, my eyes looked as if they'd sunk back in my head, and I had a yellowish purple bruise on the right side of my jaw from where Richie had punched me. It was a good thing I wasn't going out on a date this weekend, I decided as I rinsed my mouth out and patted water on my face and neck. I was studying the bruise on my jaw when the pounding on the door started again.

"You got thirty more seconds," Angie yelled.

"Hold it." I took off my jeans and T-shirt and slipped on the dress Fast Eddie's mother had given me. It was a red-and-yellow-checked, long-sleeved smock and could easily have accommodated at least two of me, maybe even three.

A moment later the door flew open. "Let's go," Vinnie said and motioned for me to step outside.

"Jesus, is that Teresa's dress?" Angie asked Fast Eddie's mother as I stumbled out into the hall. "She's going to be pissed."

"What do you care?" Fast Eddie's mother snapped, and Angie shut up. She put her hands on her hips, clicked her tongue against the roof of her mouth, and shook her head as she surveyed me. "Come on," she said and pushed me toward the door. "You think my son has nothing better to do than wait for you?" Her fingers were bony and they hurt as she prodded me in the ribs to keep me moving.

Fast Eddie was sitting in a wheelchair in the second room. It was all dark wood and velvet furniture and yellowing prints. An oxygen tank was strapped to the wheelchair's side. A thin plastic tube ran from the cylinder to Fast Eddie's nose. The sound of his breathing filled the air. His head was small but his body was big. His stomach bulged out from underneath the flowered Hawaiian shirt he was wearing. No wonder the police didn't want to arrest him, I thought, remembering George's story. If he wouldn't walk, they'd get a hernia carrying him down the stairs. As he motioned for me to come in I noticed that he was wearing five gold chains around his neck. The bright metal highlighted his skin's pallor.

"You have to come closer," he whispered. "It's hard for me to talk. I'm having a bad day."

When I didn't move fast enough Angie and Vinnie pushed me over. Despite his mother's cleaning efforts—the room gleamed—the smell of sick bodies permeated the air.

"So what happened to Tony and Richie?" he demanded of the two men ignoring me for the moment.

"Tony called and asked me for help," Angie said. "When I got over to the Colony she"—Angie pointed to me—"was climbing out the window. I just hit her one in the back of the head, threw her in the trunk, and came on over."

"You didn't look for Tony and Richie?"

Angie shrugged. "I figured you'd want me to bring her over ASAP. I figured those two clowns would be right out." Fast Eddie didn't say anything. "You want, I'll go back to the Colony and get them," Angie offered.

Fast Eddie shook his head. "Don't bother." He turned to me. His eyes were blue and watery and gave the appearance of protruding from their sockets. "What happened?"

I gave him a detailed rundown of the evening's events. Vinnie and Angie snickered throughout my recitation.

"They were supposed to ask you to come talk to me," Fast Eddie said when I was through. He sounded peeved. "That was all they were supposed to do."

"Well, they did a good deal more than that."

Fast Eddie threw an angry glance at his mother.

"Sssh." His mother made a quieting motion with her hands. "Don't get upset. It's bad for you."

"I'm not upset," he said, though his expression indicated otherwise. He began to cough, a deep rumble that came from inside his chest and went on and on. By the time he stopped his face was red and he was panting for air. His mother ran over with a glass of water. He took a few sips and waved her away. "So," he said to me when he could talk again, "I hear you've been asking around about Marsha Pennington. Why are you interested in her?"

"She was a friend of mine." I wondered how he'd heard, but I didn't have the nerve to ask.

"So?"

"I'm trying to find out what happened to her."

Fast Eddie leaned forward. "Then you're not looking for the money?"

"What money?"

His eyes widened. The angry look came back on his face. His mother made a nervous little noise. He glanced at her and she shut up. "My money," he said. "She had thirty thousand dollars of mine. It's disappeared and I want it back."

Chapter
24

I stared at Fast Eddie. Except for his wheezing and the drumming of the rain on the windowpanes the room was silent. Fast Eddie's face had become more animated. Talking about the loss of his money had energized him. He made small circles with the oxygen tube while he spoke.

"She was supposed to show up here with my thirty grand the day she killed herself. But she never made it. Neither did the money."

"Maybe she didn't have it," I suggested, thinking of the way Marsha had looked when she'd been in the store. "Maybe she was lying to you."

Fast Eddie frowned. "Oh, she had it all right. She called me up the week before she died and said she'd be coming into some money, that she'd have it on Monday, and that she wanted to pay me off. She said she didn't want to pay by the week no more." Fast Eddie took a pull of oxygen and continued talking. "Why should she call if she didn't have the money?" He stared at me, waiting for my answer.

"No reason," I agreed, sorry that I'd started the conversation in the first place.

"That's right." Fast Eddie nodded, and his double chin briefly turned into a triple. "Like I said, she was supposed to show up here Monday evening, but she never did. Then two days later I read the cops fished her out of the LeMoyne Reservoir. As for my thirty grand—nobody knows anything and believe me I asked, I asked plenty."

I thought of how pale Merlin had turned when he saw the limo at the cemetery.

"Then I hear you're asking questions. Naturally I'm curious."

"Naturally," I murmured, thinking that thirty grand was a good reason to murder someone.

Fast Eddie leaned forward. "Satisfy my curiosity."

Scheherazade I'm not, but I did the best I could. Under the circumstance I didn't feel as if I had much of a choice.

"You think she was killed," Fast Eddie said when I was done.

I nodded.

He sat back in his chair and made a steeple with his fingers. "That's what I've been thinking, too," he allowed. "I've also been thinking that whoever killed her has my money."

It was the obvious conclusion, but I didn't say that.

"And you don't know anything else?"

"No," I replied.

"And you'd tell me if you did."

"Yes."

He leaned forward for the second time. "You're sure?" he asked, staring at me.

"I'm sure." I stared back at him. I was not going to let him know how much he intimidated me.

Fast Eddie smiled. "I think you would, too. I don't think you're stupid enough not to." He started making loops with the oxygen tubing again. "Which is why Vinnie is going to give you a card with my number. Which is why you're going to call if you hear of anything, anything at all, concerning my money."

"All right." Then I asked Fast Eddie the self-evident question. "How do you know one of your guys didn't take it?"

"Hey," Vinnie squawked. He took a step toward me. "Exactly what are you saying?" he demanded.

Fast Eddie silenced him with a look. "The reason I know is because I was the only one Marsha spoke to and I didn't tell anyone else. Any other questions?"

"Not at the moment," I said, even though I knew there were things I should be asking. I was just too foggy to figure out what they were.

"Good." Fast Eddie made a few more loops with his oxygen tube. He seemed lost in thought. Then he straightened up and concentrated his attention on me. "I told you what I want. Now here's what I don't want." He paused for a second to listen to the rain rattling against the windowpanes. The storm was increasing in intensity. "I don't want you making the kind of mess that comes to the police's attention. Right now the cops and I, we have an understanding. I keep things low key and they leave me alone. But if they hear that Marsha owed me thirty grand, they're gonna want to talk to me and," he paused for dramatic impact, "I will be very unhappy if that occurs. Very, very unhappy because I do not want to become involved in a murder investigation. The case has been closed and I want to leave it that way."

"I understand."

He smiled. "I thought you would." He turned to Vinnie. "Give her my card."

Vinnie walked over and handed me a white card embossed with blue letters. I glanced at it. "Santorelli Electronics?"

Fast Eddie shrugged. "My brother-in-law sells the stuff. He's into real estate, too. You ever need a new TV or a VCR or want to sell your house come to me. I can get you a good deal."

I slipped the card in my pocket.

"So you'll call, right?"

"Right." And I meant it. This was one man I didn't want to cross if I didn't have to.

"Good." He told Vinnie to take me home.

On the way out Eddie's mother handed me my clothes. "You can keep that rag you're wearing, too," she said, pointing to the smock I had on.

God. And I thought my mother was bad.

It was pouring when we stepped outside. Even though the car was parked just a few feet away, I was soaked by the time I reached it. But I didn't mind. After having been stuffed in the trunk of a car and cooped up in Fast Eddie's flat, I wasn't going to complain about getting wet. I was happy to be breathing fresh air. I asked Vinnie to drop me at the store; then I leaned back and closed my eyes and listened to the swish swish of the wipers and the tapping of the rain on the windshield.

"You better pay attention to what Fast Eddie says," Vinnie told me as we drove along. "He ain't kidding."

"I didn't think he was," I murmured. I was trying to keep my head perfectly still because every time I moved it I saw spots of light dancing in front of my eyes. After a while I began admiring the patterns they made.

"We're here," Vinnie announced some time later.

I opened my eyes. We were parked in front of Noah's Ark. I started to get out of the car, then stopped. "Listen, I have a question for you."

"Yeah?" Vinnie unwrapped a stick of gum and put it in his mouth. "What?"

"How did you get to the Colony so quickly?"

Vinnie laughed. "I was eating at Aunt Patsy's." He took in my blank look and explained. "The new place down at Armory Square. Ever hear of cellular phones?"

Duh. Feeling like a total idiot I got out of the car. Vinnie roared off. I looked at my watch. Richie had grabbed me three hours ago. It felt as if I'd been away from the store for four days. When I unlocked the door Zsa Zsa and Pickles came running out to greet me. I wanted to bend down to pet them, but I was afraid that if I did I'd pass out. Instead I carefully walked into the office and lowered myself onto the sofa. Zsa Zsa jumped up and licked my face while Pickles twined herself around my feet. I closed my eyes again. I could barely keep them open. I knew I should go to the hospital, but first I had to take a nap.

My dreams were all swirling colors and shapes and ants and bats crawling over me. No matter where I went they always found me. Then the ringing started. I wanted it to stop, but it kept going. Finally I realized it was the telephone. I opened my eyes, got up, stumbled over to it, and fumbled around for the receiver.

"Yes?" I mumbled.

"Robin?" George asked. "Is that you?"

"More or less." Mostly less I decided.

"Are you okay? You sound awful."

"I feel awful." The room started swaying. I hung up and lurched back to the sofa. I managed to sit down before I threw up. This time I brought up yellow-green bile. I closed my eyes and lay down. The next thing I knew someone was standing over me. I opened one eye. It was George. I felt bad enough to be relieved. I closed the eye and dozed off again. The next time I woke up I was being lifted into an ambulance.

Oh, God, not again, I thought as the paramedic closed the doors.

Chapter
25

"So?" George said and dropped the clothes I'd asked him to get from my house on the foot of my bed. It was eleven o'clock the next morning and the attending physician had decided I could be released—evidently the X rays had shown I wasn't bleeding into my brain—which was fine with me because I was in the middle of a nicotine fit.

"So what?" I asked.

"Are you going to tell me what happened?"

"You were there when I talked to the cops. You heard what I said."

"I repeat, are you going to tell me what happened?"

"You don't believe my story?"

George snorted. "A ten-year-old child would have come up with a better story than you did."

"I did as well as I could under the circumstances." Which was true. It's hard to come up with a convincing lie when your head feels as if someone is playing the drums on it. But better a bad lie than telling the cops the truth and having them pay a visit to Fast Eddie.

"Let's see if I have this straight." George clasped his hands in front of him and stared down at me. "You were going to your car when someone you didn't see came over and hit you over the head?"

"That's right," I said.

"But he didn't take your wallet."

"He probably didn't have time."

"Really?" My heart sank as George walked over to the chair and lifted the dress Fast Eddie's mother had given me off the seat and held it in the air. "But your assailant had time to put this on you?"

"Maybe he's seriously kinked," I suggested. "Maybe he has a fetish about women in muu-muus."

George shook his head. "Try again."

"I found the dress at a rummage sale?"

"Teresa wouldn't be happy to hear you say that."

I sighed.

"I told you I used to work that area. It's not as if you could miss the lady." George came over and dropped the dress in my lap. "Teresa never struck me as the generous sort."

"It was her mother's idea."

"Yes, Mrs. Marino is a truly delightful woman."

"Yeah, I don't think she's going to get the unsung heroine of the year award, that's for sure."

George leaned over me. I hate it when he looms. "So exactly why did Fast Eddie have you picked up?"

Since George knew half the story, I decided I might as well tell him the rest. I mean it really didn't matter. He wasn't on the force—even if he did tend to forget that once in a while. I also decided to make him wait. On principle. I don't like being crowded. Or rushed. "After I'm dressed and out of here."

"I'm disappointed. That hospital gown definitely does things for you."

I glared.

George straightened up. "Fine. I'll bring the car around."

"And get me a pack of cigarettes," I called as he walked out the door. "Camels."

He turned. "Can't you wait?"

"No. You want the story, I want my smokes."

Last night's storm had washed the gray away. The sun was shining. The branches of the two flowering crab trees in front of the hospital looked as if they were covered with tufts of pink cotton candy. I was watching a robin hopping on the grass when George pulled up. I got out of the wheelchair the nurse was holding and into the Taurus. Zsa Zsa licked my chin and ears. Her tail was wagging so fast her whole body was going from side to side.

"How'd she do?" I asked George. He'd taken her home with him after he'd left me at the hospital.

"Aside from sleeping in my bed and waking me up at five in the morning—not badly."

"I always knew she was your type. Long hair. Long legs. Too bad she's not blond."

"Funny lady. Here." George threw the Camels I'd asked him to get me in my lap. "Go kill yourself. Not that you need any more help in that department."

I opened the pack as we turned onto South Crouse and held it up to my nose. "Ah," I said, inhaling the aroma.

George snorted. I ignored him and lit a cigarette. Then I sat back and luxuriated in the sensation and the sunlight.

God it was good to be out of the hospital. Every time I'm in one I remember how much I hate it.

George glanced over. "Okay," he said. "You're dressed, you're out of the hospital, you've got a cigarette. Now give."

So I did.

"Richie and Tony always were scumbags," he muttered when I was through.

"Tell me about it." I took a puff of my cigarette and conjured up darkly detailed visions about what I'd like to do to them if the opportunity ever arose.

"Although," George continued, "to be fair, if you hadn't run away, you probably would have been all right."

"Are you saying what happened was my fault?" I asked indignantly.

"No. I'm just pointing out that you made things worse by pissing them off."

"And what would you have done if someone dragged you in a car and jabbed a gun in your ribs? Sat there?"

"I wouldn't be in that position in the first place."

"Really?"

"Yes, really." Then before I could reply George changed the subject. "So what do you think? Did Tony and Richie kill Marsha for the thirty thousand?"

We stopped at a light.

"No." I opened the window and flicked the ash from my cigarette out into the street. "And Fast Eddie doesn't think so either. Because if he did, those two wouldn't be walking around right now. They'd be buried somewhere in Utica."

"True," George replied. "One thing about thirty thousand dollars. It certainly provides an incentive for homicide. I've known people who would slit your throat for two bucks let alone thirty grand."

Zsa Zsa jumped up on my lap. I scratched underneath her

chin. "What I want to know is where would someone like Marsha Pennington get that much money in the first place? When I saw her I got the impression she was broke."

"Interesting question." George put his foot on the gas and zoomed through a yellow light just as it was turning red. "Possibly *the* most interesting question. Maybe she got an inheritance."

"You mean from some distant relative? I guess she could have, although it doesn't seem likely. At least, she didn't say anything to me when we talked." I wound my hair around my finger. It felt oily. It definitely needed to be washed. "Maybe I should give her mother a call."

"Maybe you should." George chewed on the inside of his cheek for a moment. "Of course, she could have always gone down to Atlantic City."

"She was thirty thousand in the hole. Where would she get a stake?"

George shrugged. "She could have conned someone into lending her a couple of thousand."

I took another puff of my Camel. "I'd imagine that if you're a compulsive gambler, your sources would dry up after a while."

"I don't know. In my experience there's always a loan shark out there willing to give someone enough rope to hang themselves with." George loosened his tie. "Or maybe," he continued, "she's got someone in her family who's a soft touch."

I pushed a strand of hair off my forehead. "She did go down to see her mother just before she died," I allowed. I decided I was definitely going to have to speak to the lady—if I could get the nurse to put her on the line.

George zoomed around a car and shot up Beech Street. "How about this? She embezzled the money."

"From where? Office petty cash? She taught ESL in high school for God's sake."

"I was thinking more along the lines of her husband's business."

"That makes a little more sense," I admitted.

"Or she could have been blackmailing someone."

"Who?"

George shrugged. "How the hell would I know?"

We both fell silent.

"Carpe diem," I said suddenly.

George shot me a questioning glance.

"It's Latin," I explained. "It means seize the day."

"I know what it means," he growled. "I'm not a total idiot. I just don't see the relevance."

"I was just thinking that that thirty grand gave Marsha an opportunity to wipe the slate clean and start over again. She was going to pay off her debts, get a divorce, and start a new life with Brandon Funk. She was going to seize the day."

"And everyone would live happily ever after," George observed as he drove up Beech.

"Except in this case there was no 'ever after.' " We hung a right on Westcott and went down Euclid. I tightened my grip on the door handle as we sped through the intersection.

We turned up Meadowbrook. "There probably wouldn't have been a 'happy' either," George said.

"Why's that?"

"Because your friend didn't pick the greatest guy in the world to start over with."

"You checked on Funk?"

"I said I would. Funk does have a record. He was arrested twice for assault and three times for domestic violence. All the complainants were women. One of them, a Shirley Hinkel. . . ."

"That's the name of Merlin's girlfriend!" I cried.

"If you say so. She's got an order of protection out on him."

"Why?"

"Assault. He slugged her. Pleaded guilty to a misdee and got a year probation. I talked to the other two women, too."

"And what did they say?"

George turned up Crawford. "They both said he was very nice, very kind, but then something would happen that would set him off and he'd go nuts. He was always sorry afterward. They always are," George added.

I thought about Brandon sitting there and repeating, "it's my fault" over and over. He'd definitely been referring to Marsha. What was he feeling so guilty about? "Do you think he killed Marsha in a fit of rage?" I asked.

"He could have. He's got the temperament." George pulled up in front of my house. "The only problem is there weren't any marks on your friend's body. None at all. I pulled the ME's report," he explained in answer to my glance. "I just wanted to make sure the paper had gotten the facts straight."

"He could have half suffocated her and thrown her in."

George shook his head. "There still would have been some bruises around the facial area, and anyway that sounds too complicated for him. I see Funk as the kind of guy that beats someone to death, realizes what he's done, and runs out the door."

"That's my impression, too." I clicked my tongue against the roof of my mouth. Something else occurred to me. "I wonder if Eddison would know anything about the money Marsha came into?"

"Who's Eddison?"

"He was Marsha's therapist."

"Even if he does know, why should he tell you?"

"Why shouldn't he?"

"Breach of confidentiality."

I put my cigarettes in my pocket. "Maybe I can come up with something that will make him change his mind."

"Well, whatever you do be careful." George lifted up my chin with the tip of his finger. It hurt like hell. "Because I don't want to have to call an ambulance for you again."

"That makes two of us."

Chapter
26

After George drove off I stood outside for a moment and admired the crocuses and grape hyacinths blooming in my neighbor's front yard and decided that next year I'd plant some of my own. I used to do things like that in my other life; in fact I'd even read garden catalogs, but then my other life hadn't included people like Fast Eddie and his mother or Brandon Funk. I turned and walked into my house. I still felt weak and I needed to sit down.

Zsa Zsa ran in front of me. I followed her into the kitchen, got two Snickers bars out of the fridge, poured myself a shot of Scotch, went into the backyard, uncovered one of the lounge chairs, sat down, and tried to forget about the events of the past day. Two seconds later James padded through the grass, jumped up on the deck and into my lap.

I petted him while Zsa Zsa licked his ears. He must have missed her because outside of an occasional shake he didn't do anything. For a while I just sat there eating my candy and drinking my Black Label and watching the new leaves on my neighbor's birch tree fluttering in the breeze. But little by little my mind started drifting back to the problem of Marsha's death and the thirty thousand and how she got it and who had it and whether or not that person was the one that had killed Marsha. I was willing to bet it was. Find the thirty thousand and I'd find Marsha's murderer, something that was easier said than done.

Then I started thinking about Estrella again and wondering how she fit into the equation.

If she did.

Her death could have been happenstance.

But the more I thought about it, the less I believed it.

Someone, an English playwright I think, had written about "the long arm of coincidence."

If you asked me, this arm was a little too long.

Because things weren't so coincidental after all.

Marsha and Estrella had several connections.

They both went to the same school—one as a student, the other as a teacher.

They both went to the same therapist.

Which meant what? Maybe nothing, maybe a lot.

I got up and went inside to pour myself another Scotch.

I was coming outside when I remembered something George had told me. He'd said that a lot of kids from Wellington hung out at the LeMoyne Reservoir. They went there to party and smoke and cut class. Was it possible that Estrella had been there when Marsha was killed? Could she have seen the murder? Is that why she'd been so anxious to leave Syracuse?

I sat down and finished off the last half of the second Snickers bar.

And of course she couldn't go to the police. She couldn't take the chance of having them turn her and her family in to the INS.

I wondered if she'd said anything to her boyfriend Ray. Or to her friend, Pam Tower. I was deciding I should really speak to her when I drifted off to sleep. I awoke a couple of hours later with a crick in my neck. I was massaging it when the phone rang. I went inside to get it. Tim was on the line.

"Sorry to disturb you," he said, "but the ball python we just got has really bad mouth rot. Do you want me to take him to the vet for a shot of antibiotics or do the iodine number?"

"Take him." Reptiles Inc. was definitely going to hear about this.

"When?"

"I'll be in in an hour. Make the appointment for any time after that."

"I thought you were supposed to stay in bed for three days."

"I was," I said and hung up. I would have gotten bored anyway. Then since my car was still at the store I called Ace Taxi for a pickup. They came thirty minutes later.

Tim left with the snake as soon as I walked through the door. I settled in and fed the fish. I was fixing the filter in one of the tanks when Manuel walked in.

"What do you want?" I said as I reconnected the tubing. My headache was coming back which put me in an irritable mood.

"Why do you always think I want something?" Manuel demanded.

"Because you usually do." I put the lid on the tank and dried my hands off on the back of my jeans.

Manuel placed his hands on his hips. "Well, maybe I got something you want. Maybe I came to do you a favor."

"Really? What might that be?"

"Look." He beckoned me over to the counter. "I got something for you."

I walked over reluctantly. Whatever it was that Manuel had, I was pretty sure I didn't want to see it. When he took a Glock nine millimeter out of his pocket I knew I'd been right.

"What the hell am I supposed to do with that?"

"I figured that the next time someone tried to grab you you could pop 'em with this."

I rubbed my temples. My headache was getting worse. "Manuel, just put it away."

"I can let you have it for one twenty-five."

"Forget it."

"Okay." He put the gun back in his pocket. "I was just trying to help you."

The sad part was that in his mind he was. "Manuel," I told him, "why don't you go back to school before you get yourself into some real trouble."

"I'm planning to," he said, doing sincere.

Yeah. Right. I don't know why I bothered. Manuel would do what Manuel wanted to do.

He hitched his pants up. "I thought I'd give you first crack, but if you don't want it, I know someone else who will."

"At least get a job," I continued, even though I knew what I was saying was a study in wasted effort. We'd had this conversation too many times before.

"Hey, I make more money doing this than working at someplace like Pizza Hut." Then he snapped his fingers. "I knew there was something I forgot to tell you."

"What's that?"

"You was asking about Estrella's girlfriend."

"Pam Tower?"

"Yeah. I saw her the other day. She was working at Eats Galore over on Westcott Street." And with that he left.

Tim came back a short time later without the ball python. I asked him what happened.

He bent down to pet Zsa Zsa. "The vet and I decided to put him down. His mouth was so deformed, even if we had cured the rot, he wouldn't have been able to open his mouth enough to eat. We would have had to force feed him for the rest of his life."

"How much did Curey charge?"

"Thirty."

"Thirty? We could have put him in the freezer for nothing."

"I know." Tim straightened up and handed me the bill. "He charged us for an office visit."

I threw it on the counter. "I'm sending this straight to Reptiles Inc. with a nasty note."

"You think they're going to refund the money for the snake plus the vet bill?" Tim said dubiously.

"They'd better." I went in and wrote my letter. Then while I was at it I sent Garriques a bill for the money he owed me. I spent the rest of the day cleaning cages, phoning in orders, and taking Advil to keep the pain in my head down to a tolerable level. I would have loved to have gone home, but considering the amount of time I'd been away from the store recently, I thought that probably wasn't a good idea.

At nine o'clock I locked up the shop, and Zsa Zsa and I drove over to Eats Galore on Westcott. It was on the way home and I figured maybe I'd get lucky and catch up with Pam Tower. But she wasn't there. According to the manager she worked three days a week and this wasn't one of them. I gave the manager my card and asked him to pass it on to her, but I didn't have much faith that he would. If I wanted to speak to her, I'd have to come back later.

I stopped at Nice N' Easy on the way home and got the evening paper, a package of cigarettes and a pint of coffee ice cream. The street was quiet when I parked the car in the driveway and stepped out. My neighbors were in for the evening. The only sound was coming from the Fonte house. Their kid, a pimply twelve-year-old who thought he was eighteen, was practicing his sax. It sounded as if someone was strangling a goose. It made my head hurt even more and I went inside and went to bed. I guess the day had taken more out of me than I'd thought.

I woke up at four. At four-thirty I gave up trying to get back to sleep, went downstairs to the kitchen, got the pint of coffee ice cream out of the freezer, and lay on the sofa and ate it while I watched *The Creatures From Planet Nog*. After a few minutes I found myself thinking about the LeMoyne Reservoir. What had Marsha been doing there? She must have been meeting someone. But who? Not a social acquaintance, that was for sure. Maybe it was the person she was blackmailing.

Maybe she'd arranged for the payoff to take place at the reservoir.

And maybe the person she was blackmailing decided he didn't want to pay, killed her, and took back the money.

Or maybe not.

The more I thought about it, the more I thought that arranging for a payoff to take place in a deserted area was just plain stupid.

But then Marsha never had been exactly smart.

I was stifling a yawn when I remembered something I'd forgotten, something I should have remembered earlier—Merlin's papers, the ones Marsha had never gotten around to giving me. What had Marsha said about them? That she thought he was doing something dirty and she wanted me to look at them and find out what it was. Maybe she'd found out what he'd been doing. And maybe she'd demanded thirty thousand dollars' worth of hush money and he'd killed her.

Except why had she come to me if she already knew?

The answer was obvious: when she'd come to me she hadn't known. Something had happened after we'd met to change the equation.

But what?

It seemed as if it was time to have another chat with Merlin. But before I did that I decided to call Marsha's mother. Marsha might have told her something that would help me make sense of everything. I ate another spoonful of ice cream and watched the first streaks of light on the horizon and thought about how some daughters actually talked to their mothers and about how I no longer talked to mine.

Chapter
27

Because I was still playing catch-up at the store, it was a little after two in the afternoon before I got a chance to call Marsha's mother. Once I managed to get through Nurse Ratchett, Mrs. Wise, or Nancy as she insisted on being called, was full of interesting surprises, the most interesting one being that her daughter had left late Saturday afternoon, not Sunday as the nurse had told me.

"Pearline wasn't here," Mrs. Wise explained as I wound the telephone cord around my finger. Her voice was crisp, her dictation precise. A picture of a thin, patrician-looking lady, the obverse of pudgy, rumpled Marsha, rose before me. "She just made an assumption because that's how long Marsha usually stays."

"But not this time."

"No. Not this time. She wanted to get back early. Evidently she had things to do."

"She didn't happen to say what things?" I asked as I pried a piece of paper out of Zsa Zsa's jaws.

Mrs. Wise paused for a second before continuing. "No, she didn't, and I didn't ask." Another pause. I got the feeling she was choosing her words carefully. "Over the past three years I've learned not to pry too much. But I can tell you she seemed very excited."

"She didn't ask you for money, did she?"

"No. She knew better. I'd stopped giving her any." Mrs. Wise's voice grew hesitant. "Why? Did she need any? Was she in trouble?"

"I think she may have put herself in some."

"She always made things hard for herself—always." Mrs. Wise stopped talking again. This time the pause on the other end of the line was longer. "You know," she finally said, "I thought I was doing the right thing not giving her any money. Everyone I talked to said not to. They said that no matter what she told me she'd just gamble it away. Maybe I shouldn't have listened to them."

"No. I think what you did was correct," I replied, trying to console her.

"I'm not so sure." Marsha's mother's voice cracked. "She was my only child. And now she's gone. What do I do with the money now? Just answer me that?" She began to cry. Her sobs were dry and harsh.

Before I could think of anything to say the nurse came on the line and told me I had no business upsetting Mrs. Wise like that. Then she hung up.

"So?" Tim said. He'd been following the conversation as he restocked the doggie biscuit bins that sat over by the side of the counter.

I reached for a cigarette and took a sip of the coffee I'd

poured myself half an hour ago and forgotten about. "When I first spoke to Merlin he told me that Marsha had come back on Sunday. Now it turns out she was back on Saturday night. Why should he lie?"

"Maybe he didn't." Tim emptied the last of the small doughnut-shaped biscuits out of the carton and straightened up. "Maybe Marsha didn't go home. Maybe she stayed somewhere else."

"I bet it was at Brandon Funk's house," I murmured.

"So?"

"So nothing. I just want to know why he didn't mention it." I looked at my watch. It was three. Funk would probably still be at Wellington. I was sure I could catch him among his mops and pails, but after a moment's thought I decided to wait till later in the evening. I still had too much work to do around the shop.

I spent the rest of the afternoon unpacking the shipment of dog food we'd just gotten in, listening to our macaw sing the first two lines of "When The Saints Come Marching In" over and over, waiting on customers, and fending off a salesman who wanted to sell me homemade kibble.

"Just try some," he urged. "See." He put a few pieces in his mouth. "It's good. I eat it all the time."

I resisted the temptation and gave it to Zsa Zsa instead. She spit it out.

Around five I lay down and took a nap. Tim woke me at five-thirty to tell me I had a call.

"Tell them I'll call back."

"I don't think that's a good idea."

"Why not?"

"It's Fast Eddie."

"Jesus." I jumped up and reached for the phone on the desk. I could hear Fast Eddie's wheeze through the wire.

"So how's it coming?" he whispered.

"It's coming," I said, even though it wasn't.

"Good. That's what I like to hear." Then he started to cough. "You'll call me and let me know how things are going," he said when the spasm had passed.

"Of course."

"Because I'm trying to clean up a lot of odds and ends. I don't like things messy." He hung up the phone.

"Nice company you're keeping these days," Tim observed as I replaced the receiver.

"Tell me about it." I'd been thinking of going home and going to bed instead of going out to Funk's house, but Fast Eddie's call had made me change my mind. I spent the rest of the evening wishing Marsha had never come into the store.

Nine o'clock arrived quicker than I thought it would. I said goodbye to Tim, locked up the shop, took Zsa Zsa home, and headed over to Brandon Funk's house. It was warm out and I rolled down the window. At the corner of Genesee and Cherry a police car sprang out of nowhere and sped past me, siren blaring. The Cherry Hill apartments, a monolith of poured concrete and brick, stared down from the hill. On the corner five teenagers lounged against a lamppost passing a bottle cloaked in a brown paper bag back and forth. Their hoots echoed through the night air—the only sign of life on the deserted streets. Or maybe the streets were deserted because of them.

It took me twenty minutes to get to Funk's house. He didn't look happy to see me when he answered the bell.

"What do you want?" he said. He was wearing a dirty T-shirt and smelled of beer.

"To talk to you."

His mouth took on a stubborn twist. "Why should I?"

"Because I think we have something to discuss."

"Like what?"

"Like the fact that Marsha spent Saturday here with you."

"So what if she did?" Funk crossed his arms over his chest. "She was entitled."

"I'm not saying she wasn't."

Funk's expression softened slightly. I took advantage of it. "Are you going to let me in?"

He hesitated, then shrugged. "Aw what the fuck. Why not? It don't make no difference now anyway."

Except for the fact that there were more beer bottles, the room looked the same as the last time I was there.

"Listen," he said quickly, "I'm sorry about what happened the other time when you were here. I got upset."

"It's okay."

"It's just that I get these spells sometimes."

"Spells?" I suppose that was as good a word as any for assault.

"Yeah, spells." Funk scratched his cheek with the edge of his Budweiser can. "Want any?" He lifted up the Bud. "I've got a six pack in the fridge."

"No thanks."

Funk shrugged. "Suit yourself." He remained standing and so did I.

Porter's picture seemed to stare out at me from its frame. I looked away, but the stuffed bats my eyes fell on next were equally disturbing. I went back to looking at Porter. It was the lesser of the two evils. I reached for a cigarette, then remembered Funk didn't allow smoking and stopped. "So why did Marsha come back early from her mother's house?" I asked him.

"She wanted to see me. She wanted to talk."

"About what?"

"Things," Funk said cryptically. He finished off his beer and crushed the can. It seemed to disappear in his big meaty hand.

I persisted. "What things?"

A rueful expression crossed Funk's face. For a moment his gaze turned inward. He looked as if he were a man who'd seen his dream and lost it. "The store. We talked about how we were going to open the store."

"She didn't happen to mention anything about the money she owed?"

He frowned. "I already told you she didn't."

"Or about how she was going to settle her debt with Fast Eddie?"

"Who's that?"

Funk was a bad liar. I leaned forward. "Come on," I told him, "don't waste my time—or yours."

He went for another beer. "Okay," he allowed after he'd pulled the tab and taken a sip. "Maybe she had a little problem."

"A thirty-thousand-dollar debt is not a little problem—at least not in my book."

Funk flushed. "Just because she's dead doesn't mean you can say bad things about her."

"That wasn't my intention."

Instead of answering, Funk chewed on the inside of his cheek and studied a stuffed squirrel he'd mounted on the wall. "Everyone makes mistakes," he said softly after a minute had gone by. I got the idea he was talking about himself as much as about Marsha. "Listen, she wasn't going to gamble anymore. She stopped when she met me and she wasn't going to start again either."

"And you believed her?"

"Yeah, I did. Things were gonna be okay." Funk was indulging in magical thinking, a process I knew too well. You wanted something to happen, so you thought it would. But who knew? Maybe in this case I was wrong. Maybe Marsha would have started a new life—if she'd gotten the chance.

"What about the money she owed?" I asked.

Funk looked mournful. "I wanted to help her. She wouldn't let me."

"You mean she wouldn't let you help her blackmail her husband?"

"She wasn't gonna do anything like that," Funk insisted.

"You're so certain, are you?"

"Yes, I am."

"What about the papers?"

"What papers?"

"The ones Marsha left in school."

"I don't know what you're talking about." Funk's face had taken on a mulish cast.

"Really?" I leaned closer. "Well, I think you're lying. I think you saw that Marsha had forgotten those papers so you took them home. And then maybe she called you and you told her you had them, and she decided to come back to Syracuse early and take another look. Which she did. And that's when she decided she didn't need me. That's when she decided she could get the dogs plus thirty thousand from Merlin on her own."

"You're crazy!" Funk cried.

"Am I? Tell me why?"

Brandon Funk balled up his hands into fists. "I want you out of here."

"Or you'll what? Punch me?"

Funk was taking a step toward me when the front door flew open.

Chapter
28

Enid Garriques's voice preceded her into Funk's living room.

"Brandon," she said. "Mom wants us to—" Then she saw me and stopped. A flustered expression danced across her face. For a second she looked embarrassed, as if she'd been caught doing something déclassé like reading the *National Enquirer;* then her habitual mask of poise returned and she nodded and gave the gracious smile. Like Dylan Thomas's aunt, Enid always did the right thing. "I'm sorry if I seemed startled to see you here," she told me. "It's just that you never mentioned you knew my brother." With that she shut the door and walked inside. She looked out of place in Funk's house. Her expensive clothes and carefully styled hair clashed with the surroundings.

"That's because until recently I didn't," I replied.

She looked around the room and wrinkled her nose in distaste. "People tell me we look alike. What do you think?"

I shook my head. "I don't see it." And I couldn't.

She smiled briefly. I'd given the right answer. "Neither do I, but that's what they say. I don't know why." Unconsciously, she adjusted a strand of hair that wasn't out of place before looking at her watch. "I'm sorry to intrude but I'm going to have to drag my brother away. My mom's having the dining room painted tomorrow and I told her Brandon and I would move the table and the sideboard."

Funk's anger at me had evaporated into sullenness. "Why can't we do it later?" he demanded.

"Because she wants it done now," Enid answered impatiently, taking no notice of his mood. "She's going to go to bed soon."

"Oh, all right," Funk said. Watching him I got the idea his sister ran the show.

Enid went over and straightened the pictures on the mantel. "About the tank," she said to me.

"Yes," I replied, figuring she was going to tell me the deal was off.

"I definitely want it."

"Great." At least something was working out right.

"What tank?" Funk asked.

"It's Gregory's birthday present," his sister replied. "And don't you tell him. I don't want you to ruin the surprise." Enid turned toward me. "He's always saying things he's not supposed to," she explained.

Funk flushed. "No, I don't," he protested.

Enid shrugged. "Have it your own way." She looked around the room. "How can you live like this? All these animals. Those pictures. The past is past, Brandon. You should throw all this stuff out."

"No!" he cried.

The lines were obviously the beginning of an old, well-rehearsed argument. I left them to it and walked back out to the cab. A hint of rain hung in the air. I couldn't see the stars. Clouds obscured the view. By the time I got home the wind had picked up. As I walked up the driveway I heard two cats yowling under my neighbor's laurel hedge. I put my key in the lock. Zsa Zsa was right in front of the door when I opened it. She jumped up and I rubbed her chest. Then I walked her to the end of the block and back. When I returned I ate a handful of Hershey Kisses, swallowed a couple of vitamins, and went to bed. I fell asleep immediately but woke up again at two with bad dreams, and even though I tried, I couldn't get back to sleep. This no sleeping thing was getting boring.

I ended up sipping Scotch, watching TV, listening to the rain, cataloging my deficiencies—which were legion—and wondering how I'd come to make such a mess of my life. Then I started thinking about Marsha and the mess she'd made of her life, and I decided that maybe I hadn't done so badly after all. At least I hadn't been terminally stupid. Why the hell had she been out at the reservoir anyway? That really bothered me. And it kept bothering me. I couldn't let go of the problem. Finally I decided that seeing the site in the daylight might help me make sense of what had happened. Then because I was feeling the kind of lonely you get to feeling right before the sun comes up, I called George and asked him if he wanted to come along.

"Do you know what time it is?" he groaned.

"About five-thirty."

"Jesus, I went to bed at three."

"Go back to bed." Maybe this hadn't been such a good idea after all.

"No." He sounded resigned. "As long as you got me up I might as well come. I'm curious, too."

"You sure?"

"Of course I'm sure."

"Good. I'll be over in ten minutes."

"Make it fifteen and bring some coffee."

"You got a deal."

I went upstairs and changed into jeans and a black cotton turtleneck. Then I went back downstairs and put on my sneakers. Zsa Zsa wagged her tail as I went by, but she didn't get up. I guess she was sleeping in. It was cool and damp outside. The sidewalk was still wet from last night's storm. Rain drops dripped from the leaves of the flowering crab trees. Its downed petals littered the grass. The sky was streaked with purple-edged clouds. In a few minutes the sun would be up. A crow hopped along the grass. He ignored me till I got about five feet away; then he cawed and flew up to the roof of the house across the street. I got in the cab, drove to the AM Mini Mart, bought two cups of coffee, and cruised over to George's place.

"Be careful. It's hot," I warned as I handed him his cup.

He grunted and took a sip. "God this stuff sucks."

"I know." It tasted as if it had been brewing for the past four hours.

"Where'd you get it?"

"From the Mini Mart over on Delphi."

"It figures." But he took another gulp anyhow.

I snuck a look at George out of the corner of my eye. He hadn't shaved yet. I could see the stubble on his cheeks in the early morning light. He was wearing a stained sweatshirt and a pair of torn jeans. I realized I'd never seen him so disheveled. For some reason the thought that he could actually look like this cheered me enormously.

"Have a hot date last night?" I asked. I kicked myself as soon as the words left my mouth.

George frowned. "Actually I was working on my paper."

"How's it going?"

"Not well." He took another sip of coffee. "Listen," he began.

"Yes?"

"You know the offer you made?"

"About helping you?"

"I don't want you to write it for me."

"I wasn't intending to."

"But maybe if you could show me a couple of things . . ." His voice trailed off.

"Sure. Anytime."

"I'll call."

"Whenever you're ready."

I couldn't see the expression on George's face because he was looking out the window.

"Beginnings are always hard," I told him.

He grunted and I shut up. The conversation had gone about as far as it was going to go. We finished the drive to the turnoff in silence. In the pale morning light the path and the trees surrounding it looked sad, as if they knew they'd been abandoned. The scarred white birch trunks leaned this way and that, anemic matchsticks surrounded by puddles of stagnant water and small middens of beer cans, potato chip and Taco Bell bags.

"Watch the rock," George warned when we'd gone about fifty feet.

"I see it."

How could I not? It was right in the middle of the road. I could have probably gone over it—the cab's suspension was higher than that of most cars—but I didn't want to take the chance of ending up with a broken spring.

"I guess we walk," I said, stepping on the brake.

We got out. For some reason it felt colder here and I shivered in the chill morning air. We walked along the path in silence. It was muddy and my sneakers made a squishing sound whenever I took a step. When we got to the reservoir I stopped to study the ground. It was littered with Styrofoam cups and beer cans and small blackened areas where kids had lit camp fires.

"What are we looking for?" George asked.

"Some sort of evidence that Estrella was here."

George chewed on the inside of his cheek while he thought. Then he pointed to a cluster of scrub trees on the other side of the water. "That might be a good place to start."

George was right. It would be. The murderer wouldn't have been able to see Estrella, but she could have seen him. We walked over. The place had obviously been in use for a while. There were indentations in the ground from where sleeping bags had lain. Someone had made a fireplace with a circle of stones. The earth in the middle was blackened. I kicked one of the beer cans scattered along the ground. An edge of something blue hidden in the bushes caught my eye. I pulled it out. It was a folder with Wellington scrawled across the front. I opened it up. Aside from the words "social studies" written on a blank piece of paper it was empty.

George nudged a Southern Comfort bottle with his foot. "I used to drink this when I was a kid."

"I think we all did," I said as I squatted down and began to search the ground.

George joined me, but after twenty minutes he and I were forced to concede defeat. The only things we'd come up with were sodden take-out containers, one size-ten Nike sneaker, a pair of jeans, and a dirt-encrusted green sweatshirt.

"Did Estrella have any friends?" George asked as he stood up.

"Only one that I know of. A kid by the name of Pam Tower."

"Do you have an address on her?"

"She's a runaway."

"Great."

"Could be worse. Manuel spotted her working at Eats Galore over on Westcott Street."

"Have you spoken to her yet?"

I shook my head. "She wasn't at the restaurant when I dropped by."

"Estrella might have told her something."

"The thought had occurred to me." I turned and began walking along the reservoir's outer perimeter. Estrella had to have left some evidence she'd been here somewhere. I'd gone halfway around when I saw an opening in the woods. "Where does that go?" I asked George.

He shook his head. "I didn't even know it was there."

"Well, let's find out." I started down. George joined me a moment later.

The path gave evidence of being well traveled. It was littered with broken beer bottles and more torn cups. Graffiti stained the rock where it forked. We followed both branches. One led to LeMoyne College while the other let out farther down onto Thompson Road. From there it was just a two-minute walk down to Erie Boulevard.

Suddenly I had an idea. "The Pancake Palace is right near where the path comes out," I told George.

"So?"

"So maybe Marsha and her murderer met in the restaurant's parking lot. Remember you said a lot of teachers from Wellington eat breakfast there."

"It's possible," he agreed. "The place does open early. People come and go there all the time. A car in the lot wouldn't excite much notice."

George and I exchanged glances and headed back to the car. It looked as if we were going to pay a visit to The Pancake Palace on our way home. The parking lot was almost empty when I pulled in. Sea gulls strutted back and forth looking for scraps. It was odd seeing them so far from the ocean, but they'd been on Erie Boulevard for years. Maybe they'd gotten stranded up here the same way I had and couldn't find their way home.

"Let me do the talking," I said to George as I turned off the engine.

He shrugged. "It's your show."

To emphasize the point, once we got in the restaurant he headed over to the counter and ordered two cinnamon rolls and a couple of coffees to go while I asked the two waitresses on duty if anyone remembered seeing Marsha.

Both of them had. It turned out Marsha Pennington was a regular.

"She came in two to three times a week and got an English muffin, orange juice, and coffee," the waitress with a strawberry birthmark across the lower part of her left cheek informed me. I noticed that she kept that side of her face slightly tilted away from me. "She used to sit over there." She pointed to an empty table over by the far window. "It's too bad about what happened."

"Yes, it is," I agreed.

Unfortunately neither of the waitresses could remember if Marsha Pennington had been in the day she died.

"The days all kind of run into one another," the waitress I was talking to explained. "I mean, I can't even recall what I had for dinner last night let alone whether or not someone was in a couple of weeks ago."

"Did she have any specific days she came in on?"

The waitress shook her head. "Not that I can recall."

I cast around for another way to help her remember. "Did she usually come in with somebody?"

"Once in a while, but mostly she came in alone." The waitress looked around the room checking to see if anyone needed her. "She'd order her breakfast and read her paper. Then she'd leave. She didn't tip real well. None of these teachers do."

"Anything else?" I asked, grasping at straws.

"Well, there was something." The waitress tapped her nails on the edge of the chair she was standing next to. "It wasn't a big thing. I just remember it because I had never seen the other lady before. She didn't wait to be seated or anything. She just walked over to Mrs. Pennington's table and stood there. The next thing I know they was arguing."

"About what?"

"I don't know. I couldn't hear."

"Then how do you know they were fighting?"

"I could tell from their faces and the way they were waving their arms."

"Then what happened?"

"Nothing. The other lady turned around and walked away."

"What did she look like?"

"Cheap clothes, frizzy hair, big belly."

There was no doubt about it. The woman the waitress was describing sounded liked Shirley, Merlin's girlfriend.

It would be interesting to find out what they'd been arguing about.

I decided it was time Shirley and I had another talk.

Chapter
29

I passed five kids and their parents, coffee cups in hand, waiting for the school bus as I pulled into the apartment complex where Shirley lived. Despite the early hour the children were giggling and wrestling while their parents chatted away. It looked like a pleasant scene, something I might have enjoyed doing, and suddenly a visceral ache for the children I was never going to have washed over me. God, I'd really blown it in the baby department. I'd gotten pregnant a year after Murphy and I started sleeping together. Murphy had been happy when I'd told him. He'd offered to marry me, but I'd said no and gone to Puerto Rico and gotten an abortion instead.

The world was just opening up and I hadn't wanted to be tied down. I wasn't ready for motherhood. I don't know if Murphy was ready for fatherhood, but I do know he never forgave me for what I'd done because later when I told him I wanted to have a kid he'd looked at me and said, "You should have taken your chance when you had it." I figured he'd change his mind, but he never did. It was amazing really that our sense of timing was always so bad. Whenever he wanted something I didn't and vice versa. Lately for some reason I can't help thinking a lot about how different my life would have been if I'd had the kid. Jesus, how could I have been so wrong about so many things? I sighed and tried to concentrate on what I'd come to do instead. It was less depressing. By the time I'd parked the car, walked to Shirley's apartment, and rung the bell, I'd gotten myself under control.

I hadn't called Shirley to tell her I was coming when I'd dropped George off. I wanted to surprise her instead. From the look on her face when she opened the door I'd say I'd succeeded.

"Here." I handed her the morning paper I'd picked up off her stoop and stepped inside before she could stop me.

She hugged the *Herald* to her as I closed the door behind me. Her movements were slow. Her eyes were swollen with sleep. She must have just gotten up.

"What are you doing?" she said in a voice thick with early morning phlegm. "You can't come in here like this."

"I just did."

She plucked at the edge of her robe. It was ripped along the left side seam. "I have to go to work."

"So do I."

"I'm going to be late."

"Not if you answer my question." I sat down on the sofa and crossed my legs.

"I want you out of here now," Shirley cried.

"This will just take a couple of minutes."

She moved toward the phone. Her movements were a little sharper. She was waking up. "If you don't leave, I'm going to call the police."

I shrugged. "Go ahead. But if you do, I'll tell them you were seen arguing with Marsha Pennington near where she was killed."

Shirley glared at me. "Says who?"

"Says the waitress at The Pancake Palace." I played a hunch. "I'm sure they'd be interested. Especially since it happened the morning Marsha was killed."

Shirley put the newspaper down on the coffee table. "That's not true. We met on Friday. And we weren't arguing."

"Then what were you doing?"

"Talking."

I leaned forward. "That's not what the waitress said."

"Well, she's wrong." The daylight wasn't kind to Shirley, I thought as I watched her. It highlighted every line and wrinkle in her face. "What do you care anyway?" she asked in a aggrieved tone. "Why can't you just leave this alone? Marsha's dead."

"Exactly."

"Even when she's gone she makes trouble for me," Shirley said bitterly.

"But I thought you were friends."

"I thought so, too," Shirley snapped. "But we weren't. I don't think we ever were. I was just too dumb to see what was going on." The corners of Shirley's mouth twitched. "All I wanted her to do was leave Merlin alone," she told me. "She didn't love him. She didn't care about him. She never cared about anybody but herself. Ever."

"That's not an opinion other people share."

"That's because they never knew her like I did," Shirley said. "All those years we lived next to each other and all she ever did was lord it over me. She thought she was so much better. I got a new coat, the next week she got a more expensive one. I got a new sofa, she got one, too—only hers was better. The only reason she wanted Brandon was because I had him."

"From what I understand she did you a favor. You were well rid of him."

Shirley shook her head. "You don't understand, do you? Women like you don't."

"Women like me?" I asked.

"Yes." She pulled at a thread on the sleeve of her robe. "Attractive women. Women men like."

I looked down at myself. "I don't think so."

"No." Shirley pointed an accusatory finger. "You wanna look the way you do. I used to see you all dressed up to go to work when you lived here. Those tight skirts you used to wear. All that makeup. The men used to watch you walking out of your car. You can look like that again any time you want. But nobody has ever looked at me that way. Even when I was younger they didn't. Brandon was all I had. Marsha knew that and she took him away anyway."

"He hit you," I reminded her. "You had an order of protection taken out on him."

Shirley looked down at the floor. "I only did that because I was angry at him. I didn't mean it. I was gonna go to the court and get it lifted. But then Marsha comes along and takes him."

"So you go after her husband?"

"She didn't want him, but she wouldn't let him go," she said softly. "Marsha didn't want me to have anything."

"He could have just walked away," I told Shirley. "He is a big boy."

"He wanted to, but she was threatening to go—" Suddenly Shirley stopped talking.

"To go to who?"

"To nobody," Shirley said and changed the subject. "She

always thought she was so smart just because she was a teacher. But who was she teaching? You answer me that."

"Who was she threatening to go to?" I asked again.

"Nobody. She wasn't going to go to nobody." Shirley's voice rose a notch.

"Is that what you were arguing about?"

"I want you to leave now. I want you to go."

"Are you sure you don't want to tell me?"

"Get out!" she screamed.

I rose. There was no reason to stay. I'd learned as much as I was going to for the time being.

"I don't want you coming back here. I've got nothing more to say to you." Shirley's voice had gone up again. She sounded as if she was on the verge of hysteria.

Suddenly I heard Brandon's voice in my head. "Ask her what she did to the cat who peed on her doorstep." So I did. She threw an ashtray at me by way of an answer. Fortunately her aim was bad. I left before it got better.

One thing was for sure, I thought as I walked toward the cab. Shirley had gained by Marsha's death. Now she had Merlin all to herself. I guess there really is no accounting for taste.

I lit a cigarette. But then where did the blackmail come in?

Maybe it didn't. Maybe I'd been wrong. After all, it had been known to happen.

On a frequent basis.

I got in the cab and drove home. I took Zsa Zsa out for a walk and checked my answering machine for messages. There weren't any, which was probably just as well. These days the only messages I was getting were dunning ones from credit card companies. Then I went to work. A flock of geese was passing overhead as Zsa Zsa and I were walking up to the store. They were flying low and their honking bounced off the houses and echoed in the air. Zsa Zsa wagged her tail in excitement and went after them before I could stop her. I cursed and ran after her. Half a block later I caught up with her and carried her back to the store.

"She looks embarrassed," Tim said when I set her down on the floor.

"She should be." I made a pot of coffee and got down to work.

I couldn't get Shirley off my mind, though. I kept seeing her, hearing her voice. Could she actually have murdered Marsha in a fit of jealousy? It seemed unlikely, but stranger things had been known to happen. And what exactly had Marsha been threatening Merlin with? Going to the IRS? Going to the police? I was turning the possibilities over in my mind when Angie, one of Fast Eddie's lowlife scum, walked through the door.

I reached under the counter to where Merlin's twenty-two was and patted the gun. Maybe it wasn't much, maybe it couldn't make a very big hole in someone, but knowing it was there made me feel better anyway. I didn't know what Angie wanted. I just knew I didn't want to go on any more rides with him.

He looked around as he strode over to where I was. The short-sleeved teal shirt he was wearing showed off his tan. "Nice place you got here," he said.

"Thanks." I made a big show of lighting a cigarette.

"So how things going?" He rested an elbow on the counter with the easy familiarity of one who is used to being in charge.

"Fine. Listen, I already told Fast Eddie I'd call him if I found anything out. He doesn't have to send you around to check on me."

"He didn't send me. His mother did."

I groaned.

Angie smiled. "She's really something, ain't she?"

"Yes," I replied with feeling. "She certainly is."

"She just wanted to make sure you understood not to keep the money if you happened to find it."

"I'm not a moron," I told him.

"That's what I said to her. But she worries a lot. Especially with Eddie being sick and all."

I spun my lighter around with my index finger. "Is that it?"

"So what should I tell her?"

"Tell her I'm no closer to finding her son's money than I was before."

"You talked to everyone?"

"I talked to everyone."

"Because I thought that therapist guy . . ."

"Eddison?"

Angie nodded. "I thought he was holding out on me. Maybe you should go speak to him again."

"Maybe you should," I snapped, losing patience.

Angie raised an eyebrow. "Is that what you want me to tell Fast Eddie's ma? I will if you want me to."

I sighed. Even though I would have dearly loved to tell her to fuck herself, it wouldn't be worth the price. "No. I'll go talk to him," I told Angie.

"Good." He straightened up. "See. I told her you was sensible."

I wasn't. I was just tired, but I didn't say that.

Chapter
30

Angie's visit bothered me. I thought about why it did while I opened up a can of cat food for Pickles and gave Zsa Zsa a bath.

The whole thing was just too pat. I was being steered in a specific direction and I didn't know why. Of course, I could always choose not to take that road. But if I didn't, I'd never find out what was going on. On the other hand that might be a healthier alternative.

"What do you think I should do?" I asked Zsa Zsa as I dried her off with a towel.

She licked my finger by way of an answer.

I decided that meant I should call Eddison. At the very least I'd get Fast Eddie's mother off my back, and at the most I might find out something else about Marsha. I dropped the towel in the hamper and spent the next twenty minutes combing the tangles out of Zsa Zsa's coat. Then I put the comb down and called Eddison, but he wasn't in. According to the message on his answering machine he was gone for the day. I looked up his home address in the phone book. Surprisingly he was listed. A lot of times therapists aren't. I decided to drive by his house on my way home. He wasn't that far away.

His house turned out to be a neatly kept, unremarkable green and white Cape Cod in the outer university area. It was one of those houses you'd pass by without a second glance. There was nothing wrong with it—but there wasn't anything terribly right with it either. I was feeling irritable by the time I arrived there because none of the houses on Overbridge Street seemed to have visible numbers and I had to keep on stopping the cab, getting out and looking, getting back in, and driving on. Since it was drizzling I was damp by the time I rang Eddison's bell. I got even damper standing on his front stoop because Eddison didn't invite me in.

"What do you want?" he asked, carefully closing the door behind him. The gesture made me wonder if he had someone in there that he didn't want me to see.

"There's something we have to discuss," I told him while I let my glance linger on the nearby picture window. But I couldn't see in. The blinds were too tightly drawn.

"Make an appointment," he snapped. "I'm busy." He turned to go.

"I don't think Angie would like your attitude."

Eddison halted. He turned back around slowly. His face, haloed under the streetlight, seemed to have collapsed in on itself. I'd hit a nerve.

"I already told him I don't know anything about the money." He wrung his hands while he talked. I was fascinated. I'd never actually seen anyone do that before.

"That's not what he thinks," I replied. "And," I added, "that's not what I think either."

"I don't understand." He looked at me blankly. "I don't understand how you come into this."

I nodded to the door. "Why don't you let me in and I'll explain."

"No," he stammered. "I'm sorry. The place is a mess. It's better if we talk out here."

I shrugged. "Suit yourself." The man was obviously lying, but I wasn't going to tell him that—at least not yet. "It's like this," I said, quickly coming up with a story. "Fast Eddie is giving me a ten percent finder's fee for locating Marsha's money."

"Why's he doing that?" Eddison's face was twisted with incomprehension.

"Because I told him I could get the job done faster and easier than he could. Now, if I can't, he'll send some of his associates back to talk to you again." I leaned forward slightly to emphasize my next point. "You've met one of them already—wouldn't you rather speak to me instead?"

"But I don't have Marsha's money," Eddison wailed. His voice was shrill with fear. "I swear it."

"I never said you did. I just think you know something about it."

"But I don't."

I shook my head. "I'm sorry, but I can't buy that. You're acting like someone with a guilty conscience."

Eddison bit his lip.

"You know, one way or another the truth is going to come out," I told him. "The way it does is up to you." Then I waited to see what he'd say next.

"She was blackmailing me," he finally mumbled. "I was giving her money."

"Come again?" This was not the answer I'd expected.

"Marsha said she needed it." He started wringing his hands

again. "She said this was her last chance and she was going to take it."

"Her last chance for what?"

"Happiness."

The folly of the middle-aged female, I thought, rubbing my arms. The temperature was falling and the drizzle had penetrated my shirt. It felt cold against my skin. "What did she have on you?"

Eddison turned his head away, but not before I had a chance to see his eyes brimming with tears. I felt ashamed for him and for me. "I didn't mean to do it," he whispered. "I didn't know what I was doing."

"Exactly what didn't you mean to do?" I asked.

Eddison swallowed. His Adam's apple bobbed up and down. "Estrella and I . . . we had sex," he said in a barely audible voice.

"How did Marsha find out?"

"Estrella told her."

"Why did she do that?"

"Because she thought it would be funny."

"I bet Marsha didn't think so."

"Marsha was going to report me. I was going to lose my clients. Maybe even go to jail. It's taken me so long to build up my business . . . I just couldn't bear the thought of its disappearing." His voice rose. "It wasn't like Estrella wasn't willing either because she was. She was the one who came on to me. She said she liked older men." From the little I'd seen of Estrella, I thought Eddison was probably telling the truth. He looked up, his eyes pleading for absolution. "Everyone is entitled to a mistake once in a while, aren't they?"

"I guess it depends on what it is," was the best I could do. "How much did Marsha want?"

"Five thousand." I couldn't help thinking that was a lot of

money for a couple of fucks. I hoped Eddison had enjoyed
them. "She wanted five thousand dollars," he repeated.

"Or?"

"She was going to go to the authorities and complain."

"What else?" I said. From the look on his face I knew there
was more.

"She wanted to look at my files."

"And you let her?" Screwing Estrella had been bad, but
somehow this was worse.

Eddison's shoulders slumped under the accusation in my
voice. "What else could I do?" It was the kind of question weak
men have asked down through the ages.

"What did she want with them?"

Eddison shook his head. "I don't know."

"Whose files did she look at?"

"I'm sorry, but I can't help you. I showed her where they
were; then she told me to leave, so I did. When I came back
about three hours later she was gone." Eddison started rubbing his hands together. "What I did wasn't so bad, was it?"
A glint of hope blossomed on his face. I killed it with my next
words.

"As compared to what?"

Eddison pulled back as if I'd struck him. Then he word-
lessly turned and hurried into his house, closing the front
door behind him as though it could be trusted to keep the
world at bay. I knocked on it, proving him wrong.

"Go away," Eddison cried.

But I didn't. I asked for his client list instead.

"I can't do that," he replied.

"Oh, yes you can." After all, he'd done it once, he could
do it again. "I'll pick the list up tomorrow afternoon."

"And if I don't give it to you?"

"Does the phrase talking to Fast Eddie mean anything to you?"

"Oh, God." I heard a muffled sob coming from the other side of the door. Then I heard another voice and Eddison shushing it.

"Who else is in there?" I asked.

"No one," Eddison answered.

I didn't believe him, but I wasn't going to press the issue. There was no point in doing that when I could just repark the cab and wait and see who came out of his house, so I said good night and walked back toward my cab. My encounter with Eddison had left me with a bad taste in my mouth. I didn't like him, and more importantly I didn't like myself too much either—but I guessed that would pass. It usually did.

I hurried to the cab as much to get out of the rain as to get away from him. By now the fine mist had turned into thicker rain drops, and I watched them reflect under the streetlight while I dried my hair off with a paper towel that was lying on the passenger seat. Then I started the cab, drove around the block, parked out of eyeshot of Eddison's house, and settled down to wait.

It didn't take long.

Ray Diamond emerged thirty minutes later.

Like Ichabod Crane, Estrella's boyfriend seemed to belong to the night. When I'd seen him during the daytime he'd been a skinny, awkward-looking, twenty-five-year-old man with a bad case of acne, but now as he loped toward the car, his gracelessness was gone, discarded like the husk of an insect.

As he pulled out I wondered if he'd been talking to Eddison about Estrella and if so what he'd said. It was with an eye to answering that question that I decided to follow him. I was hoping to catch Diamond as he went in his house, but he didn't go home. Instead he took a right on Comstock and headed toward East Genesee Street. I followed him anyway because I was curious to see what he was up to.

Diamond drove like a man in a hurry. The speed limit on East Genesee in the city is thirty miles an hour, and he was exceeding it by a good twenty; but then so was everyone else on the road. The unmarked police car that patrolled this particular stretch was only there in the mornings. The rain was still falling, and it gave the shuttered buildings on either side a forlorn quality. As we passed by Wegman's Supermarket I noticed a shopping cart slowly drifting down the margin of the road on the other side of the street. Maybe it had just decided to see the world.

I almost lost Diamond when he turned at Fayetteville Mall. Because I assumed that he'd keep on going straight I wasn't paying strict attention, so it wasn't until the last minute that I realized he'd veered off to the left. A car honked at me as I switched lanes. A couple of miles later Diamond took a right onto a country road. I tried to stay far enough back so he wouldn't become suspicious and close enough so I wouldn't lose him; but it was difficult to do, and I found myself either riding the brake or pumping the gas.

Occasionally I'd spot another car in my rearview mirror, and for a few seconds I entertained the fantasy that he was doing to me what I was doing to Ray; but then I decided I was just being paranoid and forgot about it. Instead, as I sped along I thought about Marsha's request to Eddison. The five thousand I could understand, but the request for his client list was a little odder. Was she on a fishing expedition, looking for new information? Or was she looking to confirm something she already knew? Too bad I couldn't ask her.

A few minutes later the road broadened out and we hit a clutch of stores. Diamond slowed down and pulled into a gas station on the right side of the road. I didn't want to follow him in and call attention to myself, so I parked about one hundred feet down and checked out what Ray was doing from my rearview mirror. First he pumped some gas; then he went inside, paid, came out and made a phone call. Whoever he was speaking to must have angered him because when he got back in his car he roared out of the lot, missing an incoming car by a matter of inches. In another minute or so we were back on the open road.

I was wondering if Diamond was taking a back road to Cazenovia, one of those quaint towns where everyone has a fit if you plant the wrong color petunias, when he made another turn. It's a good thing I was paying attention because otherwise I never would have seen the turnoff. It was narrow and obscured with trees. In the daytime it would have been difficult to see, but on a moonless night such as this one it was impossible. I pulled in and killed the engine and the lights. There was no way I could drive in and not have Ray be aware that he was being followed. I could hear his car up ahead, and then I didn't hear anything at all.

I whispered for Zsa Zsa to stay in the car. Then I got out. I took care to close the door as quietly as possible, but the silence magnified the sound, making it louder than it would have otherwise been. The same was true of my footsteps. Every twig I stepped on crackled in the dark. To make matters worse, the path I was on was extremely rutted and I kept tripping over rocks and branches. Water from the trees dripped on my head and shoulders as I walked. I was cold and wet and uncomfortable. After about ten steps or so I decided it made more sense to come back in the daylight when I could see something.

And anyway I had something I wanted to do besides trip over rocks in the dark and fall and fracture my wrist. I wanted to break into Eddison's office.

Chapter
31

I'd been toying with the idea ever since I'd left Eddison's house. Even though I was pretty sure Eddison would give me the names of his clients, I'd decided as I'd been sitting in the car outside his house that I needed more than that. I needed to see what was in the files. Who knew? Maybe Marsha had found a juicy little tidbit and was blackmailing someone else besides Eddison. I knew I was playing a long shot, but I figured it wouldn't hurt to look. Of course, I could have just asked Eddison for them, but I didn't think he'd say yes. Or maybe I was hoping he wouldn't.

Besides, it wasn't as if the building his office was located in was going to be that hard to break into. It was set in an industrial park well off Erie Boulevard. The other buildings around it were also office buildings. Most of the people who worked in them had cleared out by six o'clock, eight at the latest. The only people who would be coming by would be the security patrol, and they probably did a round every one or two hours at the most. As I headed back toward Syracuse I decided to drop Zsa Zsa off at the house, then drive over and check out the situation. I didn't want to take the chance of having her bark at a patrol car.

Wide Waters Plaza was deserted. I could have killed ten people—slowly—and their screams wouldn't have brought anyone running. I didn't see another living soul as I drove through the industrial park. There were no cars in the lots or patrol cars on the road. I began to feel as if there had been a terrible disaster and I was the only person left alive in the world. Or at least in Syracuse. When I got to Eddison's building I stopped and did a pro forma inspection of the front doors. They were locked and alarmed as I'd expected they'd be. That didn't concern me. I wasn't planning to go in through the front anyway. I was banking on the fact that this type of building usually had a fire escape in the rear and that I could climb up it and get in through a window. Of course, the windows could be hooked up to the alarm system, too, but I was betting on the fact that the management hadn't wanted to spend the money.

I got back in the car and drove around to see if I'd been right. I was. The back did have a fire escape. Even better there was a Dumpster just underneath it. I wouldn't have any problem at all. I could just climb up on the Dumpster and go from there to the fire escape and from the fire escape to a window. My biggest problem was going to be where to leave the cab. I didn't want to attract any more attention to myself than necessary. Finally I decided to park it a couple of buildings down. That way if the cops found it, at least I'd have a little more time to get out. And if they turned up later at my door I could always claim the cab had been stolen.

I jogged back to the Dumpster, took hold of the chain around its lid and worked myself up. Now comes the hard part, I thought as I jumped up and grabbed on to the slats on the bottom of the fire escape. The metal cut my palms. For a moment I just dangled there. Then I pulled myself up. It took all my strength, and my shoulders ached liked crazy when I finally got there. I wondered if I'd pulled something as I climbed the ladder to the third floor and began trying windows. None of them budged. I was just starting to think I'd have to break a pane of glass when I found a window sash that moved. I pushed it all the way up and slipped inside. I was standing in a bathroom.

My heart was fluttering as I walked across the bathroom, opened the door and peeked outside. No one was in the hall. Of course. I was just suffering from a bad case of the heebie jeebies, I decided as I stepped out and scanned the numbers on the wall. Eddison's office was down the hall to the left. I made my way to it as quickly as I could. The lock on his door looked simple enough. I hoped it was because that was the only kind I could pick. I took my Swiss Army knife out of my pocket, pried out the nail file, and inserted it between the door frame and the lock. Then I pressed down. I heard a click and the lock gave.

As I entered I wondered why Eddison had bothered with the lock at all. It gave the illusion of safety and nothing more, but then that's all any of us ever have anyway, I decided as I made my way through his waiting room into his private office. It was furnished the same way his waiting room was— cheaply. I skirted his desk and headed straight for the cabinet on the far wall, figuring that's where he kept his patient files.

The top drawer was full of business-related items such as rent receipts, insurance forms, and telephone bills. Nothing of interest to me. I opened the second drawer. Except for a folder lying on the bottom it was empty. I took it out and looked at it.

A Mr. William Dean was afraid of flying. Recommendation: hypnosis to reduce anxiety. I threw the folder back in the drawer and slammed it shut. While I'd been following Ray, Eddison must have come up here and moved his files. He'd figured out what I was going to do and beat me to it. I was so mad I kicked his desk, but all I got for my troubles was a sore toe. Even though I knew it was useless, I checked the other room anyway. The files weren't there. As I closed the door to his office I decided that maybe Eddison had more scruples than I'd given him credit for, a fact which, given the situation, annoyed the hell out of me.

I climbed down the fire escape and walked to my car without encountering any difficulties. I roared out of the parking lot and sped down Erie Boulevard. I knew I should slow down, but I didn't want to. I was too pissed. Instead, I went faster. I was doing fifty in a thirty-mile zone when the cop pulled me over by Springfield Gardens. He gave me a ticket and a long lecture which put me in an even worse mood than I was already in. As far as I was concerned the whole evening had been a waste of time and I hate wasting time. Although truth be told, it was ridiculous for me to feel that way. If I hadn't been following Ray around and breaking into Eddison's office, I would have been sitting home watching TV. Oh, well, I decided as I turned onto Genese Street. Maybe next year I'd work on my social life.

When I got back to the house I took care of the animals and listened to the messages on my answering machine.

There were three. Two were hang ups and one was a call from George telling me to call him. I did, but the line was busy, and after a second try I gave up and went to bed. Somewhere along the ride home my anger had given way to fatigue. My legs were aching and my eyes felt as if pieces of grit were lodged under my lids. I had to sleep. As I was drifting off I realized that one of the reasons I was so exhausted was because I hadn't eaten anything since twelve o'clock in the afternoon.

Next morning when I woke I was ravenous. I ended up finishing the only thing I had in the house—a package of Oreos—before I got dressed and went to work. Once I opened up the shop and reconciled the drawer I made myself a pot of coffee and called George. The line was busy. I tried again at ten. This time there was no answer. It looked as if I'd missed him. I was just about to leave a message when Enid Garriques walked in.

"Do you think it would be possible to set up the aquarium today?" she asked when she reached the counter.

This was typical Enid, I thought as I hung up. Delay, delay, delay, and then, Bam. Do it now.

"I know it's short notice," she said as she shifted the clutch she was carrying from one hand to another.

"No problem," I replied, even though it was. Then I reminded her that we couldn't put the fish in today.

Enid nodded. "Yes, I remember." She opened her pocketbook, extracted a check from her wallet, and gave it to me along with her keys which she told me to leave in the mailbox when I was done.

"Where do you want me to put it?"

"In my husband's study over by the wall opposite the bookcase. I'm sorry I can't be there," she explained, "but I have a doctor's appointment. That's the problem with having diabetes. You have to spend all your time in doctors' offices. Or at least I do." She sighed. "Then I have to go over and have lunch with my mother and my aunt." She wrinkled her nose, indicating she wasn't going to enjoy that too much either. "I hope I don't get like them when I get older."

"It's scary, isn't it?"

She gave a genuine smile, the first I'd ever seen. "Yes. It sure is. Why do families want to hang on to you so tightly? Why don't they want to let go?"

"Sometimes the other way isn't so good either," I said, thinking of my experience.

"I guess you're right," Enid replied, but she didn't seem convinced.

We chatted for another couple of minutes about how to take care of a salt water tank and then she left.

"Who are you going to get to help carry the stuff in?" Tim said after she'd left.

"I don't know. Maybe Manuel."

Tim rolled his eyes.

"You have any better suggestions?"

"No," Tim admitted. "I don't."

It took seven phone calls and the promise of thirty bucks, but I finally got Manuel up and functioning. He was at the store three-quarters of an hour later, and we loaded up the cab and drove over to Garriques's house.

"Nice place," Manuel commented as we pulled into the driveway.

I nodded my head in agreement. The house was a large, well-kept Tudor. In a another community it might have cost two hundred and fifty thousand or more. Here it would go for one hundred and eighty. One of the advantages of living in Syracuse is the cheap price of housing.

"I wouldn't mind camping out here," Manuel told me as I unlocked the door.

"Me either." We stepped inside. The hall floor gleamed so brightly I almost felt guilty stepping on it.

The living room was furnished with good English antiques and Oriental rugs. Enid had told me that the study was across the hall. It proved to be equally tasteful. A large desk took place of pride in the center of the room. The walls were covered with Garriques's collection of antique maps while the mantel was lined with photographs. Most seemed to consist of two youngish women now sitting, now standing, in front of a house. Something about them and the house looked very familiar, but I couldn't think what it was. I was still trying to figure it out when Manuel tugged at my sleeve.

"Are we going to get going or not?" he said.

I turned away reluctantly and studied the site Enid had proposed for the aquarium. Everything seemed to be fine. There was no reason the fish tank couldn't go in there.

"All right," I told Manuel. "Let's do it."

By the time we were done we were both hot, sweaty, and irritable.

"God, I didn't think it would be this much work," Manuel said as we walked out the door. "I don't suppose you could add another ten to the thirty you're giving me."

"Not a chance." I put Enid's key in the mailbox. "As it is I'm already giving you too much."

Manuel shrugged. "Oh, well. It was worth trying."

I paid Manuel, dropped him off at his house, and went back to the store.

"I hope Garriques likes it," I told Tim as I bent down to pet Zsa Zsa. "I'd sure hate to have to take it back."

"He will once the fish are in," Tim promised. "How could he not? They're gorgeous."

"True." I looked through the day's mail. "Did George call?"

Tim shook his head. I tried George again. No one was home. I left a message telling him to call and hung up. It looked as if George and I were playing telephone tag.

Chapter
32

I'd planned on taking an hour and dashing back out to where I'd followed Ray and having a look around, but things didn't work out that way. First the store got busy, then Tim had a dentist appointment, and then when he got back I got a call from Hancock. A shipment of lizards I'd ordered three weeks ago had just come in. Somebody had to pick them up. That someone was me. By the time I got done with that and Tim and I housed the skinks, it was time to close up. My little trip would have to wait till tomorrow. It was too dark and I was too tired to go. Instead Zsa Zsa and I went home.

James was waiting for me. I let him in and opened a can of tuna for him. While he was eating I called George. Still no answer. I was now beginning to feel annoyed. The least he could do was call me back, I decided as I poured some Cocoa Krispies and milk into a bowl. I took it into the living room, turned on the TV, and sat down on the sofa. Zsa Zsa jumped up beside me. We sat there together as I ate my dinner and watched reruns of 1950s sitcoms. I have to get a life, I thought as I put the bowl down on the coffee table. A moment later I was sound asleep. I awoke at four with a stiff neck. I took a couple of Tylenol and stumbled upstairs and went to bed.

I must have been making up for all the sleep I'd been missing recently because I slept through my alarm. I awoke at eight-forty-five took one look at the time, pulled some clothes on, called to Zsa Zsa and ran out the door. The rest of the morning was equally annoying. One of the new lizards escaped and it took forever to find it. Then some guy I'd never seen walked in and wanted his money back for a sick fish he claimed he'd bought in the store. I knew he hadn't because we don't carry fancy goldfish, but when I explained he'd made a mistake he started yelling and screaming. I had to call the police and have him thrown out. And to top everything off Tim was late.

By the time two o'clock rolled around all I wanted to do was get the hell out of Noah's Ark. Finding out where Ray had gone seemed like the perfect excuse. I told Tim to mind the store and took off. The drive back out to where I'd followed Ray took longer the second time around, mostly because I had trouble finding the last turnoff. I drove up two dead ends before I located it. Or at least I thought I had. The road looked familiar, but it was hard to tell since everything always looks different at night. I kept going anyway. The worst that could happen was that I'd made a mistake and would have to turn around. After about fifteen feet the paving gave out and turned to gravel, and then a little later the gravel turned to dirt. As the cab jounced along I began wondering if this was such a good idea after all—my shocks were in bad enough shape as it was—but I managed to make it without a damaged spring or a flat tire.

Here and there I saw signs of civilization—a discarded

soda bottle, a white porcelain sink, a pair of torn under-pants—but mostly I saw sumac and honey locust. The after-noon sun slanting in through the trees gave the scene a nice bucolic quality. Normally I would have enjoyed it, but I was too keyed up about what I was going to find to pay much at-tention. After about seven minutes of driving the trees gave way to an open field. A house stood a little ways away. When I saw it I jammed on the brakes.

I couldn't believe it.

I was looking at the house Estrella's mother was supposed to have been living in.

I must have come up the back way.

What the hell had Ray been doing here?

This didn't make sense.

I drove up to the farmhouse and got out.

It was still deserted.

No one was here.

I knocked just in case. When there was no answer I tried the door. It was open. I went inside.

The place felt damp and chilly—as if the house didn't know that spring had come. Strips of wallpaper dangled from the hall walls. It looked as if someone had started stripping the walls and then gotten tired of the job and walked away. I went into the living room. A sagging sofa sat in the middle of the room. Some old newspapers were spread out on the floor along one wall. The wall itself had brown water stains on it. The plaster was beginning to buckle along the inter-section of the wall and the ceiling—the bathroom upstairs must have overflowed. I turned and walked into the kitchen. The counter was bare. I opened the cupboards. Except for a few boxes of Kraft's macaroni and cheese, they were empty. So was the inside of the refrigerator. I was turning to leave when I spied a bag of garbage over by the door that led to

the outside. I went over and sniffed. It didn't smell. Someone had bagged the trash fairly recently. I didn't know
whether that meant anything or not.

I climbed the stairs to the second floor, but didn't get any
more answers up there. There were four small bedrooms,
each of them filled with three or four sagging, dirty mat-
tresses. From the look of them whoever had slept on them
hadn't slept well. I opened each of the room's closets. Except
for a baseball hat hanging on a hook in one, they were all
empty. I turned and went down the stairs. Garriques had said
he thought that Estrella's mother was working as a migrant
laborer. Well, if she was and she'd been here, she'd moved
on. I closed the house door behind me and went to check
the barn. Even though I knew I wasn't going to find anything,
I wanted to be able to tell myself I'd done a thorough job.

As I walked along I was aware of the silence surrounding
me. The only noise I heard was the crunch of my footsteps
on the gravel path that led to the barn. When I got to the entrance I stopped and looked. My impression was one of desolation. I stepped inside. The place smelled of lost hopes.
Orb spinners' cobwebs decorated the walls. Bird droppings
lay splattered on the hay-strewn dusty floor, though when I
looked up I couldn't see any nests on the eaves overhead. I
went through the stalls. They were all empty except for the
last one. It contained several large yellow and blue metal
drums. They were the kind chemicals were stored in. Some
stood upright; others had fallen over on their sides. As I drew
closer I saw the caution signs scrawled along their tops. Something told me I didn't want to get too near to whatever was
inside them, and I backed away.

When I'd gone a little ways I stopped and stood there hoping that enlightenment would strike; but it didn't, and after
a few minutes I left. I was almost at the main door when a glint

of gold on the floor caught my eye. I stooped to get a better look. A pen lay half-hidden beneath a fallen metal rake. I picked it up. It was a Mark Cross, an expensive one from the look of it, the kind that belonged on Fifth Avenue, not in this kind of place. I turned it over in my hand and wondered who owned it and what its owner had been doing here. I'd ask Ray, I decided as I slipped it in my pocket. Dollars to doughnuts he'd know the answer.

I was still thinking about the pen as I got in my car and drove off the property. This time, though, I went out the front way. As I passed the gravestones standing on the slope of the hill I thought that soon, with no one to care for them, they'd be completely covered over with weeds. It seemed sad to be neglected like that, and then I reminded myself that I hadn't been back to Murphy's grave since he died. I lit a cigarette and looked at the flame on my lighter. Maybe cremation had a lot going for it after all. Especially if you had your ashes scattered to the winds. You couldn't be neglected if you weren't there.

"Tell me, how do you want to dispose of your body when you die?" I asked Tim when I stepped inside the door.

He looked up from the hamster food he was shelving. "It's not a question I've given a lot of thought to. Why? Are you planning on dying soon?"

Pickles rubbed herself around my ankles. "Not as far as I know," I replied.

"Good." Tim went back to rearranging the shelf.

I picked up the cat and rubbed under her chin. She began to purr. "Would you feel bad if you were dead and no one came to visit your grave?"

Tim snorted. "At that point I don't think I'm going to care.

If I were you, I'd be giving more thought to increasing the sales in here and less to this kind of stuff."

"Maybe you're right." I banished the gravestones from my mind, walked out back and poured myself a cup of coffee. Then I came back in and looked over the mail. It was all bills and circulars. The usual. I dropped the circulars in the garbage can.

"Where's Zsa Zsa?"

"She went for a walk with Lucy. She'll be back soon."

I grunted. Lucy was eight going on twenty-five. Once in a while when things got rough at home, which was usually once a week, she came over and took Zsa Zsa out.

"Anything else?"

"Yeah. A guy named Eddison phoned. He said he wanted to speak to you."

"Did he say about what?" As if I couldn't guess. I should have been more careful replacing things when I'd gone through his office. What had Grandma always said? Neatness counts.

"He didn't leave a message," Tim replied. "You want to do the rabbits or should I?"

"I will after I call this guy." I was curious to hear what Eddison had to say.

What he said was, "You were in my office, weren't you?"

"Are you accusing me of breaking and entering?" I countered. Over the years I've learned the best thing to do when you're challenged is to throw the challenge back.

"Yes, I am," Eddison replied.

Tim stopped dusting the shelf behind the counter and listened.

"Now, why would I want to do a thing like that?" I demanded, even though I knew what Eddison was going to say.

"To look at my files." He took a deep breath, then exhaled.

"I know what you're thinking, but Marsha wasn't using my files to blackmail anyone. I was the only person she was doing that to."

"So you say," I observed, even though I suspected he was telling the truth.

"You'll have to take my word."

"What if I don't want to?"

"I'm not giving you my files," Eddison reiterated.

I lit a scrap of paper and put it in the ashtray. As I watched the edges curling in on themselves I tried to decide how badly I wanted to see what was in them. I knew I could get Eddison's client list if I pushed a little, but I had a feeling getting the contents of their files might take more pushing than I was willing to do right now. It might make more sense to look at the list first and go from there.

Eddison coughed. "Don't you understand I can't betray people's confidences like that?" he cried.

"I think I'd be more sympathetic if you hadn't done it the first time around," I told him. Eddison didn't reply. I guess he couldn't think of anything to say. "Listen," I continued. "I want that list over at my store in half an hour. Otherwise I'm calling Fast Eddie." I hung up.

"Would you really do that?" Tim asked.

"I don't know," I replied.

Fortunately I didn't have to make the decision.

Eddison slunk in the store with five minutes to spare. I scanned the list as he was leaving.

I don't know what I'd been expecting, but none of the names leaped out at me.

I thought about them on and off during the day with a mounting sense of frustration.

But no matter how many times I looked at the list I didn't recognize any of the names. I finally decided that I'd check them out if nothing else panned out, but for the time being it made more sense to concentrate on Merlin and Shirley and Ray and Eddison. I lit a cigarette and spent the next couple of minutes watching the smoke rise toward the ceiling.

Around eight-thirty I called George. I wanted to fill him in on the latest.

I got his answering machine instead. Even though I didn't have any right to be, I was annoyed and I hung up without leaving a message.

I spent the next half hour mopping the floor. At nine I closed up the store and did some paperwork. When I was done Zsa Zsa and I had a couple of Big Macs and I dropped her off at my house. Then I headed over to Ray's. I had a few questions I wanted answered. A slight breeze was blowing and the air smelled as if spring was here and meant to stay. As I got near Ray's house I could see that he was home. His car was in the driveway and one of Merlin's vans was parked on the street. I pulled up behind it and got out. The van's back doors were open.

The interior light was on. It silhouetted Ray.

His back was to me. He was hunched over a low table.

Whatever he was occupied with must have involved him completely because he didn't turn when I stepped inside.

"Ray," I said, tapping him on the shoulder.

He whirled around.

I gasped when I saw what he was holding.

Chapter
33

A brown bat lay cupped in Ray's hand.

It looked exactly the same as the ones Tim and I had been taking out of people's houses for the past couple of weeks. Something told me I'd stumbled on their source.

"That's a rather odd pet," I said, aiming for wry.

Ray didn't answer. I guess he wasn't doing banter—not that he ever had.

As I walked over for a closer look I became aware of a cacophony of high-pitched squeakings coming from a cardboard box in the far corner of the van.

"I bet you didn't know that it's illegal to kill bats in England," I observed pleasantly. "If there's a colony in your attic, you have to apply to the council for permission to move them." I knew this because I'd researched an article several years ago on rental rights in the United States and England and the fact had stayed in my mind.

Ray glowered. "Who gives a fuck about England?"

"Obviously not you, but it's illegal to kill them in New York State, too." It wasn't true, but it seemed like a good thing to say.

"No, it's not."

"Yes, it is," I insisted.

Ray got a mulish expression on his face. "I ain't killing them."

"That's good." I pointed to the bat in his hand. Some people said they were cute, just small cuddly mice with wings, but I couldn't see it. It was probably their teeth that made me feel that way. They were little and jagged and reminded me of the kind of teeth gremlins would have—if gremlins existed. "Would you mind telling me exactly what you are doing with them?"

Ray took two steps back. I took two steps forward. The bat stayed still.

"This wasn't my idea," he whined.

"Let me guess, you were just following orders."

Ray touched his upper lip with the tip of his tongue. "I got bills to pay."

"Don't we all." I took out a cigarette and lit it. For some reason the smoke made the smell of chemicals coming from the canisters stored along either side of the van worse. I sighed and scotched the Camel on the floor with my heel. I guess I'd have to wait till later. "You know," I continued, "when I followed you . . ."

The corners of Ray's mouth quivered in suppressed alarm. "You followed me?" he cried.

"Last night." By now I was close enough to smell his breath. He'd eaten something with garlic and onions not too long ago. I glanced at the bat in Ray's hand again. It looked forlorn. Then suddenly something occurred to me; the droppings I'd seen in the barn earlier in the day were from bats not birds. That was the reason I hadn't spotted any nests in the rafters. "You got that in the barn, didn't you?"

Ray didn't answer. As if roused by my thoughts, the bat in his hands began to shiver.

"Let him go," I said.

"What if I don't want to?"

I shrugged. "Have it your own way, but it looks to me as if he's getting ready to bite."

Ray quickly uncupped his hands. The bat flittered around the van. I instinctively ducked. So did Ray. A few seconds later the bat found the opening and disappeared into the night. As I watched him go I wondered if he'd be able to find his way home. Then I turned to Ray.

"I think we have a lot to discuss," I told him.

Ray briefly touched the top of his hair with an unsteady hand, then brought it back down and brushed a nonexistent speck of dirt off his black T-shirt. "Look, all I know is I was supposed to pick up these bats at the barn, they was supposed to be outside the barn in this carton, but I didn't see no carton. No one was around."

"That must have been annoying."

Ray didn't respond to my sarcasm. His glance had turned inward as if he was communing with himself. "I don't like it out there," he said, more to himself than to me.

"Why not?"

"It's too quiet. It gives me the creeps, especially at night. Merlin thinks it's funny me feeling that way."

"Anything else?" I prompted.

Ray wiped his hands on his pants. "Well, I thought I heard someone . . ." he allowed. Then his voice trailed away.

"Someone where?"

"Inside the barn. But when I called out no one answered."

"And you didn't get out and investigate?"

"No. I left."

"In spite of the fact that you hadn't done what you'd come to do?"

"I got nervous." Ray glared at me, daring me to make a crack. I managed to resist the temptation. "Who the fuck knows what was in there?"

"Maybe it was a ghost."

"Maybe it was." Ray sounded defensive. "The place is supposed to be haunted."

"By who? Casper?"

"No. By this guy that got himself killed out there. They never found the body."

"Where'd you hear that from?"

"People."

"What people?"

Ray looked embarrassed. "I'd rather not say."

"Fine." I pointed to the bat-filled carton. "So how did those get into the van? Did they just materialize?"

Ray let out a short bark of a laugh. "Very funny. No. Merlin went and got them. He had to 'cause I told him I wasn't going out there no more."

I reached out my hands. "Give me the box."

Ray took a step back. "Merlin won't like that."

"You're right. He won't."

"What happens if I don't?"

"Then I'll call the police."

"Go ahead. They won't care about some bats in a box."

"That's true, but they will care when they find out you've been breaking into people's houses."

Ray turned even paler. "But I never took anything."

"It doesn't matter. It's still breaking and entering."

"But Merlin said it would be all right," Ray whined.

"You shouldn't believe everything Merlin says."

"But then he's in trouble, too."

I painted a half circle in the air with my hand. "I can see it all now. The DA asks Merlin, 'Did you tell your employee to do this?' 'No,' Merlin says looking outraged. 'I never would suggest anything like that.' What do you think? Does it play for you?"

In answer Ray turned around, walked over and picked up the carton. "Here," he said, handing it to me. "I guess I'd better start looking for another job now."

"Well, Merlin never exactly did strike me as the charitable type." I nodded toward the carton with my chin. "How many bats are in here?"

Ray shrugged. "I'm not sure. Maybe five or six."

"Whose houses were you supposed to be putting them in?"

"Merlin was going to call me up and tell me."

"Do you know how he gets the names?"

"I think out of the phone book." Ray scratched his cheek. "I got a sister out in Phoenix. Maybe I should go visit her."

"Maybe you should."

"I hear they got lots of bugs down there."

"Not to mention scorpions and snakes."

Ray chewed on his cheek. "I wonder how much I'd get paid for killing them?"

"You like killing things?"

"I like killing stuff like this. It's fun watching them scurrying around trying to get away."

"I prefer video games myself."

Ray paused to scratch his chin. "I wonder if that's the way God feels?"

"I sincerely hope not."

Ray grinned. "I bet he does."

Suddenly I thought of something else. "Did Estrella know

about the bats in the barn?" I asked, changing the subject to something a little less metaphysical.

The grin vanished from Ray's face. "Why?"

"I was just curious. You took her up to the house . . ."

"To visit her mother . . ."

"Exactly. And now her mother is gone and she's dead. It makes me wonder."

"What are you saying?" Ray demanded.

"I'm asking what the connection is."

"There isn't any."

"Are you so sure? Did Estrella know Merlin?"

"I think they met a few times," Ray stuttered.

I raised an eyebrow. "You think?"

Ray looked at the floor. "Sometimes she'd do stuff for him to earn a little extra cash."

"What kind of stuff?"

"Stuff. Like answering the phones."

"Did she know about the bats?" I repeated.

Ray shook his head. "I don't think so."

"Does the farm belong to Merlin?"

"Maybe. I don't know." Ray turned his back to me. He was finished talking.

"You want my advice," I told him as I left. "Get on that bus to Phoenix."

When I got into the cab Ray was still standing where I'd left him. I had the feeling he'd stay that way for a while.

The squeaking of the bats filled the cab as I drove over to Merlin's house. He wasn't home, so I continued on to Shirley's place. I cruised around the complex's parking lot till I spotted his car; then I drove over to Shirley's town house, parked the car out front and got out. I was humming as I rang the bell. Merlin answered the door. He didn't look pleased to see me. Shirley joined him a moment later. She looked even less happy than he did.

"You again," she snarled.

I allowed as to how it was.

"Go away."

"I'm afraid I can't do that."

Standing there together in the door they reminded me of a pair of trolls guarding the bridge to the castle.

"This time I'm calling the police," Shirley threatened. The house light was shining down, and I could see patches of scalp under her frizzy hair. "You can't come in here and bother us anytime you feel like it. That's harassment."

"Go ahead and call," I told her, "but I think your boyfriend here may be interested in what I have to say."

Merlin jabbed his finger in my direction. "Nothing you say could interest me."

"That's too bad, because I have something of yours."

"What's that?"

"I'll show you." I went back to the cab, got the box I'd taken from Ray, and held it out to him. "A carton full of bats."

Merlin's eyelids began twitching so fast they looked as if they were sending out semaphore signals. "I don't know what you're talking about."

"They were in the company van. I just got them from Ray Diamond."

"You can't hold me responsible for what that kid does," he told me. The tics had stopped. He'd gotten hold of himself again.

"He said he got them from you."

Merlin made a dismissive gesture with his hand. "The kid smokes too much dope. He's delusional."

"I wonder if the DA will think that."

"The DA won't believe anything that kid says. He's got a record. I was being a nice guy hiring him." Merlin's smile was smug. He did smug well.

"Tell me, do you own the farm or do you just trespass when you get the bats?"

"Screw you."

"I can find out easily enough," I told Merlin while I watched Shirley out of the corner of my eye to see what her reaction was.

She looked confused. "Sweetie," she asked him, "what's this all about?"

"Nothing. It's about nothing. She"—he pointed to me—"is making a big deal about nothing."

"Why don't you tell her what you're doing," I urged.

"Tell me what?" Shirley asked. Her eyes were bright with worry.

Merlin nodded toward me. "Don't pay any attention to her. She's crazy."

I turned to Shirley. "Your boyfriend has been having his help break into people's homes and put bats in them. Then he comes and charges them about a thousand dollars to bat proof their house."

Merlin shrugged. "You got a complaint, take it up with the Better Business Bureau. Don't bother me with it."

I leaned forward. "Tell me, did Marsha find out about what you were doing? Did she try and blackmail you?"

Merlin sniggered. "Blackmail me for something like this? Don't be stupid."

He was right. What he was engaged in was penny-ante stuff, really not worth anybody's while. But then I thought of the papers Marsha had found, the ones she'd wanted to show me. Those could be a different matter. "Actually I was thinking more of the second set of books you've been keeping," I said, playing a hunch.

Merlin's eyelids twitched again and I knew I'd hit home.

Shirley looked at him with consternation. "You haven't been doing anything like that, have you?" she asked anxiously. "You told me Marsha was—"

Merlin turned on her before she could say anything else. "Keep your yap shut," he snarled.

"You said she was lying," Shirley bleated.

"I told you to shut the fuck up." He raised his hand to hit her.

Shirley flinched in anticipation of the blow to come. Evidently the two of them had played this scene before. Why wasn't I surprised?

"Don't do it," I warned Merlin.

He whirled around and faced me. His lips were pulled back, showing his teeth. I was thinking he needed to see a good dentist when the blow came. I caught his wrist in midair.

"I'm just going to say this once," I told him. "I'm not Shirley and I'm not Marsha. Hit me and I'll hurt you."

We stood there locked together, each waiting for the other to make the first move. Out of the corner of my eye I watched Shirley tugging on Merlin's shirt.

"Please come inside," she begged. "Please. Remember the neighbors."

"Fuck the neighbors," Merlin hissed.

But even as he said it I could feel the tension going out of Merlin's arm. The crisis was over. I let go. Shirley put her arm around his shoulder and shepherded him into her town house and closed the door.

I stood there for a moment remembering the time Murphy and I had done this. Only our scene had been worse.

I couldn't even recall what we'd been fighting about. Just

that we'd had too much to drink and we were arguing. Then before I knew it Murphy had punched me in the stomach and the mouth. I was standing in front of the hall mirror looking at my split lip when the cops rang the bell. Our screaming had been loud enough to alarm the neighbors. I should have told the police what had happened, but I'd sent them away instead. I'd been too embarrassed.

I shook my head in amazement. God, how could I have been such a jerk?

It was a question that didn't have an answer, or at least one I wanted to pursue, so I lit a cigarette and thought about Merlin instead.

Marsha had tried to blackmail him. Of that I was sure.

Was that the last straw? The thing that drove him to commit murder?

Merlin had everything to gain and nothing to lose from Marsha's death.

Had he done it?

I thought it was a distinct possibility.

Chapter
34

Three men were sitting at the bar nursing their drinks when I walked into Pete's. I could feel their eyes on me as I sat down.

Connie nodded and came over. She lowered her voice and put her mouth next to my ear. "Did you ever see such losers?" she whispered, indicating the men with a roll of her eyes. She straightened up without waiting for my answer. "George ever get in touch with you?"

"No. We've been busy playing telephone tag. Did he say what he wanted?"

"Let me think." Connie clicked her tongue against the roof of her mouth while she tried to remember. "It was something about you being interested in what this girl had to say."

I lit a cigarette. "What girl? Does she have a name?"

"It was . . ." She put out her hand. "Hold it. It's coming. It was Pam. Pam something." She poured me a shot of Black Label.

"Pam Tower?"

She snapped her fingers. "That's it. Who is she?"

"A friend of Estrella Torres."

"The one that got killed?" Connie asked.

"That's right."

"I'm glad I'm not growing up now," Connie observed as she put my drink down in front of me.

"Me, too," I agreed. "Things were simpler then, well maybe not simpler, but they were safer."

"That's for sure." Connie paused to light a thin black cigar. It was her latest affectation. "I wouldn't want to be a cop these days."

"Me either." I took the conversation back to George. "When was he in here?"

"A couple of days ago. Why?"

"I can't get hold of him."

"So?"

"It's starting to make me nervous."

"Maybe he's busy."

"No. This thing with Pam is important. He would have called me back by now."

Connie leered. "Maybe he found something even more important."

"Jesus. Can't you think of anything else but sex?"

Connie batted her eyelashes. "You mean *there* is something else?"

"Gimme a break." I took a sip of Scotch.

"No. Think about it. There's sex and death."

"How about art, music, and literature?"

"Sublimated sex." Connie warmed to her topic.

I listened to her with half an ear. I was too busy thinking about George and wondering if something was wrong. The more I thought about it, the more I became convinced that something was. When Connie paused for a breath I asked her for the phone.

"I take it you're calling George," she said as she handed it to me.

"You take it correctly." I dialed his number. He didn't answer. As his answering machine clicked in, the sense of unease I'd been experiencing grew. I handed the phone back to Connie. "I think I'm going to go drive by his house and see what's up."

"Go ahead if that will make you happy, but if you're asking me, I think he just got tired of the school thing and is shacked up somewhere with one of his bimbos."

"In this case I hope you're right."

She sniggered. "Sure you do."

But I wasn't lying. Connie's scenario was preferable to some of the others I was conjuring up. I paid for the Scotch and left.

I could feel the wind gusting when I stepped outside. It had set the canvas awnings dancing and the trash can covers rolling. I could feel the temperature falling. Another storm was sweeping in. As I got in the cab I thought about what Connie had said back in the bar. Maybe she was right. Maybe I was making a big deal out of nothing. What if I got to his house and he opened the door? I'd feel like a total jerk. But then I decided, so be it, at least I'd stop worrying.

On the drive over I tried to think about where George could possibly be, but I didn't have much success. The truth was, even though I considered George my friend, when I thought about it I realized I didn't really know that much about him. I didn't know who his other friends were or how he spent his time. It was a sobering thought, one I didn't very much like, and I was still contemplating what that meant when I pulled up in front of his house.

I'd been hoping against hope that by some miracle George's car would be sitting in the driveway, but God must have been busy elsewhere because the Taurus wasn't there. As I walked from the curb to the house I noted that the lights in the living room were on, not that that meant much. I always left a light on when I wasn't home. As I went through the motions of ringing the bell I noticed the mail box was stuffed with letters and magazines. My sense of disquiet grew.

I lit a cigarette and thought about my options. I could go home and wait for a couple more days and see if George showed up, or I could go downtown and file a missing person's report. But I didn't see much point in that. Since there was no evidence of foul play the police wouldn't do much—at least not for a while. And I didn't want to wait. Which brought me to option number three. I took a look at the door and tried to remember whether George had ever said anything about his house having an alarm system. I didn't think he had. Usually there was a decal warning that the house was protected. I didn't see one here, but then it would be just like George not to put it on. I sighed. Oh, well. I'd find out soon enough. The worst that could happen was that I'd spend a night in the PSB before my lawyer bailed me out.

George's house proved to be easier to break into than I anticipated. For someone who was always after me to be more careful, he was amazingly lax about security when it came to himself. Keeping to the shadows thrown by the arborvitae, I walked around to the rear. First I tried the back door, which was locked; then I tried the kitchen window, which wasn't. It took a little effort, I had to slam the sash with the palm of my hand a couple of times to get it moving, but I managed to open it up. I held my breath waiting to see if an alarm went off. Nothing happened. I glanced around. No one seemed to be up. The houses on both sides of me were dark. Everyone was asleep for the night.

I said a silent prayer, raised the window, and pulled myself in. When my heartbeat slowed to normal I glanced around. Everything looked the way it should. The kitchen was neat. Nothing was spilled or broken. I went over and listened to the messages on the answering machine. Most of them were from me. It was odd listening to my voice rolling out into the silence. I glanced at the message pad next to the phone. "Call Robin" was underlined. I thumbed through the rest of the pages, but there was nothing else written on them. I picked up his engagement calendar. It was an expensive one. The leather was a dark, rich brown, the pages edged with gold. I usually use the giveaways you get in the gas station myself.

I sat down and went through the book. According to what George had written he should have met with his adviser yesterday afternoon and gone out with a guy named Ron last night. I looked up their numbers in George's phone book and called. George hadn't made either appointment and he hadn't called to cancel. The knot that had taken root in my stomach grew. I got up and went into the living room.

It was tastefully furnished in Mission Oak. The only jarring notes were the treadmill, the stationary bike, and the free weights sitting in front of the large screen television. I went over and glanced at the videos on the shelves that branched off from the fireplace. There must have been at least three hundred, maybe more, all carefully alphabetized and arranged by category. The titles ranged from science fiction to the old classics. I took out the *Caine Mutiny* and stared at the box. I hadn't even known George liked movies all that much. The thought depressed me and I reshelved the film and turned to the desk.

It was an old rolltop. The top was littered with note cards

and textbooks and papers filled with George's neat writing. I sat down and went through them. If there was anything here that would shed light on George's disappearance, I couldn't see it. I checked the cubbyholes next, but all I found were stamps and rubber bands and paper clips and White-out. Fighting a growing sense of disappointment I opened the top drawer. Two black pen cases lay nestled next to a bottle of black ink and a blotter. I took the cases out and opened them up. Both of the pens were black. Both of them had gold tips. I stared at them for a minute, not daring to believe what I was seeing.

I got up, retrieved my backpack from the kitchen and pulled out the pen I'd found in the barn. It could have been the brother of the two I'd found in the desk. I twisted a lock of hair around my finger. Of course, the pen could have been somebody else's. It could have been, but it probably wasn't. What the hell had George been doing in the barn? What had he been looking for?

I'd bet anything it had something to do with Estrella.

But what?

I leaned back in George's chair and stared at a blank spot on the wall. Somehow it reminded me of my mind at the present moment. I shook my head to clear it.

Maybe Pam Tower would know.

She'd been the last person George had spoken to, at least the last person I knew of.

It was time she and I had a little chat.

There was only one problem.

I had to find her.

I stood up and took one last look around George's house. Then I opened the front door and left. It was easier and a good deal less conspicuous than climbing back out through the window. It had started to drizzle. I turned on the wipers and headed over to the house on Deal. When I got there I rang the bell and waited. I heard footsteps. A moment later the door opened. A girl I hadn't seen before was standing there stifling a yawn. I must have woken her up.

"I'm looking for Pam Tower."

"Sorry. You're too late. She's gone."

"Can you tell me where?"

The girl shrugged. "She didn't say."

"When did she leave?"

The girl scratched her neck while she thought. "A couple of days ago. Right after this big black guy talked to her."

"What did he look like?" I asked, wondering if she was describing George.

"He was wearing a pink button-down shirt. Actually he was kind of scary-looking."

It was George all right. "Did Pam say anything at all before she left?"

The girl rubbed the sleep out of her eyes. "Just that she was going to say goodbye to her parents, and then she was catching a bus out of town."

"I don't suppose you have their number?"

"Her parents?"

I nodded.

"Maybe." The girl turned and I followed her into the kitchen. She rifled through an old stack of newspapers sitting on the kitchen table while I watched impatiently. Finally she tore off an edge from the sports section. "I knew it was here somewhere," she said as she handed it to me.

I could barely read the scrawled numbers. As it turned out, I could have saved myself the trouble of deciphering them because Pam's mother didn't know anything either. When I got her on the phone she told me her daughter hadn't told her where she was going or when she'd be back.

As I listened to the pain in her voice I began to think that maybe I was lucky not to have children after all.

I let myself out. Two men looked up at me as I stepped out the door and onto the street. They were standing huddled together a little ways away from the cab. I skirted them and kept my gaze averted so they'd know I had no interest in the business they were in the middle of transacting.

"Want something?" one of them asked as I passed by.

Nothing you can help me with, I thought as I shook my head and got in the cab. As I drove away I decided I had two choices: I could either go home and do nothing or I could go back to the farm and take another look around. There was no contest. I opted for the farm. Before I left, though, I swung by the store and picked up Marsha's twenty-two. I didn't know what I was going to find, and I didn't want to take any chances.

As I looked at its ridiculous pink mother-of-pearl handle, I decided that Tim was right. It wasn't much of a gun. On the other hand it was better than nothing at all. I said goodbye to Pickles, told the cat to wish me luck, then got back in the cab and took off.

The road out to the farm was almost empty and I drove it fast. My heartbeat seemed to be keeping pace with the swish swish of the windshield wipers. I tried to use the time to think. Something was at the farm. Something important. Something relating to Estrella. Otherwise George wouldn't have gone out there. But what? I had a feeling I already knew. All the pieces of the puzzle were spread out on the table. All I had to do was put them together.

I lit a cigarette and reviewed my conversations with Brandon Funk, Merlin, and Shirley. I thought about what Eddison and Ray had said. By the time I got to the farm I almost had the answer, but it kept slipping away, dissolving back into the recesses of my mind whenever I tried to put it in words.

I was so frustrated I wanted to spit. Instead I put out my cigarette and made myself think of other things. The answer I was looking for would come once I stopped searching for it. At least that's what I told myself.

By the time I reached the turnoff the drizzle had changed into a downpour and I had to slow down because of poor visibility. As I drew closer I began to make out the farmhouse. It was dark. No lights were on. No cars were parked in the farmhouse's driveway. I didn't know if that was good or bad.

I slowed down as I passed, but then I changed my mind and sped back up. I'd start my search in the barn. After all, that's where I'd found George's pen. Then after I was done I'd go through the house.

I parked close by the barn, turned off the engine, smoked a cigarette and watched the rain streaking down the windshield. When it was done I stubbed it out and took Marsha's gun out of my backpack. As I studied it Ray's comment about the place being haunted popped into my mind. I shook my head to clear it and told myself that whatever had happened here hadn't been caused by ghosts. I slipped the twenty-two into the band of my jeans, grabbed a flashlight from under the front seat, got out, and ran to the barn.

I was soaked by the time I stepped inside. The air smelled of damp hay and mildew. I wiped the water off my face with my sleeve. Then I turned on my flashlight and called to George as I played my light over the walls and the floors. A cat, caught in the beam, meowed and ran out the door. Other than that, the creaking boards and the sound of the rain, the place was silent. I walked around the bales of rotting hay and looked behind the pieces of sheet rock lying against the walls. Then I climbed up on the first rung of the ladder and shone my light around the hayloft. The only thing I saw were cobwebs. I sighed as I stepped back down. George wasn't here, but then again I hadn't actually expected he would be. The truth was I was doing this because I didn't know what else to do. I turned and left.

The wind had picked up and the For Sale swung back and forth while the branches of the oak tree tossed and turned, weaving themselves into a canopy of leering faces. Raindrops stung my face and dripped down the back of my neck onto my T-shirt as I went up the path. I had to blink my eyes to keep the water out as I climbed the three steps to the porch. I didn't bother to knock. Instead I turned the handle. The door swung open. I took out my gun and went inside.

I felt for the light switch and clicked it on. Nothing happened. The power must be shut off. It had probably been off the first time I'd been here. I just hadn't realized it because I had been here during the day. As I took a couple of steps in, I heard scratching and scurrying. The noise seemed to come from the walls. Probably just a few squirrels living between the support beams, I told myself as I played the light inside the entrance hall. The strips of hanging wallpaper seemed to beckon me forward. I shuddered as I got too close and one of them brushed against my face. It felt as dry and powdery as the hand of death. I walked quickly through the living room and the kitchen. They looked the same as the last time I was here. I went up the stairs. They groaned under my weight, and I had to fight the irrational sensation that they were going to give way under me and pitch me to the ground.

George wasn't in the first bedroom. He wasn't in the second, third, or fourth ones either. Nor was there any sign that he ever had been.

I went back out into the hall.

"Where are you?" I screamed.

The rooms mocked me with their silence.

The house smiled when I left.

I slammed the door on the way out.

I'd done the best I could and it wasn't good enough.

I dropped to my knees and began to sob.

When I was finally done I got back in the cab, rested my head on the seat, and closed my eyes. I was too tired to drive home. I was too tired to do anything. I just sat there listening to myself breathing and feeling the water dripping off my hair and onto my shoulder and looking at the For Sale sign swinging back and forth in the wind.

And that's when the revelation I'd been waiting for hit.

My God. I sat up and put my hand over my mouth.

I couldn't believe I hadn't seen it before.

Suddenly everything began to come together.

I started up the car.

There was something I had to check out.

Chapter
35

I knelt down and traced the outline of the letters on the tombstone with the tip of my finger. M A R I N O. Marino. Now that I knew what I was looking at, the letters were easy to read. I rocked back on my heels and considered the implications of what I'd just found. This place was the Marino homestead. This was the place Garriques was trying to sell. I shut my eyes and thought about the photograph I'd seen in Garriques's study of the two girls standing together in front of a house. The house had been the farmhouse, but then it had been a bright, cheery place, not the rundown ruin of today. No wonder I hadn't recognized it. You would have had to have looked very carefully to see the similarities.

Then I thought of the two girls. They'd both looked lively and bright in the picture. Like the house, they gave no hint of what they would become. I shook my head as I thought about Enid's and Fast Eddie's mothers and the unhappy women they'd changed into. Over time deep lines of discontent had etched themselves into their foreheads and mouths. The only things that had remained from their youth were the deep-set eyes and the slightly receding chins. No wonder Enid hadn't wanted to meet her mother and aunt for lunch that day. Who would?

As I wiped the rain out of my eyes my thoughts went back to Garriques and the real estate agent he was always meeting with. I bet it was Fast Eddie's brother-in-law. What had Fast Eddie said when he'd given me his card? Something like, "You want to buy a VCR or sell a house come to me." That must have been why Garriques was always so concerned with being prompt. I wondered what it must be like to marry into a family like that. Maybe that's why he was always so nice to Enid. Maybe he was afraid not to be. My legs were starting to ache and I got up. As I did I caught a glimpse of the barn out of the corner of my eye and I remembered the picture on Funk's mantel of Funk and his friend Porter in front of the barn.

Of course. This was the barn where he and his friend Porter had caught the bats he'd preserved and hung on his walls. What had Funk said? I tried to remember the conversation. It had been something like, "Porter came and he went and then one day he just went." And I'd said, "Where'd he go?" And Funk had replied, "I don't want to talk about it."

At the time I'd thought he didn't want to talk about it because the memory was too painful. Now I wondered. I chewed on my fingernail. Ray had said this place was haunted. Usually people say that because something violent has happened there. Had Porter been murdered and buried here? It was unlikely, but as I turned my gaze back to the four tombstones I wasn't so sure. Then I noticed the tangle of sawed-off tree limbs a couple of feet away. Had they been there the first time

I was here? I didn't think so. I put my flashlight down and dragged the branches away. The earth underneath was freshly dug. I kicked a clod of dirt with my sneaker. Well, there went that thought. If Porter was buried here, he'd been buried a long time ago. Unless of course someone was digging him up. And then I had another thought. George.

"Dear God," I whispered as I got down on my knees and began frantically scooping the dirt out with my hands. The pebbles in the earth scratched at my fingers. In a matter of minutes they were numb with cold. I kept going. The pile of dirt in front of me was growing, but it wasn't growing fast enough. I remember thinking I was going to have to go faster when I heard a noise.

I stopped digging and listened.

I heard it again. It sounded like a moan. I jumped up and headed toward the sound. It seemed to be coming from behind the harvester. I raced around to the back of the machine.

"George?" I yelled.

My yell was answered with a thump. It was George. I knew it. He was alive. But where was he? My heart was racing as I glanced around, but I couldn't see anything in the dark. I took a deep breath and concentrated. After what seemed like minutes but was probably just seconds I spotted a rectangular shape over to the left. As I moved nearer I realized the reason the shape I was seeing lacked definition was because it was covered up with a tarp. In no time at all I was standing in front of it. I said a silent prayer and jerked the canvas back. George's Taurus was underneath.

By now the thumpings had increased. The sounds were coming from the car's trunk. I remembered what I'd felt like when I'd been locked in Teresa's car.

"Hold on," I yelled as I ran over and tried to lift the trunk lid. "I'll have you out in a second."

It was locked.

I picked up a rock and smashed it down as hard as I could on the lock. Nothing happened. I tried again. This time the lock gave and the lid popped up.

George was lying in a fetal position. His knees were almost up to his chin. "You certainly took your time," he whispered. "I was afraid you weren't coming."

"Don't be silly. You know what they always say?"

"No. What?"

"Bet on red."

He started to laugh and ended up coughing.

I felt his cheek. His skin was cold and clammy. "Where are you hurt?"

"My shoulder. The bastard shot me in the shoulder." He closed his eyes and groaned.

I thought about what to do as I stroked his hair. I had to get George to a hospital, but the nearest phone was a ten-minute drive. Ten minutes there and ten minutes back. Twenty minutes in all. I didn't want to leave him alone for that length of time. It was too dangerous. Who knew what could happen?

"Listen," I said. "If I help you, do you think you can climb out of here?"

"I'm not sure. My legs have gone numb."

"Well, let's see what happens." I was reaching in to straighten out one of his legs when I heard the sound of a car approaching. Somehow I didn't think it was the real estate agent.

George bit his lip. "You'd better get out of here," he told me.

"It'll be all right," I reassured him. "I'll just close the trunk and duck down in back. Maybe whoever's coming won't see us." Then I remembered that my car was parked out on the side of the road and realized that was an unlikely possibility.

"Hang on," I told George as I brought the lid down. I squeezed his hand. "Don't worry. I won't close it all the way." Then I took out my twenty-two, crouched behind the Taurus, and waited.

"Robin." George's voice was a ghost in the darkness.

"What?"

"I'm sorry."

"Don't be a jerk," I told him, trying to keep the tremor out of my voice.

The car was very close now. I could hear the gravel crunching under its tires. Its headlights illuminated the slanting lines of rain. Then the car stopped and the lights went off.

"Who is it?" George whispered.

"I don't know. I can't see." I leaned over and peeked. For a moment everything was dark; then the interior of the car lit up as the driver opened the door.

"It's Brandon Funk," I hissed as he stepped out.

But George didn't answer. I put my hand through the space I'd left open and gently shook him. There was no response. He must have passed out. I had to get him to a hospital soon. While I was wondering how I was going to do that Brandon Funk cupped his hands over his mouth and yelled my name. When I didn't answer he came around the car and walked onto the grass. He'd taken another couple of steps when I heard gravel crunching again. Another set of lights broke the darkness. Funk turned to look. I could see his body growing rigid. He reminded me of a deer caught in the glare of the headlights. A moment later the new car pulled up behind Funk's. As the driver killed the engine Funk spun around and started running toward the farmhouse. I heard a pop and saw a pinpoint of light. A moment later Garriques got out of his car. He was still holding in his right hand the gun he'd used to shoot Funk.

"Robin," he cried, looking into the dark for me. "Are you all right?"

My throat felt dry. The word "yes" came out in a croak. I should have been relieved. But I wasn't. I was confused. What I'd just seen didn't make any sense. Something told me it would be better not to mention George.

"Funk was going to kill you," Garriques explained, even though I hadn't asked. I suppressed a shudder.

At first I'd thought so to. But now I wasn't so sure. I hadn't seen a gun. Funk hadn't drawn one. But if he hadn't come to kill me, why else was he here?

"Come on," Garriques said. His voice had taken on a cajoling quality. "Let's get out of the rain. I'll explain everything in the car."

I took another look at Funk. There was no gun in his hand and none lying on the muddy ground nearby. Then I heard him moaning. He was still alive, but I had a feeling that like George, he wouldn't be unless he got to a hospital pretty soon. He moaned again. Garriques didn't seem to notice. Maybe he hadn't heard.

I swallowed before I spoke. "We'd better call an ambulance," I said.

"Of course," Garriques replied, hesitating a second too long before speaking. This did not give me confidence. I wanted desperately to believe he was telling the truth, but I didn't think he was.

The bad feeling I was getting grew. Things weren't fitting together. The way Garriques had acted didn't make sense. Unless . . . unless he'd shot Funk to keep him from talking.

"I'm waiting," Garriques said. He sounded impatient. I realized he hadn't lowered his gun.

I could hear my heart pounding. It was keeping time with the falling rain. "You make the call," I suggested. "I'll stay here and take care of Funk till you get back." I was surprised at how confident I sounded.

"I don't think so." I watched Garriques take a step in my direction. He had an ugly expression on his face. The more I thought about the way things were going, the less I liked them.

I raised the twenty-two and considered firing. There were only three problems: I was a lousy shot, I had three bullets left, and unless I hit Garriques in exactly the right spot the odds were the wound wouldn't stop him.

"Robin, you're being ridiculous," Garriques said. The rain had plastered his shirt to his chest.

"Am I?" I crept away from the Taurus to the harvester. I wanted to put as much distance between George and myself as possible.

"Yes, you are." Garriques's voice had turned querulous. "Now stop this nonsense and get in the car."

"Go call for an ambulance," I repeated. "I'm going to stay here." I moved my hands and feet to try and restore circulation. The rain had numbed them. I realized I was shivering from the cold.

This time Garriques didn't reply. Instead he raised his gun slightly and took another step onto the grass. I moved around the harvester. Maybe if I could get him to come close enough I could get a good shot.

"You know Enid's not going to like what you did to her brother," I told him in the ensuing silence.

Garriques didn't say anything.

And then my stomach clenched as the knowledge I'd been trying to deny rose up and hit me. "She's not going to know, is she?"

"No, she's not," Garriques agreed.

"Because I'm going to be dead, too, aren't I?" I said, hoping against hope that Garriques would say no. But he didn't. I guess the time for charades was over. "You've got a lot of bodies you're going to have to get rid of."

"Oh, I'll figure something out." Garriques's voice was flat. "I was kind of thinking that maybe I'll work it out so it looks like you killed Funk. Then I killed you when you tried to get away."

"Very inventive."

"I think so. And then, of course, I've got the woods to bury Samson in."

I looked at the twenty-two I was holding and wished I had something like a .357 Magnum. The only thing I had going for me was the fact that Garriques didn't know I had the twenty-two. That should balance the equation a little.

"My dear brother-in-law always did have a talent for being in the wrong place at the wrong time," Garriques mused as he took another step toward me. "He's been a thorn in my side ever since Enid and I married. I told Enid he'd be better off in the army, but she wouldn't hear of it. She even made me get him a job at Wellington. I had to see the moron every day."

I crept to the other side of the harvester. I'd be less visible there. "There never were any jewels, were there?"

"None at all." Garriques had stopped moving. He was trying to pinpoint my voice. I decided to oblige him.

"You just wanted me to find Estrella so you could kill her," I told him.

Garriques smiled. I could tell he thought he had me. "She'd seen me kill Marsha at the reservoir. There was nothing else I could do."

"I guess you're just a victim of circumstances."

"You can put it that way if you want." He took another step This time he ended up behind a tree. The man wasn't taking any chances.

"How did Marsha find out?" I asked to keep Garriques talking. I wanted to distract him because I'd have just one opportunity to shoot him. If I missed, George and I would both be dead.

"About Porter? Simple. Funk told her. The moron. I guess she saw it as her chance out." Garriques's voice rose. "Pennington was a gambler, no matter what she said, she wasn't going to reform. Sooner or later the itch would return and she'd come back and see me. She'd bleed me dry. I couldn't have that."

"You could have turned yourself in."

"For killing Porter?" The distain in Garriques's voice was palpable. "He was an animal. Sleeping in the barn. Never changing his clothes. He stole things, you know. I told him to stay away from my stuff, but he wouldn't listen."

"Is that why you killed him? Because he stole from you?"

"I found him in my room going through my drawers looking for money. The week before he'd taken eighty bucks. This time it was my camera. I'd told him then he'd better keep away, but he thought he was entitled. He thought I should work my ass off and he could just come in and take whatever he wanted."

"Did he offer to put it back?"

"No. He started to run, but I caught him. 'This time,' I told him, 'I'm going to teach you a lesson. This time I'm going to teach you to stay out of my stuff.' "

"So what did you do? Shoot him?"

"I punched him in the face—hard. The funny thing is I always had trouble with my right hook in the ring." Garriques paused for a minute. "I guess I must have rammed his cartilage up into his brain. He just dropped dead."

I thought about his wife. "What did Enid think?"

"She didn't think anything because she didn't know. She wasn't here."

"If it was an accident, why didn't you call the police—your friends on the force would have hushed it up."

"I didn't have that many friends." Garriques paused for a few seconds. "I thought about it, though. But it seemed simpler to just bury the body. I figured everyone would think Porter had just wandered off like he usually did. And that way I wouldn't get Enid's family involved. I wasn't exactly on their good side right then."

"How come?" I asked as I crouched down.

Garriques shrugged. "I'd roughed up one of Fast Eddie's boys. I mean, I didn't know who the asshole was. I told him to move and he gave me some lip. What was I supposed to do? You don't know what it's like out there. You ain't got respect, you ain't got nothing. Fast Eddie should have understood that."

"It's a good thing you were family," I observed.

Garriques gave a dry little laugh. "Yeah, wasn't it, though?"

"So what about Brandon? How did he find out about Porter?"

"He saw me bury him."

"Why didn't he go to the police? Porter was his best friend."

"The same reasons I didn't. The family. He didn't want any problems either. And anyway, I told him I'd make sure that everyone thought he'd done it."

"And he believed you?"

"I guess you've noticed that intelligence isn't his greatest asset."

"Why did he tell Marsha?"

Garriques shrugged again. "He said it just slipped out one night. Who was it that said, 'Love makes idiots of us all'?"

"Does that apply to you, too?"

"No. I knew who Enid's family was. I knew what I was getting into," Garriques replied as he stepped out from behind the tree trunk.

"Tell me, were you going to add George to the other grave-yard inhabitants?"

But Garriques didn't answer. He was trotting toward me, using my voice as a guide. Evidently he'd decided the time for conversation was over. I flattened myself against the muddy ground and waited. For some reason I kept thinking about the time my grandmother had spanked me for playing in the mud. I wonder what she'd say if she could see me now. Finally when Garriques was about fifteen feet away I raised the twenty-two and fired.

Garriques shrieked and clutched his right shoulder. I waited for him to fall, but he didn't. He stayed on his feet. I fired again. Nothing happened. I'd missed. Garriques kept coming.

"You and your friend are dead," Garriques said. He tried to raise his gun and groaned. "Fuck," he cursed as he switched hands.

I figured it was now or never and started running.

I headed for the barn. As I ran I could hear the crack of Garriques's bullets whenever one of them hit something. By the time I reached the barn my breath was coming out in short, hoarse bursts and I had a stitch in my side. I'd gone a couple of feet when I tripped over a bale of hay and went sprawling on the floor. I'd just crawled around to its far side when Garriques sidled through the doorway. He wasn't going to make himself an easy target.

"If you come out, I promise I'll make it quick for you and Sampson," he said.

What a guy. I didn't say anything. Instead I waited for him

to come closer. I had one bullet left and I wanted to make it count. Garriques took another step and another. When he took his third one I fired my last shot. Garriques let out a shriek and went down on the floor face first. His body twitched for a few seconds and he lay still. I waited for a minute, and then I waited for another minute before I went over. I felt as if I was moving in slow motion. I could hear the rain rattling on the roof and each one of my footsteps as it hit the floorboard. Garriques wasn't moving at all. He wasn't making any sounds. I'd just about convinced myself that I'd killed him when he rolled over and lifted up his gun. I kicked at his hand. The gun wavered. I kicked again and the gun went flying and disappeared in the dark. Now we were both out of weapons.

"I guess I'll have to do this the hard way," Garriques said and grabbed for me again.

As I twisted away it occurred to me I'd fallen for an old trick: I hadn't hit him. He'd been faking.

I ran for the ladder. I could hear Garriques behind me. I had my foot on the second rung when he pulled me down.

"Oh, no you don't," he said.

I turned and jabbed my fingers into where I thought his eyes would be. I hit something soft, and he groaned and his grip loosened. I started back up. Then I heard a loud crack. I could feel my footing go. The rung under me was giving way. I managed to hang on and pull myself to the next one. Then I heard another sound. Garriques was climbing again.

I climbed faster.

I was almost at the top when I heard a series of high, shrill squeaks. The shrieks got louder and louder till the sounds seemed to fill the space around me.

Something brushed against my cheek.

Something else brushed against the other one.

Suddenly the air was swirling with small, frantic shapes.

I closed my eyes and kept climbing through the bats.

"They won't hurt you," I repeated to myself as I kept going. "They're more scared of you than you are of them."

Bat wings touched against my forehead as I reached the loft. The books were wrong, I thought. They do collide into you after all. Then I felt a pull on my leg. Garriques. I grabbed hold of the ladder railing and stomped on his head. I heard a grunt, felt a slight loosening. I stomped harder. Garriques groaned and let go. I pulled myself up onto the loft. The air was thick with bats. Their noise filled my ears. Their smell filled my nostrils. I wanted to curl up in a ball and cover my head with my hands. But I couldn't, not with Garriques right behind me. Instead I reached out and grabbed a bat. Its body felt soft and lumpy under my fingers. I shivered and suppressing the urge to drop it turned toward the ladder. Garriques's forehead appeared. In another minute he'd be in the loft with me, and I couldn't have that. Even wounded he was stronger than I was. I waited till I could see his mouth. Then I shoved the bat in his face.

He screamed and clawed at it with both his hands.

I reached over and pushed.

Garriques tottered and fell.

I heard a thud as he hit the floor.

I looked down and caught a glimpse of him through the swirling bats.

This time he wasn't moving.

Chapter
36

George grinned when I walked into his hospital room. "Did you bring the beer?" he asked.

I patted my backpack. "In here."

George's "roommate" made a disapproving noise as I went by. Harold Root had been brought in half an hour after George had come up from the ICU, and all I'd seen him do the past couple of days was watch TV and complain to the nurses about having to share a room. I didn't know what he'd been admitted for and frankly I wasn't interested enough to ask.

"Maybe this isn't such a good idea," I said when I reached George's bedside.

"Trust me," George replied. "It is."

"I hope so." I brought out the first bottle of Sam Adams, uncapped it, and handed it to him.

George took a long swallow. He groaned with pleasure. "Ah. There is a God after all."

"Then I'd say you owe him some prayers. You should be dead."

"Listen," George told me, "why do you think my last name is Sampson? It'll take more than being shot in the shoulder and stuffed in a trunk to kill me."

Root coughed. George and I turned toward him. "Do you mind?" he snapped. "I'm trying to watch TV."

"Sorry," I murmured. I pointed to the beer. "You want some?"

Root sniffed. "Alcohol's not allowed in here. This is a hospital **not** a bar." He had a long, pinched face and looked as if he hadn't enjoyed his life and wanted to make sure no one else enjoyed theirs either. "I shouldn't have to deal with the likes of you in the state I'm in."

"You're right, you shouldn't." I got up and drew the curtain around George's bed. Suddenly we were cocooned in white.

"Do you think it's a race thing?" George whispered.

"No. I think it's an idiot thing," I whispered back.

Root raised his voice. "I'm calling the nurse and demanding my own room right now."

"You do that," I told him. Then George and I looked at each other and burst out laughing.

"Sssh." George put his finger to his lips.

"I'm trying." And I went off into another fit of giggling. When I'd gotten myself back under control I moved the IV pole and perched on the edge of George's bed.

"Did you bring any more of this stuff?" George asked hopefully, indicating the beer with a tilt of his head.

"Three. Wait until you see what else I brought you." I dove into my backpack and came out with a joint.

"You're going to get us arrested," he hissed.

"Then you don't want me to light it?" I didn't think that George was as straight as he pretended to be, but maybe I was wrong.

He hesitated.

I offered to put it away.

"No, don't," he said after another couple seconds of hesitation. "What the hell." He moved over and patted the space he'd just vacated. "Come on. There's room."

I lay down next to him and lit up.

"I haven't done this since Murphy died," George said as we passed the joint back and forth.

"Me either. He was definitely a bad influence."

"That's for sure," George agreed.

"How come you're so much more uptight with me than you were with him?"

"I don't know." George was about to say something else when Root started talking.

"What's that I smell?" he demanded. His voice seemed to be coming from a long way off. "Are you smoking in there?"

"Don't be ridiculous," I told him. "There are rules against that kind of thing."

"We'd better put it out," George whispered.

"It would probably be a good idea," I agreed.

"I guess I really was lucky," George reflected as he snuffed the joint out with his fingers and handed it to me.

"I'd say so." I put the joint back in my pocket and took a sip of beer. "I still don't understand how you knew it was Garriques. What put you on to him?"

"Mostly luck. You know when you started talking to the waitresses at The Pancake Palace?"

"Yes."

"Well, that got me thinking about the fact that everything

in the case—Marsha, the reservoir, Estrella—had one thing in common. Wellington. Everywhere I turned the school popped up."

"Which was when you went to see Garriques."

"Actually what I did was walk in and ask if I could see the principal. I just wanted to get some general background information on Marsha and Estrella, and I thought that talking to the headman would be a good place to start; but the longer we talked, the more I got the feeling that this guy was hiding something, and I wanted to know what it was."

"I wished I'd gotten that feeling."

George grinned. "People see what they're accustomed to seeing. He'd always been a good guy to you, so that's what you saw him as. I was just more open to impressions." George took another sip of beer. "I think one of the things that flagged him for me was he got into this buddy-buddy mode."

"Buddy-buddy?"

"You know. Us ex-cops got to stick together. Something about it felt phony. Which was why I went downtown and got one of my friends to pull his record."

"I'm impressed. They still had it after all this time?"

"Oh, yeah. You'd be amazed at what they've got."

"I'm sure I would be. So what was on Garriques's file?"

"A fair number of excessive violence complaints."

"He was a boxer," I said, thinking about how Garriques had killed Porter. "Maybe he just liked hitting people."

"He was the subject of two internal inquiries," George continued, ignoring my interruption. "Garriques was cleared, but reading between the lines, I'd say the department was looking to get rid of him. He'd grown into a liability."

"I wonder if they knew about his family connections?" I mused.

"It wouldn't surprise me at all," George said. "This place really is a small town. It's hard to hide things."

"I don't know. Garriques did pretty well in that department," I observed.

"Yes, he did, didn't he?"

George and I both lapsed into silence for a minute.

"So you went back and talked to Garriques?" I finally said, taking up one of the conversational strands.

George shook his head. "No. I went and found Estrella's friend, Pam. I figured if Estrella said anything to anyone she'd have said it to her. Well, she had. Unfortunately Estrella was dropping lots of acid at the time, so Pam wasn't inclined to take Estrella's story too seriously. Then when Estrella got killed, Pam figured maybe Estrella's story was true and that if she didn't want to be next, she'd better pretend she hadn't heard anything."

"Then why did she talk to you?"

"Because I pointed out she could serve a couple of years for dealing. In the nicest possible manner of course . . ."

"Of course . . ."

"After that she got a little more conversational. The description she gave me, the one she got from Estrella, matched Garriques in a general way. But given Estrella's possible mental state it wasn't enough to move on. I needed more." George paused and asked me for the second beer. After I'd opened it and he'd taken a sip he continued. "I went to talk to Ana Torres next. I was hoping Estrella had told her something."

"Had she?"

"No. She said the two of them hadn't talked ever since Estrella started running with a bad crowd. Which is why I ended up following Garriques. It was my last shot. I figured maybe I'd rattle him. Well, I did. I just didn't get the result I wanted."

I sighed. "We could have saved ourselves a lot of trouble if we'd gotten together."

"I know."

"Why didn't you answer my messages?"

"At first I was too busy to, and then I couldn't. It's hard to phone from the trunk of a car."

"Not if you have a cellular phone."

George laughed. Suddenly I became aware of the fact that his body was pressing up against mine. God, I shouldn't have brought the pot. I'd forgotten how horny it makes me feel. To distract myself I told him about Porter and the farm and Brandon Funk.

"How is he anyway?" George asked.

"Worse off than you are. He's going to be in here for a while."

"Why did he come out?"

"He told me he and Garriques got in a fight about Marsha. It must have been bad because Garriques told him to get out of town. When Funk said no, Garriques told him that the same thing that had happened to Porter was going to happen to you and that he was going to leave him holding the bag. Again. But this time Funk decided to do something. He was going to the farm to try and help you."

"Except Garriques followed him."

"Exactly."

"He should have gone to the cops."

"He was still scared about being blamed for Porter, and he didn't want to get involved in all the family stuff that was going to go down. After all, Garriques is his brother-in-law. I think he was hoping that if he rescued you, you'd get Garriques and he could stay out of it."

George reached over and took the beer. Our fingers

touched. A tingle went through mine. "Too bad you didn't shoot Garriques in a more strategic area."

"I'm just happy I hit him at all."

George's expression darkened. "I hope that sonofabitch goes straight to hell. You know he shot me and left me to die."

"I know." I put my hand on George's arm.

"It was like being buried alive. I wouldn't do that to anyone."

"Don't think about it," I murmured.

"I can't help it. It sneaks up on me. I shouldn't have followed Garriques out there. No, what I shouldn't have done was come back the next day and looked around without telling you. Or Connelly. Or somebody."

"You didn't expect he'd be there."

"That's no excuse. I knew better." I could see George's jaw muscles clenching while he remembered what had happened. Then he told me the story again because he needed to talk. "I'd just gotten out of the car when he'd pulled up. He asked me what I wanted and I gave him some bullshit answer, and looking at him I knew that he knew I was lying. That bastard pulled his gun on me before I could get to the car. I grabbed for it. I got it away from him, too, but the damned thing slipped out of my hand. It went off when it hit the ground." George blinked. "You know what Connelly told me?"

"What?" I asked, even though I already knew the answer.

"He said the reason Garriques shoved me in the trunk instead of finishing me off was because a real estate agent was coming out with his client and he didn't know what else to do with me. I guess he didn't have another change of clothes. It's hard to show a house when you've got blood all over your pants."

"I think it was more a matter of his not wanting Fast Eddie

to find out what was going on. People like that tend to frown on unscheduled killings."

George frowned. "Fast Eddie. What the hell does he have to do with this?"

I explained about the real estate agent and the homestead.

George snapped his fingers. "That's right. Fast Eddie's last name is Marino."

"It certainly is."

George shook his head. "It's lucky you came out before he finished the job."

"I would say so," I agreed as I tried not to think about the two I hadn't been able to save.

Even though I didn't want to, I found myself picturing Marsha's death. Had it been gray or sunny the morning Marsha died? Was she listening to the radio when her world came to an end? She'd been sitting in the back of the parking lot at The Pancake Palace waiting for Garriques to bring her her money and probably thinking about how her life was going to take a turn for the better. She must have been happy to see Garriques, pleased when he got in her car. Finally something was going to work out right. Only instead of giving her the thirty grand, he jammed one of his wife's hypodermics in her. At least that's what Connelly had told me. I guess he felt he owed me something.

It must have happened so fast Marsha didn't have time to react. She certainly wouldn't have been expecting it. And then all Garriques had to do was hold her and wait until the insulin took effect. How long would it have taken? Twenty minutes, half an hour at the most. In his confession Garriques had said she hadn't fought much; she hadn't tried hard to get away. After she'd become unconscious he'd driven her car over to the reservoir and tossed her in. Then he walked back, got in his car, and went to work.

"What are you thinking about?" George asked when another minute of silence had gone by.

I sighed. "Mostly about Marsha and Estrella."

"What about them?"

I shrugged. "I don't know. I guess I was just thinking how one bad deed can give birth to so many. Porter steals a camera from Garriques and Garriques loses it, kills him and buries the body. Then Marsha finds out about it and tries to blackmail him."

"And he kills her," George said.

"And then Estrella sees the murder and he kills her."

"She could have gone to the police," George said.

"She was afraid to. She was afraid she'd be deported. And anyway you told me her friend said that she didn't think Garriques saw her."

"That's true," George murmured. "According to Connelly Garriques didn't. But later that morning he decided to go back to the reservoir and make sure he hadn't left anything lying around. He saw her backpack . . ."

"So he came and got me," I said bitterly. "He wanted me to find her for him. And I did. I told him where she was and he went and killed her."

George reached over and drew me to him. "It wasn't your fault." He stroked my hair with his good hand. "You didn't know."

"But I should have."

"And Estrella should have been home. If she hadn't been sleeping one off, she never would have seen what she had and she'd be alive today."

I drew back. "So what's the moral of the story here?" I said angrily. "Lead a virtuous life or else? I refuse to buy that."

"Sssh." George raised my chin with the tip of his finger. "Come on. Let's smoke the rest of the joint."

I nodded in Root's direction. "What about him?"

"Too bad."

I lit up. We got about three puffs each before Root started complaining.

"You're smoking in there again, aren't you? Aren't you?" he cried.

"You're imagining things," I told him.

"Oh, no I'm not."

George grinned. "I guess we'd better put it out."

"One more hit each and we will." I took one and passed the joint along to George. He took in a big lungful and held it for a moment. Then he exhaled and pinched out the roach.

"This is pretty good stuff," he said as he handed it to me.

"I only get the best," I told him as I put it away.

"I just have one question for you."

"What's that?"

"How did you know that I was at the farm?"

"Your pen."

George looked puzzled. "My pen?"

I elucidated. "You dropped your pen in the barn."

"How'd you know it was mine? It wasn't monogrammed."

"I didn't. But when I was looking through your desk . . ."

"My desk?" George's voice rose. "You were in my house?"

"I just said I was."

"And you went through my stuff?"

I nodded. "It was pretty interesting. Especially your dresser." Now why had I said that?

"Was it now?" George said softly. "You know what happens to women when they break and enter?"

"What?"

"This." He leaned over and kissed me. I kissed him back.

"What are you two doing in there?" Root cried as the hospital bed groaned under George's and my weight.

We didn't answer.

We had better things to do.